The Last Moonstone

By Alex Buzzard

Acknowledgements

This novel would not have been possible without the help of a number of extremely kind people who have supported me throughout.

In particular I would like to thank:

My partner and soulmate Gaynor for her love, support, understanding, patience, and belief.

Jules Clark for introducing me to Reiki and sharing her insight.

Cat, Denise, Dave, and Janice from the Millom Reading Group for wading their way through the early draft and sparing the reader from a plethora of plot, spelling, and grammatical errors.

1

Kharmudi, the last Hyksos king, knelt before the polished obsidian volcanic glass crystal. It was set into a large solid granite altar in the Temple of Sutekh the Merciless. The crystal was almost totally black with just a hint of redness, rather like the colour of congealed blood. Oval in shape its maximum width was approximately the span of a human hand and about half its overall length. At auspicious times in the solar and lunar cycles the High Priest of the Temple would stare into the Black Crystal and summon the malign servants of Sutekh to appear before him and bid them to carry out dark acts at the bidding of King Kharmudi.

The origins of the Black Crystal were obscure, but it had been in the possession of the Hyksos rulers since the beginning of their known history. One legend said that the stone was the crystallised heart of a giant who had fallen in love with the reflection of the Goddess of the moon as he gazed in a magic pool. Each day he visited the pool to see the object of his love but each day her brightness diminished until one day her reflection was gone.

The giant, in complete despair at his terrible loneliness tore out his own heart and threw it into the water to take away the pain of his loss. The next day the light of the Goddess began once again to shine upon the pool, but the torn-out heart was unable to hold love anymore. Its resentment and anger shrivelled and hardened it into the Black Crystal. The Crystal brought the giant's power to those who owned and worshipped it, but it also brought a curse that the power gained came at the expense of the ability to be influenced by love and compassion. Those in the possession of the Black Crystal were destined to lose the power of empathy and be utterly consumed by the selfish desires of their ego.

Despite the power of the Black Crystal and his evil conjuring, Kharmudi had been unable to resist the growing military might of the Theban King Ahmose and had lost a final futile battle outside the city of Avaris. Retreating within the Temple he listened as the bronze axes of the soldiers of Ahmose frantically chopped away at the timber frame that held in place the immense hinges that suspended the great doors. These doors were now all that stood between the King and his inevitable torture, sacrifice and death.

His personal guard had slaughtered the members of his royal household and its slaves in a last act of sacrifice to the Lord Sutekh before marching out to meet their own deaths at the hands of the army of King Ahmose. The bodies of more than a hundred men women and children lay in pools of blood around the

Temple walls in a hideous contorted tableau. Kharmudi looked at the body of his eldest daughter. It was clutched in a futile protective embrace by her mother whose head had now fallen back revealing the gaping neck wound that had caused her death.

Kharmudi was not going to give the victorious Theban King the satisfaction of taking him into slavery or using him in a public spectacle by offering him up in sacrifice to the Gods. He knelt over the Black Crystal and with a final prayer for Sutekh to embrace his evil heart as he journeyed into the underworld, he plunged his dagger under his rib cage into his heart before collapsing over the altar. His blood flowed around the Black Crystal as had the blood of hundreds of others before him, sacrificed by the Temple priests to appease Sutekh's anger and to secure his favour.

Moments later, with a deafening crash the hinges of the great doors finally gave way and collapsed inwards to reveal the bloody carnage within. As King Ahmose followed his personal guard through the doors he briefly recoiled in horror at the sight before him. He was no stranger to death; he had fought many battles to claim his empire, but there was something deeply disturbing about all these bodies piled up within this place of death.

Ahmose and the Theban people worshipped the God Amun, the Sun God. His first instinct was to raze this blighted Temple to the ground and to allow the light of the blazing sun to purify the cursed ground, removing all traces of its malign existence. He was however wary of the terrible power of Sutekh and feared any act of desecration could bring the wrath of the dark lord of the underworld upon him.

Ahmose was also troubled by the Black Crystal inserted into its polished granite altar. If he stared at the obsidian for more than a few seconds the surface of the rock crystal seemed to move and contorted hideous faces began to appear before his eyes. There was powerful magic at work here and he decided that his best course of action was to contain the evil rather than suffer the consequences of retribution from Sutekh should he attempt to destroy it.

Thirteen priestesses of the Goddess Mut were called into service, one for every new moon that might occur in the year. Mut was the mother of the world and her child, the Moon God Khonsu was called to protect the kingdom from Sutekh's power. Into the walls of the Temple were set thirteen beautiful, polished fire opals, each the size of a duck's egg. These were selected and brought by the high priestess of the Goddess Mut from the mines of Ethiopia. The high priestess and the twelve other priestesses of the Temple sanctified the stones in the name of the Goddess and called for Khonsu to grant them the power to calm and placate the anger of Sutekh. The power of the Black Crystal was at its greatest when the Moon God's eye was turned away but diminished when the Moon was full, and its silvery light shone down upon the Temple.

Over centuries of war and changing dynasties the Temple was almost forgotten, just a tale in a myth told on dark nights to send a shiver down the spines of the audience and scare children. Throughout this time, over countless generations, the daughters of the priestesses of Mut dutifully maintained their watch. The evil of the Black Crystal and the wrath of Sutekh remained constrained by the power of their magic and the love of the Goddess manifest by the presence of the thirteen Moonstones.

After the passing of nearly 1200 years Egypt fell under the control of a Greek army led by the Macedonian King Alexander who was pronounced by the priests as a deity, the living son of Amun. Alexander was fascinated by the mysteries of the religions of Egypt and his unquenchable thirst for power attracted him to the dark God Sutekh. Priests of the cult of Sutekh told Alexander of the story of the lost Temple and its powerful Dark Crystal. Alexander yearned to possess this powerful stone and ordered several parties of soldiers and priests of Sutekh, commanded by his most trusted officers, to seek the Black Crystal.

The mighty deity Sutekh could, through the portal of the Black Crystal, sense the power of ambition growing in Alexander's heart. He reached out to one of the Priests of Sutekh in a vision revealing the Crystal's location. The priestesses sensed the growing unrest within the Black Crystal with dismay and sent out spies who alerted them to the approach of the Greeks.

The priestesses knew there was no hope of removing the Black Crystal embedded in its heavy granite altar and they were forbidden by sacred oath from destroying it. One of their number was tasked with saving the precious Moonstones so that the power of Sutekh might yet be constrained. She managed to escape with the thirteen precious Moonstones before the Black Crystal fell into the hands of the Greeks. The priestesses knew that the power of the Moonstones would be dissipated by separating them but if they were found and destroyed there would be a far greater danger to the future of the World. They believed that the power that had built up within the stones over the centuries could still emanate the boundless love of the Goddess. Each precious stone represented a small reservoir of hope against the evil and anger that surged and raged within the depths of the Black Crystal and within the hearts of the men that served it.

One priestess was captured as she was attempting to flee the Temple and was taken with the Black Crystal back to Alexander. Under torture at the hands of a High Priest of the cult of Sutekh she revealed the existence and purpose of the thirteen Moonstones and the love held within them that could act as a balance against the malign power of the Black Crystal.

The priestess who had been given the task of guarding the precious Moonstones travelled to the port city of Rosetta. There she met a Phoenician trader who traded Egyptian goods with the Celtic tribes who bordered the Mediterranean and the Atlantic coasts of Hispania, Britannia, and Hibernia. The trader was enchanted by the mysterious priestess, and he readily agreed to take her with him on his travels. Love quickly grew between the priestess and the Phoenician trader and they were joined in a ceremony on the island of Sicilia. Many of the Celtic tribes they met on their travels honoured the Goddess under her many different names. As the priestess journeyed with her lover, she slowly gifted the moonstones into the care of the wise women and priestesses that she befriended amongst the Celtic tribes. Each Moonstone brought blessings to the tribe but back in Egypt an ancient evil was steadily growing.

Alexander was obsessed with the Black Crystal as he felt its extraordinary power surging through his veins. It fed the ambition of his ego, encouraging him to hunger for ever more prestige and glory. He was however wary of openly showing his growing relationship with the cult of Sutekh who was known by Alexander through translation to the Greek language as Seth. Worship of Seth could compromise his identification as the deity son of the God Amun and cause unrest amongst his Egyptian subjects. He ordered the secret construction of an underground Temple where the priests would use the Crystal to communicate with the God of the underworld. They asked for Seth's blessings for Alexander's ambitions and to ensure his success upon the bloody battlefields of his future campaigns.

Alexander was furious that he was not also in possession of the Moonstones as he resented any challenge of the Goddess that might limit his future glory. He sent out spies and emissaries to try to locate the stones, but they had already left the shores of Egypt and were for the time being safe from his grasp.

Three centuries later the Roman Emperor Augustus stood in the Temple of the Black Crystal in Rome. It had been discovered in Egypt after the defeat of Marcus Antonius and Queen Cleopatra of Egypt at the naval battle of Actium. It was already seeping its malign influence, corrupting his mind and slowly fuelling his ego and ambition. The Temple was moved stone by stone and exactly reconstructed under the streets of Rome where the Temple was re-dedicated to the worship of Seth to access his blessings and power through the portal of the Black Crystal. Priests from the Temple in Egypt were brought to Rome to practice the ancient dark magic associated with the worship of Seth and who could channel its power to support the Crystal's new masters.

Augustus created the secret Order of the Black Crystal. The total membership of the Order was set at thirteen and stood as a balance against the maximum number of times in the year that the Goddess chose to defy the darkness of the night through the rebirth of the moon. The members were sworn to secrecy under the threat of being slowly tortured to death should they ever betray the Order. Being a member of the Order guaranteed riches and the ability to wield enormous power within the empire. This power went beyond the mere acquisition of material wealth although greed was a powerful motivator for most of the members. The members were also indoctrinated into the mysteries of the cult of Seth. With the help of the priests, they developed enhanced powers of divination, intuition and enchantment, skills they used to increase their power and influence. With the help of the Order and the power of the Black Crystal, the Roman Empire rapidly grew to encompass the whole of the Mediterranean. It was now on the brink of colonising the island of Britannia and suppressing its population of Britonic tribes.

The Order of Seth and the Black Crystal celebrated patriarchal power and wealth as the ultimate human destiny and used all the means at their disposal to defeat any opposition that stood in their way. Their malign influence ensured the imposition of a strict patriarchy in Rome and all the lands that they conquered. This culture deliberately undermined the influence and prestige of women and any challenge by the Goddess through her daughters exercising the gifts of empathy, love, and compassion which the order despised. If a member of the order died, one amongst them would be tasked to find a replacement who was ruthless and ambitious enough to join their number. If a leader died the other twelve members would elect a new leader from their number. The Emperor was not always a member of the Order and seldom its leader. Some emperors were considered too weak to be considered to be invited into the Order as members and emperors seldom lasted long if their actions hindered the Order's ambitions.

One of the most malevolent qualities of the power of the Black Crystal was the ability to inhibit the creation of conscious thought within the human population. The power of the human mind to balance the cravings of the ego with the qualities of empathy and compassion became increasingly inhibited, particularly within the male population. Few voices were raised against the hegemony of the worship of wealth and the entitlement of the wealthy to exercise influence over others. Increasingly the disparate populations within the empire began to accept this malign influence over their societies as the lust for wealth began to erode their traditional values and cultures. Rather than celebrating their unity with nature within the realm of the great Goddess, humanity began to seek out material trivialities instead. Increasingly they treated the natural world as just an exploitable asset in the service of human greed rather than a beautiful manifestation of the divine presence.

There were however fragile pockets of resistance to the power of the Black Crystal on the fringes of the Empire. This was where the influence of the remaining Moonstones still held sway and drove back the darkness of ignorance with the enlightenment of wisdom and the power of love.

The Order held a deep hatred for the Moonstones and those who used their power to stand in opposition to their will. As the Roman Empire spread, the agents of the Order set about the task of destroying all the Moonstones and thereby the influence of love and compassion in the hearts of the peoples of the world. By the year 832 since the founding of Rome the Order held unimaginable wealth and power. Of the thirteen Moonstones, eleven had been found and destroyed and now only two Moonstones remained that could stand against the evil of the Black Crystal and the oppressive patriarchal hegemony of Rome.

The proximity of a Moonstone acted as a shield against the Priests of the Black Crystal, blocking their powers through dark magic to penetrate the minds of the local populations under its influence. This protection came at a terrible price because it also enabled the Priests to gauge where the Moonstones might be found and where its agents should be sent. By the year 832 the Priests knew that there was a least one Moonstone on the Island of Britannia and it was no coincidence that one of the most capable and ambitious members of the Order had recently been appointed to be the new Governor of the still disputed province.

2

Chyrenia was the High Priestess of the Gallancia. Like most tribes in the land known to the Romans as Britannia the Gallancia were proud and independent but years of tribal conflict and regular incursions of Scoti raiders along the coast had resulted in the development of a hierarchy of fragile allegiances. The Gallancia offered allegiance and paid tribute to the Carvetii who in turn offered allegiance to the Brigantes. These agreements largely prevented the escalation of petty local tribal squabbles and enabled effective collaboration against incursion by armed raiding parties.

In recent times a new and powerful threat had emerged from the South from Roman invaders. These Romans had once defeated Venutius, the King of the Brigantes, but Venutius had fought back and successfully driven the Romans back once more. This had occurred in the year to which the Romans had given the number of 822 since the foundation of their accursed City. This was nine years after the defeat and brutal suppression of the great Iceni Queen Boudicca and her tribal allies. The rivers of the South were said to have flowed red with the blood of the fallen. Nobody was spared, men women and children were butchered, raped, and enslaved through the ruthless efficiency of the Roman Army.

The Roman invaders had never reached as far to the Northwest as the land of the Gallancia, but the threat and the power of the Roman presence was growing. The appetite for power and the greed that possessed the Romans was limitless and military conquest was the primary way that ambitious Romans could rise in prominence in the Roman Senate. Many once powerful and independent Britonic tribes had fallen under the imperial yoke of Roman oppression. Sometimes this was by military defeat at the hands of the legions, but the bribery and corruption of tribal leaders also played its part. Some leaders were all too easily enticed to submit to the Romans with promises of wealth and protection if they accepted the Roman imperial yoke. The Gallancia could not understand the Romans' compulsion for possessing and controlling the lands of others and despised their greed. Like most of the Celtic peoples of Britannia before the Roman invasion, the Gallancia celebrated nature, living, drinking, lovemaking, and courage above material wealth.

Chyrenia shuddered briefly, dark premonitions had disturbed her dreams but today she quickly dismissed such thoughts. The fates had revealed several possible futures to her, and no path was ever certain as the future could sometimes be altered by the choices people made. Those who were attuned to the magic of the Great Mother Goddess Anu could play their part in influencing the future in the cause of love. Anu was the mother of all-natural things, and it is the fertility of her womb and the warmth of her love that had always provided for the peoples who lived within her realm.

Today was the most important date of year, the great feast of Beltane signalling the beginning of the summer, the quarter of the year when the sun was at its brightest. This was the point in the year when the forces of growth and reproduction in nature were at their strongest and when the fertility of the land and the tribe had to be secured through sacred ritual. If the summer months were poor and the crops failed there would be pestilence, hunger, and death amongst the tribes.

Chyrenia was now in her thirty seventh year and her fifth year as High Priestess, leader of the thirteen Priestesses of the Moonstone. Unusually for a Gallancian woman, her hair was auburn, with a hint of copper, gently wavy and long. It reached more than halfway down her back although when she was not on ceremonial duties she would often pin it up under a linen cap for reasons of practicality. She had been elected as High Priestess and keeper of the Moonstone after her predecessor Elevan had been slain in a raid by the Scoti. She often felt Elevan's presence, and she would sometimes come to her in dreams and visions when Chyrenia needed guidance.

The Gallancia were called the people of the stones because they were the keeper of the ancient stone circle that had been built in the shadow of the mountains by the ancient ancestors of the tribe. Long ago most of the tribes in Britannia celebrated the great Goddess and stone circles or wooden henges were constructed in her honour and venerated across the land. Over time a new culture began to dominate which focused more on the ambitions of leaders, material possessions and the egos of powerful men and women where great barrows were built in honour of the dead. Along with this culture came the rise and increasing influence of the Druidic order of priests who held the knowledge of the law, were adept at the art of divination and were the keepers of the ancient stories and myths of the people. The Gallancia were now one of only a handful of tribes that still upheld the ancient Goddess tradition, the divine female who was the source and protector of all life.

The stone circle of the Gallancia represented the womb of the great goddess Anu. Only the daughters of Anu, the priestesses of the tribe were permitted within the stones during the eight sabbats and during the other sacred ceremonies except at this one time of year. The fertility of the tribe and their livestock could only be assured through the consummation of the God Cernunnos and the Goddess Anu. This was sought by bringing the seed of a strong young man to a vibrant young woman from the tribe, the green horned God of the woods and the maiden sprung from within the Goddess's sacred womb. It was the interaction between female and male energies that sparked the creative dynamic upon which the fruitful evolution of the divine universe and all life depended.

Even the Goddess Anu needed to embrace the love of her mate, embodied in the growing power of the new sun every year, for the cycle of life to continue. The stone circle of the Gallancia had a portal, a stone vulva, which pointed directly towards the first rays of the rising sun at the midwinter solstice. Winter Solstice was the time when the dying energy of the Sun God began to be reborn, drawn up by the will of the Goddess from the underworld so that the sacred cycle of the year could continue, and nature would once again burst into life.

The night before Beltane had been dry and mild and it promised to be a beautiful day. The festival began before dawn where the whole of the Gallancia tribe from all the settlements in the area gathered in the grazing land adjoining Chyrenia's village. This was called Gallanbhir and was the largest Gallancian tribal settlement and the seat of the Tribal Council. It was situated at the north side of the estuary where coastal trading vessels could easily moor up with the high tide. Trading around the coast and up the river estuaries was much easier than trying to follow the winding tracks and trails that joined the various tribal communities. These could be impassable during the time of the winter rains and snowfall and were often dangerous without the protection of a well-armed escort.

It was from Gallanbhir that the ceremonial procession would take a track that followed the path of a stream that led up towards the Stones about one and a half leagues from the village. This was a time of joy and celebration, and the feasting would last all day until the following dawn. Chyrenia led the procession followed by twelve priestesses dressed in green woollen robes. Each of the priestesses carried a hand drum which they beat to determine the rhythm and speed of the procession.

Behind the priestesses in the procession was Kernack, the tribal chief and twelve warriors. Four of the warriors carried an ornate litter upon their shoulders upon which sat a young woman dressed in pure white linen. The precious cloth to make her gown had been obtained from Celtic coastal traders from distant lands and had cost the tribe fifty sheep fleeces from their flocks. The platform was completely covered in flowers and the young woman wore a garland of flowers in her hair. Behind the warriors was a strange figure whose skin had been dyed green who wore a deerskin cloak covered with oakleaves and a headdress adorned with an impressive set of antlers from a red deer. The rest of the tribe followed singing and laughing as they progressed up the valley towards the sacred stone.

The stones were an impressive sight, the surfaces of the stones flickered in the light of several huge bonfires that had been lit around the circle during the night. The red glow of the burning timbers was just beginning to be mirrored in the sky above the mountain to the north-east as the sun started to rise.

When Chyrenia reached the portal of the stone circle she raised her hand and all the drumming and singing stopped. Chyrenia walked deosil, the direction of the movement of the sun, around the circle sprinkling water that had been taken and blessed from a secret spring known only to the priestesses of the Moonstone. She repeated this ritual sprinkling fertile earth taken from an oak glade from a valley in the mountains. She then took a bronze vessel from one of the priestesses filled with smoking incense made from plants, herbs, and essential oils from the lands of the East. Finally, she held up a burning torch of hazel wrapped in cloth that had been soaked in melted beeswax as she circled the stones for the fourth time. As she walked Chyrenia chanted an ancient magical verse which summoned the elementals, the spirits of the four elements, water, earth, air, and fire, to join her within the circle and to witness the sacred rite that they were about to perform in honour of the Goddess.

When the summoning of the elementals had been completed Chyrenia entered the circle alone through the portal. She brought out a beautiful stone which hung from a golden cord from between her breasts and lifted it above her head. This stone was known as the Moonstone, and it had been a precious gift from a priestess of the Goddess from mysterious lands in the far East. The Moonstone had been bringing its blessings to the tribe for more than twenty generations and was their most prized possession. With the Moonstone held aloft Chyrenia walked around the inside of the circle chanting a blessing to the Goddess Anu and as she passed the portal the other priestesses followed her into the ring of ancient stones. Chyrenia stopped at a stone that was directly opposite the portal and the other priestesses continued in a deosil direction until they were equally placed around the circle. Two of the priestesses took up positions at each side of the entrance portal.

At the same time, the twelve warriors and the chief positioned themselves outside the circle, Kernack opposite Chyrenia and each warrior opposite one of the priestesses with two guarding the entrance. Kernack drew his sword and turned to face the gathering tribe in a symbolic act of protection. In one movement the twelve other warriors all followed suit. As Kernack lifted his sword into the air and the crowd fell silent. There was a pause as more than 400 Gallancians held their breaths. All that could be heard was the sound of the wind, the crackling of the burning timbers of the fires and the sound of the bleating of the grazing sheep in the grasslands below the treeline.

Then Chyrenia's powerful voice cried out, "The priestesses of the Moonstone invite the Goddess Anu to join us in this circle and to give her blessings to her daughter who has come willingly to be a vessel for her divine spirit. Melesone a daughter of the Goddess, has been chosen for she is strong in heart and wise in words. We, the daughters of the Goddess, mother of all life, ask her to fill Melesone with her love, wisdom and bestow upon her the blessing of her boundless fertility."

The four priestesses who were nearest the portal walked back outside the circle, picked up the ceremonial litter upon which Melesone was sat, and carried her into the centre of the circle. They then slowly turned the litter around so that her feet faced the portal.

Chyrenia dropped her robe so that she stood naked under the sky. She walked around the bed upon which Melesone lay, sprinkling sacred water. She then knelt on the bed before Melesone and taking the Moonstone in both hands placed it against Melesone's forehead.

Chyrenia cried out in a loud voice "We ask the Goddess to come into the body of Melesone and bestow upon her your divine love and wisdom."

The other twelve priestesses repeated Chyrenia's words three times and then struck the hand drums they were carrying three times.

Chyrenia opened herself up as a conduit to the energy of the Goddess. As she cleared her mind she could feel it begin to flow up from the base of her spine up towards her heart and then out through her arms until it was swirling within her hands as they cupped the Moonstone. The Moonstone still firmly pressed against Melesone's forehead started to radiate light as Chyrenia channelled from within it the stored energy of over a thousand of years of ritual. The radiant energy coming from the Moonstone was amplified by the presence of the great stones that surrounded it which reflected the energy back towards the figures within the circle.

The twelve other priestesses also allowed their green robes to fall from their shoulders so that they also stood skyclad in the presence of the Goddess. They each raised their eyes to the sky and opened themselves up as the energy begun to flow through them. As it pulsed and flowed around their bodies, they visualised new life growing within Melesone's womb blessed by the spirit of the Goddess.

After a long pause Chyrenia lifted the golden cord that held the precious Moonstone over her head and placed it over Melesone's head so that the Moonstone lay between Melesone's firm young breasts. It rested at the point on her breastbone beneath which the joy of divine love was most intensely felt.

Two of the priestesses then went to Melesone and helped her to stand up so that they could remove her white linen robe leaving her naked except for her headdress and the Moonstone necklace. Then the priestesses gently supported her as she lay back upon the litter on the bed of flowers.

"The Goddess calls out for her God to join her so that woman and man may become a united whole in the act of divine creation. There is one amongst us in which the spirit of the God Cernunnos the wild spirit of the woods has grown strong. He has proved himself in battle by defeating our enemies and the lust of the horned God flows powerfully within his loins. I call upon Garraculous son of Arras to enter the circle. This sacred space is forbidden to all men except the chosen one who has absorbed the courage of Cernunnos. He is ready to join with the Goddess whose love is boundless but whose judgement is fierce. Beware any man who enters with a false heart as he shall be found wanting and shall face the terrible retribution of the Goddess's anger."

The words that Chyrenia uttered were words that had been used in this ceremony for as long as the oral traditions of the tribe had been collated. They were relayed through countless generations, held in trust through the memories of the elders and they were not empty words. If any chosen man was unable to satisfy the Goddess and the sacred rituals were not fulfilled, he would become an outcast from the tribe. This had happened a few times in the past, and it had brought dark times upon both the man who failed in his task and upon the fortunes of the tribe.

Chyrenia knew that the power of natural magic influences the fates through the power of visualisation. If the fertility ceremony of Beltane went well this fed into the happiness and confidence of the tribe. If it went badly then bad omens were sought and found and these in turn brought their own reality, fuelled by the fears within the hearts of the people.

Unbeknown to most of the gathered tribe, the ceremony that was taking place had not just been left in the hands of the Goddess and the God. Melesone and Garraculous were not chosen simply by chance as Chyrenia had carefully watched a deep and binding love develop between them over many moons.

Melesone was not the most beautiful young woman in the tribe. She was more curvaceous than some with large, rounded breasts and fuller in the hip than many of the women. She was not as strong and skilled as some of the women when called upon to join with the men in battle, but she was no less lacking in courage. She also had a slight gap in her front teeth and her nose was perhaps slightly more pronounced than many. She had been chosen by Chyrenia for three powerful reasons.

Firstly, she was a natural priestess, the spirit of the Goddess was strong within her. She was very powerful in natural magic. Since she was a young girl she could see and communicate with the spirits of the ancestors and the spectres, both good and evil, that shared the earth with the living. She also had the gift of healing in her hands which she used when dressing the wounds of the warriors or comforting those struck down with illness.

Secondly, she was very wise and quickly learnt the craft of creating medicines and herbs and the myths and stories of the tribe. She was also wise in her choice of friends and slow to temper and in the use of rash words.

Lastly, and most importantly, Garraculous absolutely adored her, and she adored him. After the ceremony Chyrenia would handfast them as partners to journey together in their lives. Chyrenia had noticed how the powerful warrior who strutted with the youthful arrogance of one who had proved himself many times in the fury of battle, melt into a grinning stumbling idiot at a smile from Melesone. She knew where the real power lay within their relationship. Garraculous may own the strength within his sword arm, but Melesone owned and pulled the strings attached to his heart.

Both of them had willingly agreed to take their parts in the ceremony. In order to increase their longing and the subsequent intensity of their lovemaking, Chyrenia had forbidden them to lay together for three moons. This was the time that separated the sabbath of Imbolc, that first greeted the growing strength of the spring sun, and the sabbath of Beltane when the energy of natural creation and growth was at its zenith.

Garraculous arrogantly strode in his antler headdress towards the portal of the stone circle but the two warriors guarding it crossed their swords in front of him.

"No man may enter the circle when the spirit of the Goddess is present" they cried.

"This man carries the spirit of the God Cernunnos, lord of the wild places and the forests, he comes at the bidding of the Goddess" cried out Chyrenia. "Let no warrior stand in his way. Yet he must enter without any cloak of concealment, he must come to the embrace of the Goddess skyclad in the form that she created him."

Garraculous removed his robe and antler headdress and stood naked in front of the tribe. His already tattooed body had been painted by one of the priestesses in green. It was covered with strange patterns of black and brown which accentuated his powerfully developed muscles, his groin and generously proportioned penis. Following Chyrenia's demand, the two warriors drew back their swords and took a step to the side to grant Garraculous entry to the sacred circle through the stone portal.

There was more than just customary ritual to her demand that Garraculous enter the circle skyclad. No weapons were ever permitted within the stones on pain of banishment. It was a place of love and fertility, not force and violence and the custom ensured that no concealed weapons could ever be secretly brought into the circle. It was also a thoroughly enjoyable part of the theatrics of the ceremony. It ensured that all the women of the tribe had an ample opportunity to fully enjoy the sight of the lean muscular body that would soon be in the sexual embrace of their tribal sister Melesone.

Like many tribes influenced by the culture of the Celtic peoples, the Gallancia celebrated lust, love, and the physical form. The concept that there was any shame in nakedness or sexual pleasure was a completely alien idea to them. Some warriors chose to go into battle naked apart from a shield, spear, or sword as an act of defiance and bravery. It was also believed that their wounds were less prone to corruption if the blood ran clean.

Garraculous walked to within four paces of the foot of the litter where Melesone gazed up at the warrior she loved. She gave him a smile of reassurance, but they were naturally both a little nervous about making love in front of the whole tribe. Chyrenia knew they might both need a little help with their arousal if the ceremony was to be a success. Two priestesses knelt beside Melesone, and they began to caress her naked body, as one kissed and stroked her neck and breasts, the other slowly worked her way down her body until the tip of her tongue was flicking and teasing her clitoris. In response to the attention of the priestesses the lips of Melesone's labia began to swell and glisten in anticipation. Her hips began to move, and her upper chest and neck flushed red with her growing arousal.

Chyrenia knelt down in front of Garraculous whose penis was just beginning to respond to the sight of his beloved Melesone succumbing to the attention of the two naked priestesses. Chyrenia knew the stress he was under and how much was at stake if he could not perform as expected in front of the tribe. She would not leave this responsibility to Garraculous alone.

She cupped his scrotum in one hand and took his rapidly swelling organ into her mouth. She visualised the seed in his testicles responding to her attention as they rested in her cupped hand and her lips and tongue began their work on his penis. With satisfaction she felt his penis stiffen until it was rigid and throbbing with desire and she began to taste his precum in her mouth as she took him deeper. She smiled inwardly as she heard the moans of arousal from Melesone behind her just as the first rays of the sun started to radiate over the top of the ridge of the mountain.

"Now my love" cried out Melesone. Chyrenia released Garraculous's swollen organ, and he threw himself into his lover's arms upon her floral bed.

Their lovemaking was intense and brief, within moments they cried out in unison as Garraculous shot his seed deep into Melesone. For a few precious moments, the lovers lay in each other's arms, before Garraculous withdrew his still swollen penis from her vagina and stood up. During this whole time the surrounding tribe had remained silent. The ritual was not complete, and they awaited in nervous anticipation for Chyrenia to pass judgement. She stood in front of Garraculous and cupped the end of his penis in her hand. She drew it across her palm leaving a trail of semen that was still leaking from its red swollen head. She looked Garraculous in the eyes and they both smiled. You have both done so well she whispered to him as he held up his head with pride.

"The Goddess Anu has been filled with the seed of the God Cernunnos, two have become one and the cycle of life has been renewed. The omens are good."

With this the whole tribe let out a roar of celebration and lovers were already kissing and grasping each other in lust and anticipation. There would be many new babies born nine moons after this sabbat ceremony.

The two priestesses who had been attending Melesone helped her to her feet and hugged and kissed her. With great tenderness they wrapped her in a fresh green robe celebrating the promise of new life and removed the Moonstone that was still lying between her breasts. Garraculous picked Melesone up in his strong arms and he carried her from the circle. He was met with whoops of delight and pats on the back from the large group of young warriors who were waiting to greet him outside the portal, and his eyes shone with pride and with the love that he felt for Melesone. Melesone laughed in his arms with joy and at the crazy antics of his friends. It would be several hours before the lovers re-joined the celebrations.

Chyrenia took the Moonstone and placed it around her neck. She then led the priestesses in giving thanks to the Goddess Anu, the God Cernunnos, and the four elementals that they had called to witness the fertility rite. She then closed her eyes and visualised the energy within the circle being drawn back inside the Moonstone adding to the reservoir of power that lay within.

All thirteen priestesses then knelt in a circle in the centre of the stones and joined hands, their minds became as one, filled with a blessing of love and hope for the Gallancia. They projected their inner love out into the world picturing ripples of pure white light illuminating the darkest corners of the land as if the power of their vision could make love a universal reality. The power of their love was strong, but they recoiled as dark broiling clouds began to intrude upon their vision and consume the light until they were surrounded by a shadowy wall that was barely held at bay by the power of the stones. They were kneeling in a defiant island of light surrounded by a churning sea of evil.

As one the priestesses fell back, their hands parting and with it their vision of love and hope, and their hearts began to fill with despair. They had sensed this threat approaching for many years but now its presence was imminent, it was almost as if they could feel the fetid stench of the breath of evil on the back of their necks.

Chyrenia looked at her sisters within the circle as the cries and laughter of the tribe gathered apace outside the stones. The tribal celebrations had already been lubricated by many flagons of mead and several amphorae of Roman wine. Some of this wine had been legitimately acquired through Celtic traders, others had been stolen through raids in the south upon the supply columns of the rapidly encroaching Roman army and its tribal allies.

"My sisters" whispered Chyrenia so that she could not be overheard, "it is hard not to lose hope when the storm clouds are about to fall upon us. We must not yet share our forebodings with the rest of the tribe for if they lose heart, all will be lost. At least for today we must let them enjoy their celebration of life and the joy of lust and love. Dry your tears. Tomorrow, sore heads will have to become wise heads, but for now we must live in the moment. Join your families, friends and lovers, celebrate the blessing of the Goddess and share the love that lies within your hearts."

The ceremony of Beltane had been completed although the festivities had just commenced. Chyrenia was too troubled to follow her own advice as she sought the reflective solitude of her roundhouse. She lived in an oak glade about half a league outside the main village. She found the noise and frivolity of the village distracting and she cherished the sounds and scents of nature. On a more practical note, it also meant that those who visited her for help had to be genuinely concerned enough to make the effort!

As Chyrenia entered her home she was grasped from behind by strong but familiar arms and she gave in to the warmth of the embrace. After a long hug she was released, and she turned to see the beautiful but scarred face of her lover Siabelle.

Siabelle had been out scouting and foraging in the south on her magnificent bay stallion. Her beautiful long black hair was now dirty and knotted and her face was grubby. She had obviously just arrived as she was still wearing the Roman leather body armour that she had taken from the body of a slain Roman cavalryman and adapted for her own use. She was also still wearing the Roman's spatha, the long cavalry sword which was in its scabbard at her side and her weapon of choice in battle.

Chyrenia helped Siabelle out of her armour and clothes and bathed her with clean water and soap in a shallow pool in the stream that ran down the hill past her roundhouse wincing as she noted new bruises on Siabelle's left shoulder and thigh. She lovingly combed her hair straight again and then took her back into the roundhouse where they gently made love under a warm woollen blanket.

As she lay with her head on Chyrenia's breast, Siabelle remembered the first time she had looked into those mysterious green eyes, still weak from loss of blood and the fever from the deep wound in her side made by an assassin's dagger. Her face hardened as she recalled her treatment at the hands of the Romans and felt the deep seething hatred she held for them in the pit of her stomach. Her mind flashed back to the first time she faced the harsh reality of what it was to be occupied by the armies of Rome. It was nineteen years ago when she was just fifteen years old and in the bloody aftermath at the hands of the Romans that took place after they defeated Boudicca.

Queen Boudicca of the Iceni had led an uprising against the brutality of the Roman occupiers, triggered by the rape of Boudicca's daughters. At first the uprising was successful and the Roman towns of Camulodunum and Londinium were put to the fire and sword. Eventually the Britons were stopped by the legions of the Roman Governor Suetonius Paulinus. Even though the Romans were heavily outnumbered by Boudicca's warriors, the Britonic tribes were not used to organising and fighting in large numbers. They lacked nothing in courage but were chaotic and disorganised on the field of battle and were put to the slaughter with ruthless efficiency by the Roman legions. It was estimated by the bragging historians of the Roman victors that eighty thousand Britons had died in the battle.

Siabelle was the daughter of a tribal chief of the Trinovantes and was rare in that her father had secured her a tutor versed in Roman Latin. By the time of Boudica's defeat Siabelle could speak and write fluently in the language of the Roman occupiers. Before the revolt there had been a strained but largely stable relationship between the native tribes and the Roman administrators, but the retribution of the Roman's after Boudicca's uprising was brutal and bloody.

Some of the Trinovantes had supported Boudicca in her revolt including Siabelle's father who died on the field of battle and all his lands were forfeited to the Roman victors. One evening the door of their roundhouse was smashed open and Siabelle watched as the Roman auxiliaries raped and killed her mother. Siabella remembered with horror how she too was pinned down and raped by the soldiers. The pain and humiliation was intolerable but even more repellent in her memory was the sweat and stench of the men who violated her. Eventually she had passed out through the trauma of her ordeal.

The following morning, she and her sister were put up for sale in the marketplace as slaves and she was sold to a Lanista, an owner of a gladiator school or Ludus, as part of a group lot of a dozen slaves. The Lanista, Gratianus Laevinus was pleased with his purchase. There were at least three men who might be suitable for training in his school, a couple more he could sell on to work in the fields or the mines and seven women and girls who would make domestic or sex slaves. Such a group may have cost as much as 5000 silver Denarii before Boudicca's rebellion. Now, after the brutal suppression of the rebellious tribes, there were so many slaves available that he managed to buy the whole group for just 800.

One girl in particular looked quite attractive with long black hair, a lithe body with well-formed breasts for her age. He thought she might be of some considerable value when cleaned up a bit. He had Siabelle stripped, and he examined with disgust her torn, bruised and violated body after her ordeal at the hands of the Roman auxiliaries. He crudely parted her legs and examined how badly his goods had been damaged during her systematic raping by the auxiliaries. Gratianus was a man motivated entirely by greed and he snorted in disdain at the behaviour of the soldiers. The essential aim of the Roman Empire was the exploitation of the conquered peoples, yet these legionnaires had shown no consideration about how badly they had devalued his merchandise when giving vent to their crude sexual appetites. The Roman empire ran on commerce, and it frustrated him as to how often the military seemed to forget this with their random acts of brutality.

It was only when Siabelle cried out in Latin as she protested against his rough examination of her torn vagina that he showed a renewed interest in his purchase. This did not restrain him from slapping her face hard with the back of his hand for having the impertinence to speak to him without invitation. As soon as he had her back in the Ludus he had her restrained and her shoulder branded with a hot iron to forever denote that she was now a slave. Siabelle was now merely an owned object. She was without any rights and could be tortured or killed at the whim of her master or by any civic or military authorities should she ever try to escape. She could not even seek shelter within her own tribe as they would be obliged to turn her over to the Roman authorities or face severe retribution. The Empire did not tolerate anyone who gave assistance to runaway slaves.

Fortunately for Siabelle, Gratiatus was a practical and greedy man who liked to get the most out of his assets. He decided that her command of Latin and her skills in numeracy would be best put to work in the administration of the business and financial running of the Ludus.

Gratianus was a cruel and intolerant master and Siabelle was often beaten for the most trivial of errors. One day she accidently dropped an amphora of wine whilst serving at a banquet. As a punishment Gratianus had her flung into the living quarters of the gladiators to service their lust. Siabelle was absolutely terrified as the men gathered around her, she still remembered the violent rape at the hands of the Roman auxiliaries and did not know how she would survive the trauma of what was about to happen to her.

Suddenly Siabelle heard a deep booming voice calling out in her native Trinovante dialect, "I claim this girl." A huge gladiator pushed to the front, grabbed her firmly by the arm and dragged her off to his cell like room, slamming the door behind him. Nobody argued because the voice belonged to Cervanix, the trainer of the gladiators in the school. Although still a slave Cervanix had earned many privileges after all his successes in the arena. Gratianus had now retired him from the arena. He had decided that Cervanix's skills would be better used in training his other gladiators to increase their value and further increase his own wealth and prestige.

Siabelle looked at this brute of a man in horror, but he made no move to overcome or rape her. She saw a twinkle in his eye and a faint glow of recognition. Cervanix had been taken by the Romans in a brief skirmish eight years before Boudicca's revolt. He had been clubbed on the back of his head by a Roman soldier whilst arguing with a trader over the price of a deer skin and the next thing he remembered was being in a cage taking him to the Ludus of Gratianus. There was something about Siabelle that seemed familiar to him.

"Who was your father" he asked her.

When she told him, he realised who this frightened girl was, and his expression softened. He walked up to her calmly and drew her into his bear like arms. "Hush now" he said in a quiet voice, "you probably don't recognise me, but I am your cousin, the eldest son of your father's brother who died of a fever before you were even born. Nobody here will harm you but if I am to keep you safe you must never reveal our relationship." Siabelle burst into tears of relief and the huge gladiator wrapped his arms around her protectively and allowed her to cry out all her hurt and fear.

Cervanix let it be known to Gratianus that the girl pleased him and Siabelle was regularly sent to his room when she had finished her other duties. Out of their respect for Cervanix, Siabelle was quickly adopted by the other gladiators. Often, when the Roman guards had left at the end of the day's training, Gratianus and the other gladiators would teach her how to use the dagger, sword, and spear. Most importantly, they taught her the weak points of Roman armour and how to kill quickly and efficiently.

Gratianus was however not as skilled in games of chance as his gladiators were in the arena. He was a compulsive gambler and eventually he could no longer sustain his debts and had to hand over his Ludus to his debtors. All the gladiators and the slaves were sold off in an auction. Siabelle was heartbroken to be parted from Cervanix who was quickly bought by the owner of a rival Ludus.

Siabelle was now 25 years old, and she was sold to a retired Roman army auxiliary veteran who had risen to the rank of Optio. An Optio was the second in command of a Centuria, the primary organisational unit of approximately eighty legionnaires that was part of a legion of the Roman army. He was originally from Hispania but had decided to settle in Britain after his retirement. He fancied this lithe attractive female slave and looked forward to making her pleasure and serve him when he had taken her back to his modest villa.

Siabelle had gained in confidence and cunning from her time with Cervanix and the gladiators and she convincingly played the part of a frightened submissive woman who meekly followed the commands of this arrogant fat leering man. She had developed a deep cold hatred of the Romans and it would not take long for her new owner to find out the consequences of her anger.

Siabelle was thrust into the courtyard of the villa where there were two male servants and another female slave awaiting the return of their master. The Optio threw the keys to one of the servants and her shackles were taken off. Siabelle massaged her wrists to get the circulation going again and discreetly looked around the courtyard. There was just the one entrance and all the other living quarters led off the central area.

Ahead of her were the main quarters where the Optio lived. He had never married, his life in the legions meant that he was constantly on the move and serious relationships were hard to form in such circumstances. Now he preferred to satisfy his desires on helpless slave girls or with one of the many prostitutes in the nearby town. The Optio pointed to his quarters and simply said to Siabelle "get in there and wait for me."

She meekly walked slowly into the quarters but although her head was bowed in mock subservience her eyes were quickly taking in every detail as she went. The Optio gave some orders to his other servants and then followed her in and ordered her to strip naked so that he could examine his prize. Siabelle noticed that in his arrogant disdain of this helpless slave, the Optio had carelessly left his gladius, a Roman legionnaire's short sword, in its scabbard on top of a chest at the side of the room.

The end was quicker than Siabelle's pent up hatred would have liked. She wished she had the time to make the Roman pig die a slow and painful death, but she could not run the risk of the servants raising the alarm. The Optio had pulled off his robe and strode in the nude towards Siabelle who pretended to meekly back away from him in fear and shyness whilst subtly closing the distance between herself and the gladius on the chest. As the leering Optio came towards her, his penis already stiffening in anticipation of her imminent violation Siabelle pretended to trip and stumbled backwards towards the chest.

Siabelle's thrust of the gladius was so quick that there was simply confusion on the Optio's face as he tried to comprehend how his own sword was now rammed upwards beneath his ribcage straight into his heart. Siabelle just had time to spit her contempt into his face before the light of life left his eyes and he collapsed forward onto the floor.

The Optio had been the greatest threat as he had had years of military training in the Roman army and could still have posed a formidable challenge if she had not taken him completely by surprise. The two manservants were no match for her, as she quickly took their lives, the hundreds of hours of training with the gladiators and her honed athletic body acting with ruthless efficiency. She looked down at the terrified slave girl who was now kneeling in front of her. To Siabelle's own amazement her embittered heart still had the capability for compassion as she looked into the girl's eyes. She was not much older than Siabelle had been when she had first been taken by the Romans.

The girl was no threat to her, but she realised that she was also in no position to take the girl with her as she would only hamper her escape. She knew she would have to move fast as the Romans were merciless in the pursuit of escaped slaves. She spoke gently to the girl who turned out to be a native Briton from the Iceni tribe. Siabelle told the girl that she meant her no harm, but she could not run the risk of setting the girl free as the Romans would brutally punish her if she was seen to be in any way complicit in Siabelle's escape.

Siabelle searched the villa for anything that she could use to facilitate her escape and took the Optio's gladius and his pugio, a short dagger. She knew that the Optio must have money hidden away but despite her searching she could not find it. She went back to the slave girl and, encouraged by Siabelle's fiery expression, the girl told her of a secret hoard kept in a secure box under a feeding trough for the villa's pigs. Siabelle found a significant stash of silver and bronze coins of which she took as much as she could easily carry. Speed was going to be far more important than wealth if she was going to survive.

Siabelle left the slave girl plenty of food and water and then shut her in the grain store, jamming a timber against it to keep the door secure. The Optio would soon be missed, and the girl should be discovered before her provisions would run out. One of the slain manservants was of a slight build and she dressed up in his clothes, bundled up her hair and put a woollen cap on her head. She then attached the sheath of the pugio safely to a loop inside her outer garment and hid the gladius in a backpack.

She waited until the sun was setting and then under the shadow of darkness, she crept out of the villa and headed across the fields into the woodland beyond. For the first time since her capture ten years before she was free and filled with a grim resolve focused on revenge for all the hurt and humiliation she had endured.

3

Siabelle knew she would have to move quickly and that she could trust nobody. Many of the tribal leaders had now become mere vassals to their Roman rulers and would be only too pleased to hand an escaped slave over to face Roman justice and prove their loyalty to their Roman masters.

The Optio's villa was on the outskirts of the Roman town of Verulamium and Siabelle decided that her best chance would be to head North towards the lands that were still largely unsubdued by the Roman military. She had heard that Venutius, King of the Brigantes had successfully revolted against the Romans two years earlier and she decided to attempt to join up with the tribe in their stand against the encroaching Romans.

Siabelle hid in a copse of dense woodland overnight before heading cross country using the sun to give her rough directions. Just before dusk on the first day she heard a loud commotion coming from behind a hedge that skirted one of the fields alongside the Roman road that ran between Verulamium and the Roman fort at Venonis. After the uprising, some former tribal warriors had become brigands who sustained themselves by preying on traders and travellers and Siabelle cautiously peered through a small opening in the hedge to see what was causing the commotion. She saw an ornate carriage on the road where there had obviously been a skirmish between the four Roman guards and a group of armed men who had ambushed the party. Siabelle reflected that the attacking group must have been desperate to take on the risk of openly confronting the Roman guards. Perhaps they had been enticed into their rash action by the implied wealth of the owner of such an elaborate carriage, but they had miscalculated, and it had cost them dearly. There appeared to be only two survivors left from the attacking party.

Siabelle watched as one of the men threw open the door and dragged a woman from the carriage. The woman seemed extraordinarily calm in the danger of the moment. She looked her attacker straight in the eyes as he tore off her dress, a pure white stola, to leave her standing naked before him. The other man who had been despatching one of the severely wounded Roman guards joined his companion and slapped the woman's face with the back of his hand to avert her gaze. To Siabelle's amazement the woman calmly turned her head back, her eyes blazing in challenge at the man that had assaulted her.

The two men grabbed the woman and threw her onto the bank at the edge of the road, they were obviously going to rape her, and an intense rage boiled up in Siabelle's belly fired by the memories of her own appalling abuse. There was a tree near to Siabelle and its shade had created a natural gap in the density of the hedge. On an impulse, Siabelle leapt through the gap with the stolen gladius raised. The startled men were taken completely by surprise as she stabbed the first assailant in the throat before quickly ducking under the clumsy cut at her head from the other man and burying the stabbing sword deep into his belly. She pulled out the blade before the weight of his body fell forward and brought it down in a lethal stab on the back of his neck severing his spinal cord.

Siabelle walked over to where the discarded dress of the woman lay on the road and returned it to the woman who now stood before her. She hated the Romans but many of their women were treated little better than their slaves and she hated the violence of men towards women even more.

Siabelle found herself looking into a pair of extraordinarily blue eyes that were calmly appraising her. The woman did not look at all surprised at Siabelle's dramatic appearance and to Siabelle's amazement the woman's face broke into a warm smile, the blue eyes radiating love towards her.

Siabelle scowled in confusion, nodded curtly towards the carriage, and spoke to the woman in Latin. "That's a very elaborate carriage for a single woman to be travelling in. Who are you and what are you doing on this road?"

"My name is Marciana, I am a high priestess in the service of the Goddess that is known in Rome by the name of Venus and by many other names in other lands. I have been tasked to create a temple in her name in Londinium and was on my way back from blessing a wedding in Venonis for the Legatus Legionis before meeting this unwelcome company. I thank you for my life which they would have surely taken if it hadn't been for your timely intervention." Marciana glanced dispassionately at the dead brigands lying on the road.

"You don't seem very surprised to meet me?" said Siabelle. She was astonished at how calm this woman had been in the face of imminent rape and death, and she showed no fear of Siabelle despite the fact that she had just efficiently slain two heavily armed men.

"I dreamt that we would meet and that our futures would be destined to be forever intertwined." replied Marciana. "I did not know that it would be quite such a dramatic encounter though."

To Siabelle's amazement the priestess's eyes twinkled with amusement. "What name are you known by warrior?"

Much to her own amazement Siabelle told her, there was something about this priestess that commanded her trust and she believed that the truth would be safe in her custody.

"I will always be your servant Siabelle and I will be there for you when the time is right, for the Goddess has spoken to me and we will meet again." Marciana went to the carriage and came back with a gold neckless with a pendant showing the image of the goddess. "If you ever need my help, send me this necklace. I will know that the message comes from you, and I shall do everything in my power to assist you." She also handed Siabelle an expensive Roman lady's travelling gown, finely woven from red wool as a gift to wear or sell at her discretion. Siabelle could not see the need for such a garment and almost refused it as it just added to her burden but something about Marciana made her accept the gift. If the high priestess felt the need to give her the gown it was probably wise to accept it.

Suddenly they heard shouts from a party of Roman Auxiliary Legionnaires on the road.

"Go now Siabelle with my love and blessings. I shall ensure that you are not pursued, and I shall enlist the service of these Legionnaires to continue my journey to Verulamium. They will not refuse a request from a high priestess of the Goddess Venus."

Siabelle took one last glance at the extraordinary Roman priestess, before darting back through the hedge and heading towards the safety of a coppice. True to her word, the priestess ensured that there was no pursuit of Siabelle as she slipped back off the road to continue her journey. She skirted the lands to the west where the Island of Mona was to be found and headed north. Mona had been the centre of learning for Druids for the Britonic and for other Celtic tribes. The island had been nearly overcome by forces of the Roman Governor Paulinus before queen Boudicca's uprising had forced him to turn back and face her warriors in battle. Since then, the Druids had slowly been regaining their strength and influence on the island.

The tribe of the Trinovante took counsel from the Druids and her father seldom made any important decisions without taking the advice and interpretation of the omens from his close friend the Druid Brachollis. She had been fond of Brachollis and she was saddened by the thought that he would almost certainly have been put to death by the Romans. Hundreds of Druids had been slaughtered by the Romans after Boudicca's revolt as the victors both feared and despised the Druids in equal measure.

The Romans rightly believed that many of the Druids encouraged the native tribes to rise up against their Roman oppressors and they also challenged Roman law with Celtic laws that had been handed down through oral tradition for countless generations. This was why Paulinus had been so determined to destroy the centre of learning in Mona. It could take up to twenty years for a Druid to be able to learn and recite the essential knowledge and wisdom to be considered worthy of the name. Although Siabelle was fond of Brachollis she did not generally trust the Druids. She had heard of others that were vain and corrupt and of some that practiced the dark arts of the necromancer.

As she approached the lands of the Brigantes, Siabelle decided she needed to adopt an appearance that would announce her status as a fighter and warrior. The Romans depended on mounted imperial messengers in order to coordinate the administration and organisation of the empire. There were two new Roman outposts at Eboracum in the East and Deva in the West reinforcing their presence on the borders of the unconquered lands of the Brigantes. These were joined by a major Roman track that was being rapidly developed into a proper road from both ends by the Roman military engineers. She decided that this was the best place to ambush an imperial messenger with the intention of stealing his horse and armour.

Siabelle took out the beautiful gown given to her by Marciana. She cleansed herself in a stream, put on the gown, put her hair up in a Roman style and took up a position on a hill where she could observe the road for a good distance in both directions. After several hours during which she had only seen a column of auxiliaries escorting supplies for the outposts, she saw a lone rider coming along the road at speed. She hurried down to the track and stumbled along the road towards the rider giving all the appearance of a Roman lady of rank in distress. The rider saw Siabelle and slowed his horse as he warily approached. He was an experienced legionnaire and was all too aware of the dangers of ambush on these open stretches of road. He looked carefully around for any signs of hostiles and listened carefully for movements in the bracken that lined the side of the hill.

When Siabelle called out to him in fluent Latin he allowed himself to relax and turn his attention to this lady in distress.

"What has happened lady?" he asked her.

Siabelle, pretending to be gasping for breath, explained that her party had been attacked and her guards slain before collapsing down on one knee in front of the messenger feigning weakness. The messenger dismounted and ran towards her to offer her support but as he reached his arm out to her, she grabbed it with her left hand and stabbed him in the right side of his groin with the hidden gladius severing an artery in the process.

The messenger leapt back instinctively, his combat training kicking in and he drew his spatha, his long cavalry sword and swung it at Siabelle's exposed neck. She expertly parried the blow with the gladius and leapt backwards to put some distance between them. Although fatally wounded the messenger was still a danger but she had no need to engage with him further as his wound prevented him from speedily closing on her.

Within a few seconds the rapid loss of blood overcame the messenger and he collapsed to his knees, his head falling face first into the dust of the road. As a precaution Siabelle thrust the gladius into the back of his neck to ensure that he was truly beyond resistance. She gathered the horse and tying the ankles of the messenger to the reins, she used the horse to help drag the body away from the track into a wooded area that shielded her from being observed. Then she quickly stripped the soldier of his black leather body armour. It was not a perfect size but fortunately the messenger was relatively slim and with a bit of work she would be able to tailor the armour to be a better fit.

She examined the scrolls in the saddlebag. They were largely boring dealing with the usual excuses for the late payment of wages to the soldiers and complaints about the tardiness of the garrison in completing the fortification of the outpost. There was however one scroll which was far more interesting. It confirmed that two cohorts of soldiers, about 700 men, from the Garrison of Legion IX Hispana at Eboracum would join a large supply column from Deva in ten days' time to raid and plunder deep into the Brigante territory. The Roman Governor was keen to put pressure on the aging Venutius to resubmit to Roman authority and wanted constant incursions into the lands of the Brigantes to help persuade him. There was a forward outpost where the two cohorts would be rested and resupplied before a planned week of incursion with the intention of stealing cattle, collecting slaves, damaging crops, and destroying villages.

Siabelle dragged the now stripped body of the messenger back to the track and left the saddlebag with the scrolls spilt out before it. She wanted the Romans to think that the messenger had been robbed and killed for his money, armour, and horse but that the robbers saw the scrolls as worthless. She hoped that the Romans would believe that their planned raid was still a secret and viable as very few native Britons could read Latin.

Siabelle had learnt to be an expert rider during her time as the daughter of a Trinovante chief and the messenger's horse soon responded to her confidence. She rode quickly towards the Brigante lands, skirting the Roman outposts that were springing up near the borders. She wanted to be absolutely sure that she would not be mistaken for a Roman and met with an arrow rather than a greeting as she entered Brigante territory. As a sensible precaution she discarded the messenger's helmet and let her long black hair blow behind her in the wind as she galloped into the lands where the tribes of Britannia were still free from the Roman yoke.

Siabelle had not travelled far before her path was blocked by three Brigante warriors and she brought the horse to a standstill. She glanced behind to see that her exit was blocked by two more warriors.

"Well, this is a strange sight" chuckled one of the warriors. "We appear to have a Roman messenger that has magically transformed into woman." Unlike the women of the native tribes, Roman women were never allowed to fight and so the figure of a woman dressed for combat on a Roman horse was quite an extraordinary spectacle.

Siabelle retorted in her distinct Trinovante accent, "Is this the usual Brigante greeting for weary travellers? I had heard that the Brigante were famous for the warmth of their hospitality, but it seems that they prefer to act like common brigands."

The warrior who had spoken smiled at Siabelle, he admired her spirit and the way her eyes challenged him.

"Sadly, these are not usual times" he said. "You have travelled far from your homeland, what brings a woman of the Trinovante so far to the North?" Although it was a fair question Siabelle knew she was not the first refugee from the South who had escaped from the Romans. Equally he knew that amongst their number were Roman spies and there was no way that Siabelle was going to be allowed to ride into the lands of the Brigante without being questioned.

"I have come here to kill Romans" she said.

The warrior roared with laughter at this. "I am sure the Romans will be terrified at the prospect."

"I have killed many Romans" she replied, "perhaps I also have a duty to teach a Brigante oaf some manners too." With this she expertly dismounted and stood facing the warrior with her hands on her hips in defiance.

The warrior roared with laughter again. He gestured to one of the other warriors. "Let's see if the fire in this woman is limited to her tongue or whether it extends to her sword arm too."

The warrior drew his sword and confidently approached Siabelle. Siabelle expertly drew the Roman spatha and adopted a crouched position. She knew that this was not a mortal contest but if she did not show skill, she would not earn respect. Without respect she would not get the opportunity to talk to a Brigante leader and tell them about the planned Roman raid.

The warrior thrust his sword towards her chest. She quickly parried the blow and made a cut for his neck forcing him to quickly step back. He smiled and licked his lips in anticipation. This was going to be interesting, more interesting than he had thought.

Siabelle and the warrior continued to exchange blows and test each other for a couple of minutes before she decided that she had put on a sufficient exhibition, and it was time finish it. The warrior aimed another blow towards her head but instead of parrying as he expected, she side-stepped so the blow missed and was over extended and she rolled forward slapping the flat of her blade at the back of the warrior's knee before springing upwards again in readiness. This was one of the manoeuvres taught to her by the gladiators and if she had used the edge of the blade it would have severed the tendon, completely incapacitating her opponent.

"Enough" called out the warrior who had first spoken and who was obviously the leader of the men.

He bowed to Siabelle in recognition of her skill. "Forgive my impertinence warrior" he said to her. "My name is Ceravantrix, I am one of the sons of Venutius and it is my honour to offer you our hospitality."

Siabelle bowed back and slid the spatha back into its scabbard. "I am Siabelle of the Trinovantes. It is an honour to meet the son of Venutius, whose courage and strength in defiance of the Romans has brought great honour to your people. I also bring important news of an imminent threat and would share this with your war counsel if you would permit it?"

4

Ceravantrix was impressed by this startling woman who had so brazenly challenged them and had displayed such skill with the sword. He decided that she had earned the right to be heard and leaving the other warriors to guard the track he rode with Siabelle to the hillside fortification where Venutius and the other elders were holding court.

Siabelle was in awe at the size of the huge hill fort from where Venutius and the tribal council administered the lands of the Brigantes. It completely dominated the surrounding area and she suddenly felt rather daunted at the prospect of a meeting with Venutius and her sheer audacity at asking for such an audience.

When they had ascended through the fort, they came to a large central area with many impressive roundhouses, which was dominated by a huge main hall. Siabelle made sure that her horse was well tended and accepted Ceravantrix's hospitality in his impressively large home. Ceravantrix's servants prepared a meal for her and she chatted with his wife about her experience with the Roman messenger and her meeting with Ceravantrix.

After about an hour Ceravantrix returned and asked her to accompany him to the huge hall where the counsel had been summoned. Before they entered Ceravantrix put out his hand for her sword. "I am sorry, but I have seen what you can do with that."

Siabelle stiffened and put her hand to the hilt but quickly realised that Ceravantrix was completely right in protecting his lord and she slowly pulled the spatha out of its scabbard and handed him the blade. For good measure she also handed him her pugio, the small Roman dagger that she kept concealed beneath her cloak.

They entered the hall which was built of huge timbers with a vaulted arched roof. The counsel sat around a long rectangular table made from oak planks with Venutius at its head. He gestured for Siabelle to sit in a space near the top of the table on one of the padded benches that were placed along the sides. Siabelle bowed low and took up her place on the table. Ceravantrix sat opposite her on the other side of the table. There were about twenty elders sat around the table, both men and women and many showed scars as a result of many years of conflict.

Siabelle thought Venutius looked old and tired and would possibly be not long for this world. She considered whether Ceravantrix might succeed him as tribal chief, but this was by no means certain. It was the custom amongst most of the Britonic tribes that a leader was chosen on merit rather than by any birth right, although being the son of a successful chieftain was certainly no handicap.

Siabelle explained the contents of the Roman scroll and the plan for the two cohorts of legionnaires to rendezvous at the Roman fort in ten days' time. She did not know the location of the fort, but the counsel quickly identified its probable location as there was only one Roman fortification substantial enough to accommodate two cohorts that was sufficiently close to their lands. They quickly devised a plan to ambush the Romans at their rendezvous which would require the taking of the fort before the arrival of the Roman cohorts.

One of the women challenged the decision to act on Siabelle's information. "We do not know whether this is a trap. How do we know whether this stranger is not a Roman spy?"

Siabelle acknowledged the legitimacy of the woman's concern. "I shall accompany any expedition to the fort and shall prove myself in battle. Let the blood of the Romans on my blade be my bond of good faith."

Some members of the counsel pounded their fists on the table in applause. The Brigantes valued courage above all else and this Trinovante warrior had impressed them.

Two days later 500 Brigante warriors made their way towards the Roman fort. They hid in the trees beyond the large defensive clearing that the Romans had made around the fort to protect it from ambush. There was also a small transient settlement outside the boundary of the fort where various tradespeople made a living supplying the Romans with goods and services.

The Brigante observed the movements of the garrison and estimated that it was no more than a centuria which usually numbered eighty men but even so, an assault on the fort would cause a lot of casualties which they could not afford if they were to remain strong enough to deal with the cohorts expected in seven days. They needed to find a way into the fort without alerting the guards. Ceravantrix knew that the Romans would have to bolster the forts supplies if it was to meet the needs of two cohorts amounting to about 800 legionnaires. He decided to capture one of the supply columns.

They set an ambush on the road but needed to be patient as there was no movement on the track for the rest of the day. Ceravantrix was beginning to wonder whether the Romans had been sufficiently alarmed by the ambush of the messenger by Siabelle that they had decided to call off the expedition. His fears were quickly allayed when the following morning one of the Brigante scouts rode back saying that a large supply column guarded by about twenty auxiliaries was approaching from the South. This told Ceravantrix that the Romans did not suspect that their plans had been discovered. It also revealed that they were reassuringly complacent about the threat posed by the Brigantes this far south by posting such a relatively small guard.

The Brigante warriors made quick work of dispatching the supply column guards, ambushing them with arrow and spear from the cover of the trees without losing a single warrior. Amongst the supply column was a wagon with seven prostitutes who were being sent to the fort. This gave Ceravantrix an idea. The supply column was led by a Roman Tesserarius, a junior officer who had been delegated to take command of the auxiliaries who made up the rest of the guard. One of Brigante warriors spoke a bit of Latin and with luck could pass as a Roman auxiliary. Auxiliaries were recruited from across the empire and therefore a poor command of Latin was not at all uncommon in their ranks.

The Roman supply column guards were stripped of their uniforms and the Brigante warriors dressed up as best they could as legionnaires. They would certainly not pass close inspection but hopefully they would not need to. As with the poor command of the language, rather exotic looking foreign auxiliary legionnaires were not an uncommon sight. Ceravantrix also had no intention of letting the guards in the fort get too close a look at the supply column until it was too late.

The Roman sentries at the fort were delighted at the sight of a wagon approaching the fort led by an officer with seven prostitutes laughing on top of it. The main supply wagons were following about fifty paces behind, but the sentries showed little interest in them as one of the prostitutes lifted up her top revealing an ample bosom and began to swing her breasts at him whilst winking seductively.

"She seems to have taken a fancy to you" said the Brigante impersonating the Roman Tesserarius from his horse.

"We'll try to make her comfortable" replied the guard waving for the gates to be opened so that the wagon and the following column could be admitted. The wagon rolled forward through the gate but suddenly stopped, preventing the gate from being closed again.

The sentry frowned and then cried out in alarm as seven sword wielding prostitutes leapt from the wagon screaming war cries. His cry was cut short as

Siabelle's sword plunged into his throat. Within seconds the rest of the warriors in the supply column rushed up to join the fray and the Brigante cavalry rushed in from their concealment in the trees at the edge of the clearing to rapidly join the fray. The short bloody battle was over within minutes and a huge cheer went up from the Brigante warriors as they celebrated their victory. Siabelle nearly fell over as Ceravantrix slapped her on the back.

"I think those clothes are rather becoming" he said as she turned laughing with defiance glinting in her eyes. She presented quite a spectacle with one blood splattered breast hanging out of the torn dress that she had taken from one of the prostitutes. Her face was also covered in Roman blood from the battle and she still held the bloodied spatha in her hand.

"Don't get any ideas" she retorted "unless you want your ability to seed children to end suddenly and painfully" she pointed the blade of the spatha at his groin to emphasize the point.

Ceravantrix roared with laughter again, he was in high spirits, the capture of the fort had been far less difficult than he had imagined and only three Brigante warriors were too injured to continue fighting.

There was however the small matter of the arrival of two cohorts of experienced Roman legionnaires from Legio IX Hispana to deal with, so they had little time to enjoy their victory.

The Brigantes lay in ambush for the legionnaires and harassed the column all day as it made its way towards the fort, picking off soldiers with spears and arrows and then melting back into the trees when the Romans organised to attack them. The Romans had already suffered significant losses when to their relief they saw the sanctuary of the fort with the reassuringly familiar helmets of the Roman guards showing above the parapets.

The senior Centurion in charge of the two cohorts backed them up to the gates of the fort so that any advancing Brigante warriors would be met by an invincible wall of shields. They were still being assailed by arrows and javelins from the Brigantes from the safety of the trees, but the confidence gained through years of harsh training prevailed. The legionnaires held firm in their defence formation, their shields largely protecting them from the hail of missiles. Suddenly a flaming arrow was launched from the treeline, the fort gates burst open, and two hundred frenzied Brigantes, led by a dementedly screaming Siabelle charged into the exposed rear of the cohorts.

At the same time, the remaining three hundred warriors attacked the front of the Roman formation. Although the Romans initially outnumbered the Brigantes the bulk of their number were uselessly contained, packed together within the centre of the formation so that the Roman legionnaires at the front and the back were heavily outnumbered. The victory was total, and the Romans were slaughtered to a man. Ceravantrix's last act was to torch the fort as a final gesture of defiance towards the Roman invaders.

Siabelle was left with a permanent reminder of the ferocity of the battle. The Roman gladius was primarily a thrusting weapon but in a wild backward swing from a Roman legionnaire in the close melee that followed the initial charge from the fort, the tip of his weapon had caught Siabelle's face. The blade had narrowly missed her left eye but left a deep wound which healed to leave her with a vivid scar from her forehead to the top of her cheek. The scar made her look even more formidable and intimidating to her foes but also made her far too easy to identify for those who held a grudge against her.

5

Siabelle spent the next four years fighting in the border wars against the Romans, but despite their many victories it was becoming apparent that the Romans were getting stronger, and the constant warfare was taking its toll on the Brigantes. Shortly after the slaughter of the Roman cohorts at the fort, Venutius died and Ceravantrix was indeed selected as the next leader by the council of elders. Siabelle became one of his most trusted advisors as well as his most successful commander of warriors during their frequent battles with the Romans and an increasing number of warriors conscripted into their service from vassal tribes.

Despite many attempts by the men of the Brigantes, Siabelle recoiled at the thought of any intimacy with a man, and she gained a reputation for often being cold and distant. She kept the horrors that had led her to this emotional dissonance to herself, she did not want to reveal any aspect of her past that could be seen and exploited as a vulnerability. She knew that there were wounds deep within her that would never heal but she needed to survive, and she bore emotional armour as well as the physical armour she wore in battle.

There were those within the Brigante who sought to exploit the simmering discontent that was resulting from the deprivations caused by fighting the Romans. There was one group in particular, led by a man called Aristartes who gained his influence from wealth accumulated by trading. Although Ceravantrix had forbidden overt trading with the Romans it was well known that Aristartes and many other traders largely ignored this order. The increasing demand for goods from the empire also meant that there was little desire within the tribe to enforce Ceravantrix's decree.

There was a growing minority of people within the tribe that felt that they would be better off coming to terms with the Romans and becoming a vassal tribe that accepted the authority of the Roman Governor Sextus Frontinus. Aristartes actively fomented dissent amongst the people through a combination of bribery and stoking their growing fears about the future. He was also in secret talks with the Romans about how to bring down Ceravantrix who would never accept Roman dominion.

One gloomy midwinter evening a shadow emerged from one of Aristartes's wagons that had just returned with a cargo of illicit wine traded with a Roman quartermaster. The shadow belonged to an assassin from the land of the Pharaohs who had been hired by Aristartes through his Roman contacts to solve the problem of Ceravantrix's intransigence. The shadow climbed onto the roof of the great hall and made its way towards the back where Ceravantrix and his family now had their living quarters.

Siabelle was restless that night, she felt a great unease and had, through painful experience, learnt to follow her intuition. She made her way through the round huts and checked in with the guards at the gate of the fortified compound who assured her that all was in order. She then headed back towards the great hall and saw that the guards at its huge oak doors were also in place and alert. Everything looked in order, but her sense of unease was growing.

She decided to walk around the hall and as she reached the far end, she heard a quiet scrabbling noise and she saw the shadow of a figure climbing through one of the small gaps between the roof and the wall that was used for ventilation. She rushed round to the front of the hall and ignoring the startled guards threw open the great doors and raced towards Ceravantrix's quarters at the back. As she burst into his bedchamber, she saw the body of Ceravantrix's wife with her throat cut and a shadowy figure leaning over Ceravantrix with a dagger in its hand. She screamed a warning, but it was too late to stop the thrust, although Ceravantrix's reactionary jolt upwards in response to her cry meant that the blow was not immediately fatal.

Siabelle leapt at the figure whose dagger arm had been grabbed by Ceravantrix and plunged the blade of her own dagger into the back of the assassin. The assassin instinctively wrenched his arm free from Ceravantrix's grip and managed to slice Siabelle's side with a nasty wound before his strength gave way and he succumbed to the loss of blood from the deep wound made by the blade of Siabelle's dagger which was still deeply embedded in his back.

The general alarm had now been sounded and the guards from the door had followed Siabelle into Ceravantrix's quarters and had thrown the body of the assassin to the floor. The assassin's face was covered in strange tattoos, and they looked at his north African complexion with fascination. He had travelled a long way from his homeland to carry out his warped profession. Although Ceravantrix was still alive, both he and Siabelle knew that the wound was going to be fatal. Even after the healing women of the tribe had done their best for him, he had no more than a few days to live.

Siabelle had the wound in her side stitched but it was very painful and inflamed. Ceravantrix dismissed the guards from his bed chamber but gestured to Siabelle to remain.

"Well, we've had a good run" he said to her, grimacing at a sudden stab of pain from his wound. "We could have died so many times on the battlefield together and I find it rather ironic that I am going to die in my own bedchamber."

Siabelle angrily wiped away a tear that had escaped from her eye and run down her cheek. Warriors do not cry she silently rebuked herself as another tear followed.

"Listen Siabelle, you have to get away from here tonight. I can hold the loyalty of the warriors of my personal guard whilst I am alive but when I am gone Aristartes will bribe his way to influence, and you will not be safe. He would gladly conspire to hand you back to the Romans to win their favour and the fate of any escaped slave is well understood. I would not see you end your days that way."

Siabelle started to protest but he raised a hand to silence her. He paused as another spasm of pain wracked his body before speaking. "It has been a great privilege to fight with you against the accursed Romans, but my fight here has ended, and your destiny now lies elsewhere. It will bring me some comfort to know that your blade will still be seeking out the blood of our enemies. I have fought my last battle in this life I now yearn to join my ancestors in the otherworld where perhaps our paths may yet cross again."

Siabelle said nothing more, instead she grasped his arm and they smiled to each other with an understanding that only those who have faced death together many times on the battlefield would truly comprehend.

6

Before the first light of the weak winter sun had streaked the sky to the east, Siabelle had ridden through the gates and left the hilltop stronghold of the Chief of the Brigantes for the last time. She also knew that some of the tribal leaders of the Brigantes would almost certainly refuse to give up their freedom without a struggle, but she acknowledged that Ceravantrix had been right and that she was no longer safe. Aristartes hated her influence and how she had conspired with Ceravantrix to constrain his ambition and she somehow knew that he was complicit in the arrival of the assassin.

There was uncertainty as to who would succeed Ceravantrix but the tribal bonds that had held the Brigantes together were under increasing pressure, and this suited the ambitions of the Romans and their many collaborators. It was the inability of the tribes of Britannia to join together in organised opposition to the Roman military machine that had been the greatest contribution to Roman success, despite the invaders being so heavily outnumbered. The Romans and their vassals would continue with their relentless conquest picking off one tribe at a time whilst sowing the seeds of division and dissent. There were many opportunists like Aristartes amongst the Britons to aid their cause.

Siabelle decided to head towards the remote mountainous lands of the Carvetii who she believed might continue to hold out against Romans if the Brigantes fell, their weak allegiance to the tribe being opportunistic at best. She rode through the day but the wound in her side was becoming more and more painful and inflamed and pus began to seep out between the stitches. By the following day she had a fever and had started hallucinating, she was sure that there were shadows in the forests watching her. She was now so weak that she struggled to remain in the saddle. She was also lost; her horse was instinctively following a track through the trees that grew in abundance in the fertile valleys and on the lower slopes of the mountains, but she had no idea where she was.

The horse walked into a clearing and through her blurred vision Siabelle saw the outline of a figure in front of her. Convinced that she was being ambushed she tried to draw the spatha, the sword she had kept ever since she took it from the Roman messenger all those years ago, but it felt too heavy. A look of puzzlement came over her eyes and then she fell from her horse unconscious.

Chyrenia rushed over to the fallen warrior and saw the bloodstain seeping through her clothing. She pulled out a large hollow shell attached to a long chord and began to swing it around her head until it started to make a deep thrumming noise that resonated through the woods. It was the alarm call of the High Priestess of the Gallancia and all who heard it would immediately come to her assistance.

They carried Siabelle to Chyrenia's hut where she began the task of trying to heal this startling looking woman warrior who was now so close to death. Although Chyrenia could see that her wound was highly inflamed and was seeping pus she immediately sensed that there was more to the fever than just the effect of the septic wound. It had been no ordinary blade that had made this wound, there had been an evil associated with this weapon and she sensed that the corruption had been passed from the blade into the woman's body. After dressing the wound with a compress of medicinal herbs she put the Moonstone around her neck and began to generate the healing energy within her hands, amplified by the power of the stone.

She placed her hands on the head of the wounded warrior and channelled the energy flowing from her hands into the woman's body. Immediately she felt resistance, something corrupt was trying to block her energy and she could feel it trying to push back into her through her hands. This was an evil and powerful force, whoever had inflicted this wound was a master of the dark arts but even this powerful a force could not resist Chyrenia and the power of the Moonstone. The Moonstone became translucent as Chyrenia focused the healing power of love through her hands and she felt the corruption beginning to give way. Siabelle's pulse began to grow stronger and match Chyrenia's as their two bodies synchronised and became as one.

Thousands of miles away in Rome, a blind priest in the Temple of the Black crystal smiled. It was the evil of the Black Crystal that had cursed the assassin's blade and the priest sensed the power of a Moonstone as the evil was driven out of Siabelle's body. Soon the servants of the Temple would be sent on their way to Britannia to find and destroy it. The days of the last Moonstones were numbered, and the power of the Black Crystal continued to rise in the east.

It took many weeks for Siabelle to regain her strength. At first, she was suspicious of the charismatic woman who was healing her. She sensed Chyrenia's power but did not understand it as it was a very different strength to Siabelle's own martial skill or the crushing power of the Roman oppressors. Chyrenia's power seemed to come from nature itself, as if she were a human conduit for all the energy that surrounded her in her woodland glade. There was a serenity in this place, so different from the hostile environments that had so vividly scarred and hardened Siabelle.

Strangely Siabelle found the love and kindness shown to her by Chyrenia the most difficult to cope with at first. She had been adopted and protected by the gladiators, but they were still violent men who would meet violent deaths. Siabelle had found herself physically repulsed by men after her rape at the hands of the Roman auxiliaries. Long forgotten feelings and emotions began to stir within her as Chyrenia's gentle touch and kindness not only began to heal her body but also began to heal her deep emotional wounds too.

Siabelle had buried all thoughts of love and affection and she protected her emotional wounds with the scar tissue of hate and anger which she physically expressed through acts of brutal violence against the Romans and their allies. The resurgence of long buried yearnings made her feel exposed and vulnerable in a way that she had not felt since her brutal abduction at the age of fifteen. Chyrenia's beautiful green eyes seemed to be able to look into her very soul. Siabelle felt exposed as the shadows that lurked within were driven back by the power of Chyrenia's love and compassion.

One warm sunny afternoon three moons after Chyrenia had first found Siabelle passed out in the wood, Chyrenia was bathing the red puckered scar that had now formed over the dagger wound caused by the accursed blade of the assassin. Siabelle had recovered much of her strength, and she was feeling happier than at any time she could remember since the first dark day of her enslavement. The inactivity and plentiful food had changed her emaciated stricken body, her breasts had filled out, there were many more inches around her hips and thighs and the muscles of her once taut belly were now hidden beneath a delightful curve.

Chyrenia ran her hand over the slight swell of Siabelle's belly and she took a particular delight in pointing out how delightfully rounded it had become. Siabelle responded by splashing cold water from the stream over Chyrenia's head which ran down her gently waved auburn hair and trickled down her lower back. The cold water was a shock in the warm summer sunshine and Chyrenia responded by giving Siabelle a shove that sent her backwards into the cold pool of water. Chyrenia leapt up and started to run back towards her roundhouse shrieking with laughter and with some trepidation at the inevitable retribution that was surely on its way.

Chyrenia had barely made fifty strides before she was caught, and the two women rolled in the grass together until Chyrenia was firmly pinned down on her back as Siabelle looked down on her in triumph. Siabelle looked into Chyrenia's captivating green eyes that sparkled with amusement and she had a stark realisation. She had fallen completely in love with this magical, caring, and compassionate woman who had brought her back from the jaws of death and had asked nothing in return.

She slowly lowered her lips to Chyrenia's which parted slightly in anticipation and the two women kissed. Their lips parted and Siabelle saw her own love reflected back at her from the beautiful woman that lay beneath her. These feelings were new and unfamiliar, and she was uncertain how to express feelings that she had suppressed for so long. Chyrenia raised her head and kissed Siabelle again, a long tender kiss and she ran her fingers through Siabelle's long wet hair. Gently Chyrenia turned the now yielding Siabelle over onto her back and straddled her. She bent over and kissed her again and again, first on the lips and she then progressed down her still powerful and muscular body. Her lips lingered on Siabelle's breasts, her tongue teasing nipples that had stiffened from the chill of the gentle breeze blowing across their still wet tips, and from Siabelle's growing arousal.

This was so very different to any sexual experience Siabelle had ever known. She was completely enchanted by the gentleness of Chyrenia's touch, her rounded curvaceous body, and the softness of her skin. This was a complete contrast to the brutal physical abuse from rough calloused hands and bristled faces that had always been her experience of sex with men.

Chyrenia's tongue sought out the sensitive button hidden under its small protecting hood at the top of Siabelle's vulva and hundreds of nerve endings tingled in response causing her moist lips to part in anticipation. Chyrenia's tongue eagerly took up the invitation and delved deeper. Siabelle gently clasped the back of Chyrenia's head and drew her closer still. In a few moments she was giving in to the first climax she had ever experienced, and she cried out in ecstasy as these unfamiliar sensations reached their crescendo.

Chyrenia drew away and she moved her leg between Siabelle's until their vulvas were firmly pressed together and the two women gently rocked themselves, their breathing becoming faster and the urgency of their movement increasing until they climaxed together. Chyrenia rolled onto her back and Siabelle lay down next to her with her head on the soft smooth flesh of Chyrenia's breast. Chyrenia gently caressed Siabelle's hair until she fell into a contented sleep under the warming rays of the sun.

From that moment the two women became partners and lovers and four years later Siabelle was still totally captivated by the extraordinary, magical, compassionate woman who had saved her life and revealed to her the nature of love.

The other members of the tribe were at first wary of this strange female warrior who had appeared within their midst. There were many Roman spies, and this had tested the Gallancia's natural inclination to show a welcome and give hospitality to travellers. Nobody in the tribe would however challenge Chyrenia's judgement, particularly when her partnership to Siabelle had been blessed and celebrated by the other twelve sisters of the Moonstone. Very quickly the Gallacian warriors learnt to respect Siabelle's judgement on matters of war and conflict and she soon became a trusted adviser to Kernack and eventually a member of the tribal council.

To the Scoti raiders, Romans and others who came into conflict with the Gallancia, Siabelle became known as the Shadow Warrior. Despite her discovery of the wonder of love in the embrace of Chyrenia she was still the same formidable and ruthless warrior whose skills had been forged by countless battles. Her seething hatred of the Romans in particular remained undiminished. She rapidly became a source of fear and myth to enemies of the tribe foolish enough to stray into Gallacian territory and many fell victim to her stealthy predation.

7

The Druid Drigwold seethed with indignation as he stood before the Druid Council in their stronghold on the island of Mona. The Druids on Mona had almost been wiped out by the campaign against them by Suetonius Paulinus and they were only saved by the timely rebellion by queen Boudicca of the Iceni which had forced Paulinus to withdraw his forces. In the intervening years, the Druid presence on the island had grown again. Scholars from the tribes of Brittania and Celtic peoples from distant lands that were still free of the yoke of Roman oppression, were again studying the ancient lore.

Drigwold had also learned the sacred lore, but he had always troubled the Druid Council as he had an evil heart. Most Druids used the knowledge and skills of their craft to give guidance to tribal leaders and to settle disputes between them without recourse to armed conflict. Druids were exempt from paying taxes or tributes and from armed service. Anyone harming a Druid would face severe penalties including permanent expulsion from their tribal community, heavy fines or even execution. Druids were held in high regard and were seen by the Romans as a challenge to their power and authority in the administration of the Empire. They were determined to eradicate all traces of the Druids from the lands they had conquered.

There were however a significant minority of Druids who used their art in the service of their own selfishness and ambition and were quite prepared to use evil to harm anyone who stood in their way. Some of these practiced the dark art of necromancy, the communication with the dead through ritual human sacrifice to predict and influence the future. This was a practice that had been forbidden under threat of banishment and expulsion from the order by the Druidic council that had reconvened on Mona after the Roman massacre twenty years before. Drigwold had been discovered with the corpse of a recently executed criminal in a hidden glade on the mainland, examining its entrails to prophesise the future. He had been detained by order of a Druid elder who was in the service of the local Chieftain and sent to the Council for its judgement.

The Druid Council, headed by the elder Sutillious, were about to pass their sentence upon Drigwold and despite his fear he was filled with loathing and resentment. How dare they challenge his right to practise the dark arts of the craft, knowledge of which had been passed down countless generations through oral tradition? He thought the pious banning of the traditional dark arts was making the Druids weak. Part of the respect and caution with which Druids were treated was through fear of the consequences of causing their displeasure. No wonder they were being wiped out by the Romans.

Drigwold admired the Romans, they were ruthless in their ambition and devoid of compassion for those who stood in their way. Drigwold thought compassion was a deep character flaw, a weakness in others that he could use and exploit.

Drigwold was thrown down by two of the guards who served the Council so that he was prostrate before them. Sutillious was dressed in the white robe of the Head of the Council, and he gazed with severity at the figure lying before him. Sutillious had the wisdom to know that those who projected harm towards others were creating negative fates and energies that would come back to damn them in the future. He was sure that it was the widespread use of the dark arts by many Druids that had led to their subsequent defeats by the Romans. He believed that the Romans may have been punitive unknowing agents of the gods and elementals who had become angered by such unnatural practices within the Druidic order.

Sutillious knew in his heart that Drigwold was beyond redemption and his head told him that the safest way to deal with him would be through his execution. He could feel the resentment and hatred projected towards him by Drigwold and he feared the consequences of letting him loose. On the other hand, killing a Druid, even by order of the Council, could also have grave consequences. This could undermine the authority and respect held by the Druidic order and send a signal to frustrated tribal chiefs, resentful of Druidic judgements and interference, that they could openly defy them. The respect, mystery, and awe with which the Druidic order was held must be preserved at all costs, especially in such difficult times where the might of Rome was an existential threat.

After a long pause Sutillious passed the judgement of the Council upon Drigwold. In a loud and commanding voice, he ordered that Drigwold be banished by the order and that all his rights and powers revoked. His name and description would be passed throughout the lands as the name of an outcast who should be shunned and spurned by all who came upon him. He was to be branded as a criminal upon his arm and he should be given forty lashes to drive out the evil that had corrupted his mind.

Drigwold was horrified as he was hauled up to a wooden frame, his cloak stripped from his body, and he trembled in terror before the searing pain of the first lash landed upon him. After about twenty lashes he passed out with the pain and humiliation of his ordeal. After his punishment he was dressed in the old tatty clothing of a peasant worker and taken on the ferry across the short channel of water that separated Mona from the mainland. He was thrown with contempt by the Druidic guard onto the shingle of the shoreline and left in the hands of the Fates.

Drigwold staggered a few paces before collapsing in pain and exhaustion on the muddy bank above the tideline. He awoke to the jarring pain of being kicked hard in the ribs and as he opened his eyes, he found himself looking at the riveted sandals on the feet of a Roman Legionnaire. He screamed in agony as the soldier grabbed his arm on the raw wound of his branding. After he was hauled to his feet, his wrists and ankles were shackled. He stumbled between two legionnaires as he was forcibly hauled to a cart with a wooden cage on top and he was then thrown inside with three other unfortunates who had been captured by the Roman Cavalry scouts who had found him.

A half day's ride later the prison wagon arrived at the headquarters of the Roman legion XX Valeria Victrix, part of the army headed by the recently appointed Roman Governor, Gnaeus Julius Agricola. The decurion in charge of the cavalry detail immediately reported the capture of the prisoners to his senior officer. Agricola had made explicit orders that all prisoners captured near the island of Mona should be immediately interrogated for any knowledge of the Druids remaining on the island.

The description of the wretch who had been so recently whipped and branded intrigued Agricola and the amazed decurion who had captured him soon found himself under the intense gaze of Agricola himself. "Show me the prisoner you picked up at the coast opposite the island of Mona" he demanded. The decurion led Agricola to a small wooden holding cage where the prisoners had been unceremoniously dumped on a floor to lie in their own faeces and urine which had mixed with liquid mud after recent heavy rain. He pointed to a dishevelled figure curled up in the corner.

Showing no regard for the stench, Agricola entered the cage and went over to Drigwold's body. He lifted his head and stared into a virtually lifeless pair of eyes. In a strange tongue that none of the Roman officers understood he asked Drigwold "where is the sacred spring of Aserging?"

"It is only revealed to those of true heart and courage. It is to be found at the base of the sacred mountain of the mists in the Otherworld." came Drigwold's faint reply.

Agricola smiled with grim satisfaction. The tale of the sacred spring was an obscure part of an oral teaching which had been revealed to him under the duress of relentless torture by a Druid. This prisoner's automatic reply showed that he was familiar with the Druidic lore and was almost certainly a Druid from Mona. Equally, his dishevelled condition indicated that he had fallen out of favour and Agricola was going to do everything he could to encourage and feed the prisoner's resentment.

To the astonishment of the decurion, who was certain that such a wretched creature as this useless slave would be quickly despatched, Agricola commanded "this prisoner is to be treated with the greatest of care and respect. He will be bathed, fed, clothed in fine linens, and given his own quarters near to my own. He will be assigned two female slaves skilled in the arts of healing and sexual gratification and I expect him to be recovered and ready for questioning within the week. He is to be guarded day and night and nobody else is to question him under pain of execution. Is that clear?"

As he spoke Agricola turned his head and levelled his eyes at Marcus the wizened centurion who had accompanied him. Marcus immediately raised his right arm in salute as acknowledgement. Marcus was the Primus Pilus, the commanding centurion of the XX Valeria Victrix. Agricola trusted Marcus implicitly and his faith was well placed. They had long campaigned together and on more than one occasion in the heat of bloody battle Marcus had literally saved Agricola's life.

After the brief exchange with Agricola, Drigwold again passed out through dehydration and the stress of his recent ordeals. When he slowly regained consciousness, he frowned in confusion. He had heard many tales of the Otherworld to which spirits were reborn after death, but it was always said that only the truest and noblest of souls would be blessed with such a fate. Even Drigwold had the self-awareness to accept that his warped and twisted soul was anything but noble. How was it that he now found himself lying on a comfortable bed within a spotlessly clean large canvas tent? He had been cleaned and perfumed, his long, matted hair had been combed and the ends trimmed, and two staggeringly beautiful women looked attentively down on him.

He tried to raise his head but found he was too weak, and the women immediately came to his assistance and gently lifted his head up onto a couple of pillows so that he could look around. "Where am I?" he croaked. Neither of the women seemed to understand his question. One brought him some fresh water to ease his throat whilst the other opened the tent to speak to someone outside. A few moments later the tent flap opened, and a huge Roman centurion accompanied by a native Britonic civilian entered.

Drigwold looked into the cold scarred face of the centurion and tried to draw his knees up in a futile defensive gesture, convinced that he was about to be slain. To his surprise the centurion bowed respectfully. He turned to the civilian and spoke to him in Latin. The civilian spoke with the accent of the Iceni, but Drigwold was familiar enough with the dialect to understand what was being said to him.

"Centurion Marcus hopes that you are feeling better and hopes that your quarters are satisfactory" said the translator.

Drigwold was utterly confused at this. Had they mistaken him for a tribal leader or dignitary? Surely not in the tattered soiled clothes that he had been wearing when evicted by the Druidic Council. In his very limited exposure to Roman legionnaires, he had not seen any evidence of their civility to the Britons. This was even more unexpected from the lips of a Roman centurion, widely regarded by the native population as rude, arrogant, and extremely dangerous.

Drigwold looked at the centurion who was patiently waiting for his response. "I am most comfortable and thankful for your kindness" he croaked. "Can I ask where I am?"

The translator exchanged words with the centurion. "You are in the camp of the Roman Legio XX Valeria Victrix as the personal guest of his excellency Governor Gnaeus Julius Agricola. You are to make yourself as comfortable as possible, your servants are tasked to satisfy any of your needs. You may however not leave the tent unless accompanied by centurion Marcus so that he may be assured of your safety. May I ask how you should be addressed?"

Drigwold was not naïve. He was a prisoner of Agricola, and this tent was his perfumed cell. Agricola was ruthless and cunning and Drigwold knew that he was being pampered for a reason. There was however nothing that he could do about it for the moment, so he decided to make the most of his luxuriant captivity. He was fed tender meats and breads, exquisite imported Roman wine and after a few days he began to take delight in inflicting his perverse sexual deviances on the two poor slaves who were bound to serve him.

During his visits Marcus started to note the bruising and wheals on the girls' bodies and his jaw tightened in anger. He had often taken part in the rape and abuse of captive women during his campaigns, this was an intrinsic part of the art of war, but even he was disgusted by Drigwold's excesses. He was however under strict instructions not to intervene, so he ignored the imploring eyes of the slaves and did not pass comment on Drigwold's behaviour although he did make Agricola aware. Agricola had insisted that he was informed about everything the Druid said and did and the Druid's behaviour told him a lot about the character of the man.

After a week of convalescing Drigwold was dressed in clean, new, woollen native clothing and brought under armed guard to the luxurious wooden quarters of Governor Agricola. Agricola was sat on a campaign chair and at first, he completely ignored Drigwold as he read and signed a couple of scrolls. He then ordered everyone from the room including Marcus. The only person left was a man dressed in clothing from the land of the Pharaohs in the Eastern Empire with strange tattoos covering his face and hands.

To his complete surprise Agricola addressed Drigwold in his native tongue. "I hope you will forgive the flaws in my use of your language" he said, "I have made it my business to practice it every day since coming to these islands. I suspect you are trying to guess why I have had you treated so well and what I am going to ask you in return?"

"I am your servant" replied Drigwold bowing his head low in subservience.

"Indeed, you are Drigwold" said Agricola and he looked with a cold penetrating stare deep into Drigwold's eyes. Drigwold immediately averted his gaze and Agricola smiled in satisfaction. This creature was as weak as Marcus had described, he felt empowered to abuse helpless women but was actually pathetic when challenged. This suited Agricola perfectly as he planned to manipulate Drigwold for his own ends through the Druid's pathetic vanity and very justifiable fear.

Agricola questioned Drigwold about why he was found in such a pitiable condition and how he had ended up on the shoreline where he had been detained by the decurion. At first Drigwold was reticent to share his tale with the Roman out of a lingering hostility to the invaders but was encouraged by Agricola's show of genuine interest in his tale. Agricola's relaxed conversation and Drigwold's own vanity at having the complete attention of such a prestigious person soon overcame his caution. Eventually he even talked about his necromancy and was surprised at the relaxed look on Agricola's face as he relayed his experiences of interpreting the entrails of the slain. All the time the strange Egyptian sat motionless and inscrutable whilst Drigwold told his story.

"This is what I received after a lifetime of dedicated service" snarled Drigwold as he gingerly pulled up his sleeve showing the fresh scab over the brand of the rune of an outlaw by judgement of the Druidic Council. Agricola looked at this with interest as a plan started to develop in his mind.

Agricola suddenly interrupted, "What can you tell me of the Moonstone?"

Drigwold caught in mid flow paused with his mouth open. There was just a bit too long a pause before he replied. "I know nothing of a Moonstone excellency."

Agricola glanced at the Egyptian who gave the briefest of nods, Drigwold was lying, this was excellent, the myths were true, there was a Moonstone on Mona.

"Perhaps it was called something else, a sacred stone, or perhaps a runestone?"

"No excellency, I have never heard of such a stone" said Drigwold nervously, this time his denial was too quick.

"An oval stone, perhaps the size of a duck's egg?" continued Agricola.

Drigwold squirmed, it was obvious that Agricola did not believe him, but the Moonstone was the most sacred and secretive possession of the Druidic Council and even with his sense of betrayal he was not yet prepared to share this knowledge with the Roman. The Moonstone had power and he was loath to help the invaders in their conquest of Britannia. How could Agricola even know of it? Very few had seen the stone as it was only brought out at the time of the sacred lunar esbats at the time of the full moon, a powerful time for magic. He had only seen the Moonstone once when he had crept up to witness the ceremony and he had seen the stone shining with a brilliant radiance on top of Sutillious's staff. It was an ancient stone rumoured to have come from distant lands at the dawn of time and Drigwold suddenly took a renewed interest in the silent Egyptian and gave him the briefest of glances. Agricola noted the glance and, although his face revealed nothing, his excitement grew.

"I am sorry your Excellency, I really can't think of any stone that meets your description" squirmed Drigwold.

"Oh, now that is a shame" replied Agricola, "I really am very disappointed with you. I was thinking of asking my friend here to jog your memory, but I have thought of a better plan. Marcus!" Agricola barked out the centurion's name so that it could be heard outside the doors of his quarters.

After the centurion entered, Agricola instructed Marcus to strip Drigwold, chain him and suspend him from the two rings attached to a ceiling beam. Drigwold had not noticed the restraints and his brief confidence immediately left him as he started to moan with fear. His feet were also shackled about two feet apart to a heavy metal bar making him completely helpless.

"Fetch the two slaves that have been serving this wretch" Agricola ordered.

The two terrified female slaves were brought into Agricola's quarters.

"Don't be frightened" said Agricola in a calm friendly voice, "I have been shocked to learn about your appalling treatment at the hands of this dreadful man and I have decided to offer you a chance of restitution. You can do whatever you want to him with my complete blessing, short of actually killing him."

Agricola had at first thought of using the skills of the Egyptian priest to extract the information he wanted from Drigwold. The Egyptian had never failed and was greatly skilled in the arts of torture whilst maintaining the victim's life, but he would not need such skills to get the information he needed from as weak and pitiful a creature as Drigwold. He enjoyed the thought of the additional humiliation that would be suffered by Drigwold to be tortured at the hands of a slave.

One of the female slaves just cowered in terror on the floor, intuitively aware of the danger she was in, but the anger in the other slave overcame her awe of Agricola. She walked up to a now terrified Drigwold and spat in his face. Then she walked over to Marcus and whispered in his ear and a cruel smile appeared on the centurion's lips. He went to one of the guards at the entrance to Agricola's quarters and shortly later the guard re-appeared with a large tapered wooden phallus like object that must have been a foot long and two hand widths in circumference at its fullest girth.

Marcus handed this to the slave girl, his smile now a wicked grin.

The girl went up to Marcus and screamed into his face in Latin "you remember how much you enjoyed using this on me you pig? You remember how you delighted at hearing my cries and pleas for mercy? Now I will share in your pleasure!"

Although Drigwold did not understand her words he completely understood her intentions and he begged Agricola to stop her, but the Governor just smiled.

Drigwold screamed in agony as the slave started to force the tapered end of the wooden phallus into his rectum. It was far too large to be accommodated and his flesh began to tear under the abuse as the slave redoubled her efforts, twisting the phallus as she forced it in, her rage from her abuse at Drigwold's hands driving her on.

Agricola and Marcus were completely unmoved by Drigwold's screams as blood began to trickle down the insides of his legs. Eventually Drigwold could take no more and he cried out to Agricola "I know of the Moonstone."

At first Agricola ignored Drigwold's pleas for his ordeal to end and as he begged to confess, his torment continued. The Druid had a harsh lesson to learn about the consequences of defying the will of the Governor. After Drigwold screamed out his knowledge of the Moonstone for the third time Agricola finally glanced at Marcus and gave a short nod. Marcus grabbed hold of the shoulders of the slave girl and pulled her away from Drigwold, the phallus left firmly embedded in his torn rectum. The slave continued to glare at Drigwold with pure hatred still blazing from her eyes. Drigwold's blood was now beginning to pool on the floor around his feet.

"You have a choice to make Drigwold" said Agricola with an air of indifference that hid his growing excitement at Drigwold's confession. "You can either become a true servant of Rome in which case you shall be handsomely rewarded for your service, or you will die at the hands of this slave. Be very careful how you answer because it is the only time I will make this offer."

Drigwold's residual loyalty to the Druid Council and any retribution he might face for his treachery was completely overcome by his excruciating pain and fear. Drigwold's only true loyalty was his own self-interest and he realised that his future destiny was now firmly aligned to Agricola's.

"I humbly beg to be a servant of Rome" he pleaded.

"Excellent choice" said Agricola. He turned to Marcus and calmly ordered him to kill the slaves. Marcus killed the slave in his grasp with a twist to her head that broke her neck and took out his dagger and calmly dispatched the other slave who was still curled up on the floor sobbing in despair.

It was a shame to dispose of his property in such a way, reflected Agricola. He particularly admired the spirit of the slave who had acted out her revenge on Drigwold but he was unsure how much of the Britonic language they may have picked up during his campaign. It was just possible that the slaves had heard Drigwold mention the Moonstone and he could not run the risk of this information being shared, no matter how small the risk. There were tribal spies in the Roman camp and if word ever reached the Druid Council on Mona, they would quickly move it beyond his grasp and all his efforts of extracting the information from Drigwold would have been for nothing.

Drigwold was still trussed up and although he did not realise it his ordeal was not yet over.

"Call my slave master" ordered Agricola. Marcus had already been instructed to make preparations, and a large brute of a man appeared with a copper lined bucket filled with hot coals and a branding iron. To Drigwold's horror the branding iron was placed in the hot coals until it was glowing a dark red. Marcus grabbed Drigwold's arm while the slave master over branded the Druid outcast brand that had still not fully healed, with the ownership brand of Agricola. Drigwold screamed in agony at this new assault upon his tormented flesh.

"You are now branded as my slave, and you will be identifiable across the empire as my personal property. If you try to escape you will be immediately imprisoned and returned to me and the consequences for you will be unimaginable. Secondly you will now no longer be identifiable as a Druid outcast, and I have future plans for you which will necessitate a story of a plausible hatred of Rome. The scars of the lashes inflicted upon you by the Druids will only help to reinforce this narrative."

He turned to Marcus, "take him to a holding cell and get his wounds treated. He has been pampered enough, now he will be given a chance to prove his loyalty."

He turned to the sobbing Drigwold, "you have four days to prepare yourself, you will soon be returning to Mona with Marcus to find the Moonstone. Believe me when I tell you that your life depends upon you being successful."

8

The weather was blissfully quiet, and the wind had dropped. It was a new moon and the Roman auxiliary legionnaires stood in near total darkness. They could hear the chanting coming from across the water and the flickering light of many fires. Agricola had selected a body of one hundred of his best swimmers to attempt to cross the short distance between the mainland and the Island of Mona. He did not have nearly enough boats for a successful mass crossing and what he did have had been taken from native fishermen or requisitioned from coastal traders. His only hope was to secure a surprise bridgehead across the water which could then be reinforced by rapidly ferrying more men across in the sequestered boats.

At his command, the legionnaires slipped silently into the water followed by three boats filled with swords, spears, and shields. The first on to the shore quickly dealt with the few guards who had been posted to protect the crossing. The guards were not looking out for swimmers and were dangerously complacent because their spies within the Roman camp on the far shore had assured them that the Romans lacked any capable invasion fleet. Within minutes the first group of legionnaires, and the initial bridgehead was secure. By the time the alarm had been sounded, there were over 300 fully armed Romans in defence formation awaiting the Britons. They were bloodily and efficiently repulsed whilst yet more legionnaires were ferried across to reinforce the bridgehead.

Whilst the main body of men was being transferred across the narrow straits three small boats with 26 men slipped quietly up the coast. The men wore light leather body armour and had left their helmets behind. They were especially chosen seasoned legionnaires, handpicked by Marcus. This mission would require stealth, and speed was more important than armour. Marcus sat in the bow of the lead boat, just behind him with an ankle chained to the thwart was a rather bedraggled and pathetic looking creature accompanied by a civilian translator who was fluent in both Britonic and Latin.

After about three hours Drigwold tapped Marcus on the shoulder and the three boats slipped silently towards the shore. Drigwold was in agony, his wounds were far from healed and the hard surface of the wooden thwart that he was sat upon made him feel like he was sitting on a bed of red-hot nails. The boats headed towards what looked to be a formidable rocky shoreline but under Drigwolds's direction they found the entrance to a small bay with a sandy beach. There were two substantial seagoing fishing boats on the beach belonging to the island community. Fortunately, there were no guards present and the Romans managed to land without incident.

The legionnaires hauled the boats a safe distance from the shore so that they could not be carried away on a rising spring tide. Before they left the beach, the Romans sprung a board on each of the traders' boats to prevent any close pursuit if they had to leave in a hurry. Marcus posted four guards to protect their own vessels.

By now the horizon was beginning to lighten and the small party of twenty legionnaires, the translator and Drigwold could see the gloomy bulk of a steep hill that rose about 750 feet in height before them. Drigwold led the party up a poorly defined path that wound its way up the rocky outcrop. Near the top of the hill the small party heard the agitated voices of local tribesmen behind a formidable dry-stone wall made from expertly stacked rocks. Drigwold led the party stealthily around the outside of the wall staring intently at the stonework. Suddenly he stopped and pointed at the wall. Marcus could see that in this spot the stones had not quite been closed together leaving barely perceptible hand and foot holds that could be used to scale the wall. This was an emergency exit point that could be used by the defenders, if necessary, should the main gate fail under a sustained attack. Marcus took the lead and he stealthily clambered up the face of the wall until he could carefully peer over the top.

The wall surrounded an area that was about fifty paces in diameter and in the growing light Marcus could see about twenty armed men standing on a defensive platform made of stout timbers looking over the wall towards the Southwest where the distant sounds of a violent conflict could be heard. Agricola had now transported sufficient legionnaires across the strait to begin the breakout from the bridgehead and they were now pushing the defenders relentlessly backwards from the coast.

There were a couple of small round hut shelters between Marcus and the group of armed men and one by one the legionnaires quietly climbed over the wall until they were grouped behind the huts. Only Drigwold, the translator and one legionnaire were left at the bottom of the wall and the legionnaire pulled out his dagger and held it to Drigwold's throat in case the Druid was contemplating any last-minute changes of allegiance. Although Marcus's party were outnumbered, they had caught the armed tribesmen completely by surprise as they suddenly burst out from behind the shelter huts. The slaughter was executed with brutal efficiency, the handpicked legionnaires were experts in the art of killing.

Once the guards had been despatched Marcus called Drigwold to climb over the wall and with the help of the translator he gruffly asked him if any of the men was the Druid they were looking for.

"No" replied Drigwold testily, "this body of warriors were Sutillious's personal escape guard who would have been responsible for slipping him off towards Hibernia in the fishing boats we found to prevent his capture. Their presence here in these numbers means that we can expect him soon as they obviously believe the island can no longer be defended."

"Are you sure he will have it with him" growled Marcus at Drigwold. "it will not go well for you if I am disappointed" Marcus pointed his bloodied gladius at Drigwold to emphasise his point.

"Yes, yes" pleaded Drigwold "Sutillious would never leave without it, it is the Druid's most precious possession. He believes it bestows him with great power and insight."

Marcus looked at the bloodied blade of his gladius and grimly smiled to himself. The Druid's insight obviously did not help when it came to Roman steel. Marcus also knew that there was another more sinister power at hand that was helping Agricola in his campaign. He did not understand this and in truth he was uncomfortable with tempting the Gods, but he knew that Agricola believed fervently in the special powers of his strange Egyptian priest. Marcus's job was to execute the Governor's orders, not question their source, and his experience so far in Agricola's service was that his commander's judgement had been impeccable.

It was now fully light, and the sounds of fighting had begun to abate a bit as the defenders had now broken into smaller scattered groups that were being systematically mopped up by the remorseless Roman military machine. Suddenly Marcus saw a group of ten Druids, nine were wearing black robes and one was dressed in white and they were hurrying up the track towards the hilltop fortification with only a couple of tribal warriors accompanying them. The native translator in Marcus's party called out a greeting to them as they approached the entrance. This was protected by a heavy timber barrier that was being raised by its integral rope pulley system by the Romans to give the party access into the fortification.

The party of Druids were in such haste that they raced through the entrance into the inner circle before realising that they had fallen into a trap. Despite being heavily outnumbered the two warriors launched themselves at the

Romans. It was a brave but futile gesture and Marcus's trained legionnaires cut them down in seconds.

Sutillious looked at the twitching body of one of the dying guards and then into the impassive face of the huge centurion who advanced towards him. Marcus grasped the shaft of the oak staff that Sutlliious held and slapped the Druid hard across the face with the back of his hand when he tried to resist. Carefully embedded into the stop of the staff was a beautiful fire opal about the size of a large duck's egg.

Marcus pulled out his pugio, the dagger that legionnaires carried in addition to the gladius and carefully prised the stone from the wood. He held it up to the light and admired its perfection, he had never seen a stone like it. He thought he felt a strange tingling sensation in his arm as if some strange energy was flowing from the stone but decided it was his imagination. He carefully placed the stone into a leather pouch on his waist, drew its thongs and tied them securely. He had no idea why Agricola was so determined to get his hands on the stone, but he knew his life depended on placing this stone in the Governor's hand.

As Sutillious picked himself up off the ground after Marcus's blow, he saw a familiar figure and he suddenly realised that they had been betrayed. Drigwold held no love for the Romans but his hatred of Sutillious and all the other Druids who had betrayed him burned within him like a hot coal. His eyes blazed with fury at Sutillious who realised what a terrible error he had made by showing Drigwold some leniency and not having him executed for his crimes. Sutillious knew that the world as he had known it would pay a terrible and irreversible price for his failure and his head dropped in despair. He had no pity for himself and knew that none would be forthcoming from the Romans.

The Romans had a simple policy when it came to the Druids. They were troublemakers and agitators, whipping up hostility from the tribes and challenging the authority of Rome amongst the Celtic peoples. Being a Druid was a capital crime in the Roman empire and the ten Druids already knew their fate. They were ordered to kneel and calmly did so, they believed that they were going to a better and joyous place in the Otherworld and had no fear of death. All of them were quickly despatched with a simple thrust from a gladius in the back of the neck until only Sutillious remained.

"Do it quickly" grunted Marcus at Drigwold. Drigwold glared at the Centurion, he did not want to kill Sutillious quickly at all, he wanted to torture him slowly to death. He had spent days imagining this moment, but Marcus had no interest in Drigwold's wishes and no further interest in Sutillious. Marcus had been irritated when Agricola had told him that he had granted Drigwold's wish to kill Sutillious. It was an unnecessary complication as far as he was concerned, and he was well aware that their small party was still very vulnerable.

Drigwold knelt in front of the elderly Druid and looked him in the eyes before slowly thrusting a borrowed pugio into his stomach. He watched with glee as he saw both agony and defiance in the Sutillious's eyes, but the Druid made no sound. Drigwold frowned with annoyance and was about to repeat the thrust when, following a quick nod from Marcus, a legionnaire despatched him with a quick thrust from his gladius and Drigwold's face was sprayed with blood.

Drigwold leapt up in anger and glared at Marcus with indignation. "I said quickly" said Marcus dismissively and he waved the party to depart. As the Romans hurried back down the pathway towards the boats, they could hear cries of alarm from the hill fort behind them as the Britonic warriors fleeing the Roman advance discovered the bodies of the Druids. Marcus called out to the four legionnaires guarding the beach and by the time the raiding party had reached the sand the boats were already in the water.

As the Romans frantically rowed from the shore a dozen Britons appeared on the beach and steel pointed arrows flew after the boats. One of the Romans let out a grunt and collapsed forward over his oar with six inches of arrow projecting from his throat. The threat was quickly over as the Romans were now gaining momentum and were soon safely out of arrow range and Marcus smiled in grim satisfaction as the Britons pushed the first of the fishing boats into the water only for it to immediately begin to sink from the gaping hole created by the sprung plank in its hull.

Agricola was eagerly awaiting news of Marcus's return in the privacy of his imperial quarters. He had already returned from the coast having satisfied himself that the resistance on the island of Mona had been effectively subdued. There would be many slaves taken today and he resolved to transport them back to Rome to be paraded before the people as a mark of his victory over the Druids. He felt a glow of satisfaction. He had managed to complete the task of destroying the Druid stronghold on Mona where his predecessor Suetonius Paulinus had failed through the intervention of Boudicca's rebellion. Mona was not just important to the Britons; it was the centre of learning for Druids from many of the Celtic peoples and he knew he had delivered a severe blow to the order. The Celts did not keep written records and most of the remaining keepers of the oral tradition were now slain at the hands of his legionnaires.

Marcus had commandeered a horse from the cavalry and had left the raiding party and Drigwold to make their own way back to the camp on foot. He knew that the Governor would be very anxious to know the outcome of his mission and would not appreciate having to wait for news. He rode directly to Agricola's quarters and answered the query evident in Agricola's expression by placing the precious Moonstone directly into his hand.

Agricola held the stone up to the light and examined its beauty briefly before handing it to the Egyptian priest. The priest took hold of the stone, but his face immediately grimaced in pain as every nerve in his body went into spasm and he dropped the stone to the floor. Rather than being dismayed at his experience the priest smiled in satisfaction and nodded to Agricola. Agricola thanked Marcus for successfully carrying out his mission and handed him a pouch containing ten gold aurei, a very considerable sum. It was not necessary for Agricola to pay the centurion for doing his duty, but he would be asking much more from Marcus in the future. It would do no harm for the centurion to know just how generous the Governor could be to those who served him well.

Agricola opened a small ornate chest that he always carried with him in which there was a broken corner of the original granite altar that had been taken from the ancient Temple of the God Seth where the Black Crystal had been found. The altar fragment was roughly square, about two hand widths wide with rough edges but with a smooth polished top surface. He handed the altar fragment to the priest Apophis who took it with great reverence and placed it on an oak table that had been prepared for this purpose. The table was covered with symbols and hieroglyphs most of which Agricola did not understand except for the hieroglyph depicting the great God Seth.

Apophis carefully picked up the Moonstone with a pair of iron tongs and placed it on the altar. He smiled as the translucent light inherent in the stone immediately dimmed. The granite altar stone had been infused with the properties of the Black Crystal which had absorbed the malevolence of all those who had worshipped the God Seth in its presence. Even the power of all the love and hope that had been channelled into the Moonstone could not drive back the evil contained within the granite from such a close proximity.

Apophis began to chant a ritual, summoning the spirit of the God Seth to be present with them in this moment, and Agricola sensed dark shadows appear which swirled around the priest and the altar stone as the priest's chanting rose to a crescendo. Agricola seemed to see the shadows form into grotesque figures with strangely distorted features whipping around the priest and the altar with increasing frenzy. Suddenly Apophis picked up a brass hammer that was next to the altar stone and he brought it smashing down on the Moonstone shattering it into dozens of small pieces.

The Priests of Seth in the Temple of the Black Crystal in Rome felt a surge of energy flow through them, and the centre of the Crystal pulsed a deep crimson red, like a heart that had been torn from its body yet still pulsed with life. The High Priest knew that Agricola and Apophis had succeeded in their task and that another Moonstone had been removed from the World. The power of the Black Crystal and those who channelled it was now virtually unopposed. He looked into the centre of the pulsating Crystal and entered into a trance. His mind soared up above the Earth and all was clouded in darkness except for a powerful white light that radiated from the Island of Britannia in the Northwest. One last Moonstone still remained. Agricola and Apophis had more work to do before the dominion of the Black Crystal would be complete and the wrath of Seth could rage unopposed upon the peoples of the Earth who defied his will.

Agricola looked enquiringly at Apophis after the shattering of the Moonstone upon the altar. "Is our task here done?"

Apophis brushed all the shards and dust from the shattered Moonstone. There was barely a mark upon the hard, grey granite surface of the Altar stone. Apophis frowned and allowed his mind to clear as he tried to project his vision across the land but there was still resistance, something was still blocking him although it was not as strong. He had a brief vision of a Moonstone resting between a woman's breasts until a blinding white light pushed him back and he cried aloud in anger and frustration.

"No, my Lord, another Moonstone yet remains in these islands."

Agricola sighed in frustration. He was not however surprised as he had been told by the priests in Rome that they had sensed the presence of more than one stone. Twelve Moonstones had now been destroyed and it was to be his destiny to be the agent of the Order of the Black Crystal that destroyed the very last Moonstone. He longed to return to Rome from this cold wet island at the edge of the Empire, he knew that the other members of the Order would be vying for influence and wealth whilst he was far away. On the positive side, the completion of his mission would almost certainly elevate him in the eyes of the Order. This would make him a favourite to become the next leader when the now aging head of the Order died. The prized leadership of the Order would give him virtually unlimited power to feed the cravings of his own ambition.

Many in Roman society had been surprised at just how quickly Agricola had risen from relative obscurity to such a position of prestige and power. Being appointed the Governor of a province required powerful supporters in Rome with considerable influence over the Emperor. Above all it required enormous wealth. The Romans celebrated greed and power above all else and saw a man's wealth as the best reflection of their worth and capability. The poor were poor because they lacked the ruthlessness and ambition to gain wealth and therefore lacked any human worth or respect. Any of the senior administrative posts of office within the Empire or higher ranks within the Roman army could only be achieved by those wealthy enough to buy them.

Agricola's success was far from mysterious to the twelve other members of the Order of the Black Crystal who had recruited him to their number after spotting his ruthless ambition from a young age. His path to becoming the Governor of Britannia was carefully planned and orchestrated and he now stood in the ideal position to destroy the final Moonstone.

"Where do we find the last Moonstone?" he asked Apophis.

Apophis carefully cleaned the top of the altar with a cloth dipped in essential oils infused with an extract of pressed scarab beetles. When the surface had been suitably polished and was gleaming with a film of oil, Apophis drew out a sacrificial dagger and drew it across the palm of his hand. He clenched his hand and let the blood flow onto the surface of the altar where it began to pool whilst he prayed for Seth's help in locating the Moonstone. Apophis noticed that the pooling was uneven, the blood seemed slightly resistant to move in one direction, there was a small but pronounced depression at the edge of the pool of blood. Apophis picked up a sacred iron stone that had been obtained for a fortune from a trader in the far lands to the east. The stone hung from a silk thread, and always pointed northwards in the same direction where the cold lands could be found. He could see that the depression in the blood was pointing to the north-east from the wind direction Aquilo which came from across the sea to Mona from the lands of the Carvetti tribe. "The Moonstone can be found in the direction of the tribes of the Carvetti" he revealed to Agricola.

Agricola smiled, this was ideal as his plans for the extension of Roman dominion in Britannia would also require him to subdue the Brigantes and in turn the Carvetti. He was planning to start the campaign in the spring as it was now too late in the season to plan and resource such an ambitious enterprise. The winter months would provide an ample opportunity for him to exploit the reluctant services of the contemptible Drigwold once more. Soon the last of the accursed Moonstones would be destroyed and the power of the Order of the Black Crystal would be unchallengeable.

9

In the mountains to the north a great storm had been building, and at that moment it released its incredible energy as lightning struck the mountain tops and the thunder god roared above the people in the valleys below. The door to Chyrenia's roundhouse in the woods flew open and a powerful squall shrieked around its timber frame. Chyrenia suddenly grasped the Moonstone that hung around her neck which had suddenly became hot. The stone was emitting a powerful radiant white light as it reacted to the destruction of its sister stone at the hands of Apophis.

Although Chyrenia did not know what had triggered the stone's reaction she knew that something terrible had happened and she suddenly felt incredibly sad and anxious in a way that she had never felt before. She felt a terrible sense of loss although she did not yet understand what had caused this intense feeling of hurt within her. In her heart she knew that her life and the lives of those she loved would never be the same again. Sinister forces with malign intentions were at large, and she had a terrible foreboding that these would now be focused upon the Gallancia.

Chyrenia closed her eyes to see if she could visualise the nature of the threat in her mind and she suddenly saw a pair of hostile jet-black eyes staring directly at her. Chyrenia immediately sought the power of the Moonstone still clasped between her hands, and as it responded the eyes retreated back into the darkness from which they had emerged. She tried to follow them to see if she could seek out their owner, but they retreated behind an impenetrable wall, and she could go no further. Chyrenia was deeply disturbed by this experience. She had never sensed such a powerful evil before. She would need to call the Sisters of the Moonstone together to ask the Goddess for guidance because her intuition told her that the threat was imminent.

At dusk, the thirteen Sisters of the Moonstone gathered at the Stones. The summer months had gone, there was a chill in the air and the Sisters pulled their cloaks more tightly around them. Soon it would be Samhain, the time of the year when the boundary between this World and the Otherworld was at its most porous heralding the dark days of the winter to come.

Chyrenia blessed the circle, and the thirteen Sisters began their chant in dedication to the Goddess and calling her presence to be amongst them. Chyrenia felt a familiar tingling feeling in her fingers as the natural energy began to flow within her which quickly built up until it was pulsing and spiralling throughout her body. The energy of the thirteen priestesses combined and became as one, creating a powerful cone of energy within the stones. She felt the presence of the Goddess within her, and a beautiful golden presence filled her being with love.

A scene began to unfold within her mind's eye. A wounded stag was found wandering in the forest and was brought to tribal council for judgement. Rather than taking its life for food, Kernack ordered that the stag be nurtured and healed so that it could be released once more back into the wild woods. It was taken to a roundhouse for healing but during the night the stag transformed into an enormous wolf that started savaging the livestock, tearing out the throats of sheep, goats, and cattle before disappearing into the forest. From the edge of the trees surrounding the settlement hundreds of pairs of eyes glowed red in the darkness and their voices howled in the night.

The scene faded as Chyrenia came out of her trance and she felt the chill of the autumn wind once more upon her face. The priestesses each shared their vision and although they each had their own experience; each vision shared the common theme of a terrible and powerful threat.

Chyrenia called for a meeting of the tribal council where she shared the vision of an imminent threat to the tribe, but without more knowledge about the source of the danger it was unclear what steps should be taken to mitigate the harm. Kernack was also rather dismissive of Chyrenia's vision. Although he would not openly stand against the High Priestess of the Goddess and the Stones, he had always resented their influence and their frequent constraints on his own independence. Chyrenia did not share Kernack's part in her vision with the council. She was aware of his resentment of her influence and knew she had to tread carefully if she was going to be able to help protect the tribe from the dangers it faced.

10

Siabelle shivered in the cold morning air and stamped her feet to restore the circulation to her numb toes. Although the first signs of Spring were evident with the appearance of the yellow catkins on the willows, there had been a sharp frost in the night and her breath left a misty trail in the cold morning air. She looked around at the dozen Carvetti warriors who stood with her awaiting her instructions. She smiled inwardly as she glanced at Garraculous who was second in command to Siabelle in the raiding party. He was a wild looking figure with a great mane of light brown hair and his full beard which revealed a hint of copper framing his face. His great bulk and strength was also deceptive as he was also astonishingly quick and agile for his size. He and Siabelle had spent endless hours training together and he had been quick to adopt many of the gladiatorial skills she had taught him. In return he had shown her how to use heavy timbers and agricultural tools to increase her own strength and endurance. Siabelle had seen Garraculous literally break a man's neck with a twist of his powerful hands and yet he was as gentle as a lamb when holding the tiny figure of his new-born daughter. His very public Beltane coupling with his beloved Melesone had been fruitful and his tiny daughter Daliphe now completely owned his heart.

It had not been a good start to the year. The Roman Governor Agricola had continued his campaign to subdue the rest of Britain and had started early. The Brigantes had been heavily defeated by the combined forces of the Roman legions, Legio XX Valeria Victrix which had marched north after the conquest of Mona and Legio VIIII Hispana which had joined them after marching from Eboracum. Although the Brigantes were far from completely subdued they could no longer offer serious resistance to the Romans who had already started building fortifications to permanently occupy their lands and suppress the population.

Agricola had not made any serious effort to invade the lands of the Gallancia. The difficulties of campaigning in the winding and often very narrow coastal strips of the peninsulas where the Gallancia lived were not really worth the rewards that they would gain from such a conquest. There were some Gallancians who still managed to trade with the Brigantes. These had reported that spies in the Roman camp suggested Agricola intended to progress northwards with the bulk of Legio XX up the large central valley pass to the east that separated the lands of the Carvetti from the Brigantes.

There were, however, frequent incursions from the Romans to keep the Carvetti at bay and to protect the flank of the main invasion forces. The Romans had also managed to establish a small trading port, Glannoventa, on the coast to the north of the Gallancia, protected by a local Carvetti chieftain who had decided it was better to accommodate the Romans than to fight them. The Romans intended to use the port as part of a coastal supply route to support Agricola's legions as they progressed further northwards.

With pockets of Roman tolerant Carvetii to the North, Agricola's legions to the east and the sea to the south and west, the Gallancia tribe had effectively become isolated upon their coastal peninsulas in an increasingly hostile environment. Many Brigantes had slipped into Gallancian territory to escape the persecutions of the Romans and a growing population of refugees was putting additional pressure on the tribe's resources and its ability to feed everyone who needed help. It was also becoming harder to trade effectively and to secure all the food and products they needed, so raiding parties against the Romans and their allies had now become a matter of survival.

Siabelle's raiding party had slipped stealthily into Roman occupied Brigante territory and laid in wait to ambush any Roman supply convoy with few enough guards to be overcome by their relatively small force. One of her scouts came back with the news that a party with only eight auxiliaries guarding it was approaching escorting two grain carts and a slave wagon. From her elevated position above the track the scout could not see any sign of other Roman forces close enough to intervene. Siabelle looked at Garraculous and smiled, it was becoming increasingly difficult to raid the Roman supply lines as they had become wary of frequent Gallancian intrusions. As a result, convoys were usually now much bigger with at least twenty auxiliaries in the escort. Although it was still possible to raid such parties, the risks were much greater and the Gallancians would inevitably lose warriors in the conflict that they could not afford. The Gallancians had a limited supply of experienced warriors whilst the Romans appeared to have virtually unlimited resources and Siabelle knew her adopted tribe would quickly lose any war of attrition.

Siabelle's experienced warriors quickly despatched the Roman escort, the first four were taken with arrows before they had even registered that they were under attack. Each of her party took at least one grain sack which they would carry to the horses that were safely hidden a short distance from the supply track. Garraculous and three of the others were strong enough to carry two.

Siabelle cut the rope that was securing the wooden lattice door to the slave wagon. They were now free, although their chances of survival were not good. Siabelle could not afford to bring more hungry mouths back with her, so the slaves were very much on their own. Two of the slaves remained mournfully in the cart, trusting their chances of survival as Roman slaves better than a life on the run. Siabelle looked at them with pity and contempt, she would rather die than fall into Roman hands again.

One of the other slaves had immediately taken off up the hillside but as Siabelle was about to go to the grain cart to pick up her sack the fourth slave touched her shoulder. This was a mistake as within a fraction of a second the slave had her dagger at his throat.

"Please warrior, I meant no disrespect" said the slave shakily "but I claim the Druid's refuge."

Siabelle looked hard at the face of the scrawny bedraggled creature standing before her and made no attempt to remove the dagger. She had little time for Druids, their spells and curses had been of little use against the Romans and in her experience, they caused more trouble and conflicts than they ever managed to settle. Suddenly Garraculous's huge paw gently encompassed her hand that was still firmly clenched around her dagger at the slave's neck.

"We have to respect the Druid's refuge Siabelle" he said softly. Garraculous was treading carefully as Siabelle could be quick to anger and this had self-evident risks.

Siabelle sighed in frustration and re-sheathed her blade. The Druid's refuge was an obligation on all of the Celtic peoples to grant refuge and free hospitality to any Druid that asked for it. She knew that her party would stand against her if she refused, as most Britons were terrified at the prospect of receiving a Druid's curse. She had no alternative but to take him back with her so that his status could be assessed by the Tribal Council. Just what they needed, another useless mouth to feed and two less sacks of grain as she would have to relinquish one of the supply horses to carry the Druid. If this slave were lying about his status, she would personally slit his throat and throw his scrawny body to the wolves.

Two days later the raiding party returned to Gallanbhir and handed over the Druid to the care of the Tribal Council for interrogation. The Druid claimed that his name was Glannox and that he had been on the island of Mona where the Druids had made their last stand against the Romans. He said that he had managed to escape from the island in a small boat, but the boat was in bad repair, and he had only just made it across the narrow body of water that separated the island from the mainland. On reaching the beach he had been captured by Roman auxiliaries but had managed to hide his identity as a Druid despite being whipped. He showed the Council the scars on his back which had only recently healed from a severe lashing. He had then been branded as a slave. When the raiding party had found him, he was being taken by the Romans to be worked to death as a manual labourer. This rang true as many slaves were being used in the construction of new roads and fortifications as Agricola's legions began the colonisation of the Brigante territories. He showed them the raised wheal of the branding on his arm that identified him as a slave of Rome.

Chyrenia was asked to verify his claims for having been trained in the Druidic arts. Although the Gallancia sought guidance from the Priestesses of the Stones, the magical and healing arts of the Priestesses and the Druidic order shared common knowledge that had been passed down through the generations. Glannox had extensive knowledge of the herbs and medicines and knew which trees and fungi could induce trance, which were fatal, and which were suitable for different diseases. It was quickly obvious to Chyrenia that the man before her had indeed been trained in the Druidic knowledge and was entitled to the protection of the Druid's refuge as he had claimed.

The Council granted Glannox refuge in the tribe provided he adhered to their laws and customs. Chyrenia took note that Kernack seemed particularly pleased to have a Druid in the community and he offered Glannox sanctuary in his personal household. Over the following weeks Kernack and Glannox spent an increasing amount of time together. Although Chyrenia was still shown the utmost courtesy and respect, she quickly noticed that her advice was no longer being sought by Kernack except when she was present in the formal Council meetings.

Chyrenia was deeply disturbed by the Druid's presence. Ever since she was a young girl, she had possessed the power to see a person's aura, the field of energy that surrounded all living beings and which reflected their health and nature. She had never before seen an aura like the one that surrounded Glannox. It was almost the absence of an aura, rather than giving off energy and light, the Druid was surrounded by a band where all energy and light had been absorbed. There was a darkness surrounding him and even more disturbing was that there seemed to be something blocking her ability to sense his essence. She had incredible powers of intuition and normally she could instantly sense the nature of a person's spirit and their intentions, positive or evil. The only time she had been blocked like this was when she had tried to follow the eyes that appeared in her vision during the trance at the Stones. Those eyes, like Glannox's essence had retreated behind an impenetrable barrier. She sensed the same magic at work with Glannox and it was deeply disturbing. She thought of her vision of the stag that turned into a wolf and knew that she would have to try to keep an eye on this unwelcome guest.

A couple of weeks after his arrival Chyrenia sensed Glannox's presence outside her roundhouse in the woods. She went out to see what he was up to and caught a glimpse of a furtive glance before he graciously greeted her and asked if she had any extract of rowan berries from the previous Autumn that she would part with as he had a disturbance of the bowel. Chyrenia cordially invited him into her dwelling and went to a yew wood box where she pulled out some dried berries and wrapped them in a leaf before handing them over to him.

Glannox seemed inordinately interested in her home and asked about all the different plants and herbs she had and where were the best places locally in the forests to find them. He was particularly interested in her altar to the Goddess and the stones and crystals that were placed upon it. In particular he was captivated by a very ornately carved yew wood box about a foot long and a hand width deep. The Box was reinforced with bronze bands and had a Roman lock securing it.

The Druid thought to himself that this was a very expensive box, and it was extremely unusual for the Britons to lock away possessions from each other as the tribal communities thrived on trust. It would have been unthinkable for someone to steal whatever was within the box from a Priestess and he had never before seen a Roman lock used amongst the Britonic tribes.

"That is a very elaborate box, can I examine it more closely?" said Glannox.

Chyrenia's demeanour immediately changed, and she curtly remarked that she had other things to do, and it was time that he left. It was very obvious to the Druid that the Priestess did not want him anywhere near the box and as he stepped out and walked slowly back to the village, he was quite sure that he had found what he was looking for. He saw Siabelle coming the other way and noticed how she glowered at him as they passed. Although this warrior tolerated him, it was obvious to Glannox that she did not trust him, and he would have to be very wary of her. She could be a dangerous enemy.

The following day was a market day in Gallanbhir where goods and livestock were traded with other tribes and travellers. The Romans had not yet tried to impose an embargo on trading with the Gallancia which was rather surprising. A trade ban would be difficult to enforce as the many river estuaries and peninsulas made it virtually impossible to stop coastal trading taking place, but it was still strange to the Gallancia that the Romans had not tried.

Glannox had been advised not to attend the market because if it were discovered that the Gallancia were harbouring a Druid it could bring unwelcome attention from their Roman enemies. Despite this advice Siabelle spotted him moving furtively between the stalls disguised in a brown hooded robe and she decided to keep an eye on him. There was one particular trader who seemed to have caught the Druid's attention who was selling rock crystals and coloured stones for jewellery. Siabelle had not seen him at the market before. The trader had quite a successful day as it was unusual to find such products at the Gallanbhir market. Usually, members of the Gallancia would have to travel to the market at the huge Brigante hillfort to find such exotic goods and so they were excited about his wares.

Glannox had arrived at the tribe with nothing, but he had quickly ingratiated himself with members of the tribal council and created a lucrative business offering remedies and blessings or telling stories about myths and legends from distant tribes. Chyrenia had been getting increasingly disturbed by the Druid's growing influence and she had had fewer visitors seeking her help in her woodland home. On several occasions she had had to heal people after they had taken advice from the Druid and become very unwell as a result. She had brought this up at the Tribal Council and was told by Kernack that it was probably a coincidence and he implied that she was jealous of the Druid's popularity. At the last Council meeting she was staggered to find that Glannox had been invited to attend as Kernack's guest and observed the Druid frequently whispering in the Chief's ear with advice and observations.

After a considerable amount of haggling Glannox handed over a handful of bronze coins to the trader in exchange for an impressive quartz crystal and slipped away from the market back to his quarters in Kernack's household. Shortly afterwards the trader packed up his stall, loaded his goods on to his cart and headed back along the track towards the Brigante lands. As Siabelle watched him go, her intuition was telling her that something was not right but there was nothing specific that she had seen to justify her unease. She would discuss her concerns with Chyrenia who greatly valued intuition and would want to know about Siabelle's suspicions.

11

The trader felt the reassuring weight of ten silver Denarii that had been given to him by the giant Roman centurion and he bounced the coins in his hand relishing their presence. He had been tasked with going to the Gallancian's market and a token giving an authority to trade had been obtained from Aristartes of the Brigante. At the market he was to await contact from a Roman spy who would make himself known by saying that he was looking for polecat pelts. The trader was to reply that it is not the best season to hunt them as they were up in the hills. He could expect either a reply about where and when it would be more prudent to hunt for them or a reply that perhaps he would settle for squirrel instead. After making contact he was told that he had to immediately report back to the Roman Centurion who would handsomely reward him for his efforts.

After paying the trader Marcus headed directly to Agricola's quarters where he relayed the message. "Polecat kits are reputed to be found playing around the stones at dawn on Beltane."

Agricola was delighted by the news. The message meant that his spy in the Gallancian village had managed to locate the Moonstone and that it would be at the Stone Circle of the Gallancia to celebrate the dawn of their most important festival. He grudgingly had to admit that the wretched creature had done rather well. It was just before the Spring equinox and Beltane was just six weeks away. There would be just one more market day in four weeks' time for the trader to relay their plans to 'Glannox' whose true identity was the contemptible Drigwold and whose capture by the Gallancia had been so carefully orchestrated. The eight auxiliaries that had died were on punishment duty and were a small price to pay to put on a convincing display for the unsuspecting Gallancian raiders.

Agricola had also given strict orders that no action was to be taken to interfere with the Gallancian market so that he could use it to facilitate his link to Drigwold and his plan had paid off. It was now time to destroy the last of the accursed Moonstones once and for all, with the added bonus of crushing the rebellious Gallancia into submission at the same time.

12

It was the eve of the last market before Beltane, but this was going to be a Beltane like no other. The Druid Glannox in his privileged position within Kernack's household had gained a powerful influence over the Gallacian Chief and he had successfully managed to sow discord and disagreement between Kernack and Chyrenia. Glannox had pointed out that, for all their faults, the Romans never let their women interfere in their politics or hold positions of power and influence. There were no women in the Roman Senate to limit the ambitions of men and he told Kernack that it seemed strange to him that such a powerful warrior was constrained by the opinions of a woman.

Just after the equinox market Glannox was reading the runestones on behalf of Kernack and he gave a worrying frown when he examined them.

"What's the matter" said Kernack.

"Oh, it's probably nothing" said Glannox in a voice that suggested entirely the opposite.

"I order you to tell me what you have seen" demanded Kernack.

With a look of great reluctance Glannox told him that the runes had revealed to him that the God was angry that he had been neglected for so long. The worship of the divine Goddess Anu by the Priestesses of the Stones had made the God angry. The Romans were being supported by their powerful God Mars, the God of war and lightning. If he was not appeased there was a danger that the powerful Britonic God Cernunnos might not stand with them if it came to conflict.

"But we have the Goddess, she has always protected us and will do so again in our hour of need" retorted Kernack.

"If you are happy that she can defeat the Romans and Mars their God of war on her own then I am content" said Glannox. "I am sorry to have troubled you with this, perhaps in future you would rather I keep my observations to myself as I have no wish to sow discord in the tribe?"

Kernack immediately insisted that he was to be immediately informed of anything that the gods were revealing to the Druid. He was unsure what to do about this new revelation. For weeks Glannox had been sowing seeds of doubt and this had taken its toll on Kernack's confidence. Before Glannox had arrived in the village Kernack would never have considered questioning Chyrenia's judgement. Now he questioned everything and Glannox's subtle encouragement of his male ego was also having an effect. Why was it only his tribe where the chief had to take the advice of a woman where other tribal chiefs stood side by side with powerful warlike Gods? He should be amongst their number, he felt disempowered by Chyrenia, and he was becoming increasingly angry as a result.

Chyrenia's influence had meant that all the proceeds of raids and trade were distributed amongst the tribe whilst Kernack only received a double share. He looked at the thin gold torc around his neck and remembered the size of the torcs worn by the tribal leaders of the Carvetti. They were not constrained by the whims of a priestess! Kernack should have a torc that truly reflected his position as the chief of the Gallencia. When previous male and female leaders of the tribe had died they were burned in a ceremonial fire and their ashes scattered in the woodland as a tribute to nature. When he died, he wanted to be buried in an impressive barrow with his possessions which he could take with him to the Otherworld. He threw his drinking horn against the wall in frustration.

"I can't stop the Beltane festival" he said "but I don't want to upset the horned God. I don't see what I can do."

"Well, there is a possible option, but again, I really don't want to interfere" said Glannox.

"Tell me!" roared Kernack in frustration.

"On the island of Mona, we also worshipped the horned God, but his realm was in the forests and his spirit resided amongst the mighty oaks running with the wolves and stags. Many times, we threw back the Roman invaders with our God by our side until sadly their number grew so great that even with the power of our God in the arms of our warriors, they could no longer stand against them. If your warriors were to hold a ceremony to the great and powerful Cernunnos amongst the oaks at the same time as the Priestesses called upon the help of the Goddess, then might both be appeased? Is there a place in the forest where the great oaks grow that would be suitable?"

"Yes, yes" said Kernack with increasing enthusiasm, "there is a ring of ancient oaks less than a league from the village. I could take you there to see if you think it would please our God. Would you be prepared to lead the ceremony?"

"I would be deeply honoured" said Glannox. "We would obviously have to seek the counsel of Chyrenia and the other priestesses first though. They may not give us permission to do such a thing."

"I am the Chief of the Gallancia not that interfering Priestess, and I will decide what's best for the people" roared Kernack, his face red with rage.

Glannox bowed his head in submission. What Kernack could not see was the broad grin upon his face. After their meeting, Kernack took Glannox to the glade surrounded by oaks where the Druid made a great display of honouring them and calling upon Cernunnos to bless their proposed endeavour. With great gravity he again threw the runestones and with a look of great relief upon his face he declared to Kernack that the God was pleased and would bestow his favour on any warrior who stood beside him amongst the oaks on Beltane.

Kernack wasted no time in calling a Tribal Council and he sat at the head of the great table with Glannox in his now usual position beside him. As members of the Council, Chyrenia and Siabelle were also present, and they waited patiently for all thirteen Council members to gather to hear what Kernack had to say. Although Glannox was present, he was still only a guest of Kernack and not a member of the Council and he was not entitled to vote.

With great solemnity Kernack rose to his feet and looked around the table until his eyes rested on Chyrenia. "It has been revealed to me that the great God Cernunnos has become angered at the neglect he has been shown by the Priestesses of the Stones." He glared angrily at Chyrenia in an attempt to intimidate her, but she calmly met his gaze, and it was Kernack who was the one who turned away. Kernack was anticipating some kind of direct challenge from Chyrenia, but she said nothing.

Glyderferwyn, the eldest person on the council was the first to break the increasingly awkward silence. "Just how was this revealed to you Kernack?" she asked.

"The God's anger was revealed to the Druid Glannox through the sacred runestones" replied Kernack.

Siabelle let out a snort of derision, but Chyrenia placed a calming hand on her shoulder gently discouraging a direct confrontation.

"The God revealed that he would not support our warriors in battles to come which would leave them at the mercy of the Roman War God Mars unless they pay him proper homage. I have long felt that our devotion to the Divine

Goddess and the power of the Moonstone has been misplaced. We have listened to the voices of women for far too long and it is time we listened to the voices of our warriors. I give thanks that the Gods have brought to us the wisdom of Glannox at this time of great peril." Kernack posed imperiously in front of the Council.

Siabelle thought Kernack looked pathetic, and she snorted again with derision. It had been years since Kernack had led any of the warriors of the tribe into battle. Laziness and self-indulgence had left him weak and obese, and she felt her anger rising as he claimed to be speaking on behalf of those who fought and died for the tribe. With obvious derision in her voice she replied, "Have you forgotten that many of your warriors are women Kernack? You are keen to listen to the sounds our swords make when locked in battle with our enemies, but you have decided that you no longer wish to hear the sound of our voices?"

Kernack glared at Siabelle with anger, his face becoming scarlet. He resented the fact that Siabelle had gained the respect of many of the warriors of the tribe and that increasingly it was Siabelle they turned to for leadership and advice. "Need I remind you that you are a guest in this tribe and tolerated in this Council at my pleasure?" he shouted at her. This was not strictly true, Siabelle had been elected to the Council by an overwhelming vote of its members after she had demonstrated her courage and skill in conflicts with their enemies. Although Kernack could in theory remove someone from the Council through the power of veto, it was against all custom and would be unprecedented in living memory.

Again, and slightly more firmly, Chyrenia placed her hand on Siabelle's shoulder. She did not want open conflict around the Council table, and she knew that this moment had become inevitable. She knew how susceptible Kernack was to the flattery of those who inflated his ego, and she had seen how Glannox's influence had been growing upon the ageing chief over the last few months. She also had the wisdom to know that the World was changing. An insurmountable force was bearing down upon them, like a mighty tidal wave driving all before it. If she attempted to stand against this force, she, and all of those that she loved and cared for would be destroyed. She knew that their only chance was to somehow rise above it, like a boat riding upon the waves of a stormy sea and afterwards try to build some kind of future when the tempest had passed.

Kernack was becoming increasingly nervous at Chyrenia's calm silence. He turned to her, "Have you nothing to say on this matter?"

Chyrenia deliberately left an awkwardly long pause before replying, "Sadly I did not have the benefit of examining the Druid's runestones after he threw them, so I am unable to comment upon his interpretation of the will of Cernunnos. I would make the observation that if God worshiping warriors supported by their Druids are so blessed with good fortune, why have the Romans arrived at our borders after conquering so many tribes? Why also is this Druid hiding from the Romans under the protection of the Divine Goddess worshiping Gallancia and their Moonstone?"

There was a ripple of laughter around the table which incensed Kernack and it concerned Chyrenia that such an egoistic man was being so openly ridiculed. A diminished chief like Kernack could become very resentful and could be tempted to seek restitution against his tormentor. This meeting was not going well, and she needed to change the dynamic. Trying to muster as much sincerity in her voice as she could, she addressed Keranack once again.

"I am sure that you have given great thought to this matter, and I would like to hear your wise counsel as to how we can appease the will of the God?" she said.

Kernack sat down again at the head of the great table and appeared somewhat mollified by Chyrenia's respectful tone. "I have decided that I will take the warriors at dawn on the sacred festival of Beltane to the sacred Oak ring in the forest where Glannox will hold a celebration and make offerings to Cernunnos. We shall then join you at the Stones for feasting and celebration."

For a moment there was a complete silence from around the table. Then Glyderferwyn decided to speak. As the eldest member of the Council her experience was highly respected, and her words held great weight.

"Since the earliest memories of our tribe we have always worshipped the Goddess, it is her fertile womb that grants the gift of life to all living things. This has always served us well and I fear that great harm may fall upon us if we disrespect her on the day of her most important festival."

Kernack knew better than to directly challenge Glyderferwyn as it would cause great displeasure amongst the Council, so he chose a more cautious approach. "As always the Council benefits from Glyderferwyn's wisdom" he replied. "I would never suggest that we offend the Goddess and instead I propose that the thirteen Priestesses of the Moonstone carry out the great ritual amongst the Stones as always. With the blessing of both the God Cernunnos and the Goddess Anu we shall surely overcome our foes."

Glyderferwyn looked far from convinced but said no more. "Let us put it to the vote" said Kernack. "All in favour of my proposal say aye."

In the tradition of Council votes starting with the person after Kernack in a deosil direction and five members called out their approval. The vote was repeated with those against and again there were six votes including Glyderferwyn and Siabelle. Kernack looked to Chyrenia who had not voted either way. Her vote was crucial. If she voted against his proposal the motion would be lost but if she supported it the vote would be tied, Kernack would have the casting vote and his proposal would be accepted.

"I have a request to make before I cast my vote" said Chyrenia. "I would like thirteen warriors to accompany us as the guardians of the Stones as has always been our tradition. If you agree to this request, I am prepared to support your proposal."

Siabelle stared at Chyrenia in amazement, she was sure that Chyrenia would oppose this fragrant breach with tradition, especially as it had been suggested to Kernack by the nauseating Druid Glannox. She was about to say something but a sharp look from Chyrenia stilled her tongue.

Kernack pondered Chyrenia's suggestion. He was not opposed to it in principle, especially if it meant that he got his way. The meeting was going better than he expected and he was as surprised as Siabelle that Chyrenia had decided not to overtly oppose him. He glanced at Glannox who gave a slight shrug of indifference.

"If you can find thirteen warriors who are prepared to go with you to the Stones then I will not stand in their way" said Kernack by way of compromise.

"In that case you have my support," said Chyrenia.

After the meeting broke up Chyrenia refused to speak to Siabelle until they were safely in the woods on their way to the roundhouse and away from listening ears.

"Why did you support such an idiotic idea" said Siabelle in exasperation. "The ceremony will be meaningless if most of the tribe is absent."

"If I had not supported it the tribe would be split and riven with internal conflict at a time when we are in great danger" replied Chyrenia. "We would also attract unnecessary attention from Glannox and Kernack which I am very keen to avoid as we have a lot to do. They will be so busy preparing for their ceremony that they will have little time or interest in our affairs."

"I can quickly despatch that conniving worm Glannox," said Siabelle, "nothing would give me greater pleasure."

"I know you could," replied Chyrenia with a smile, she loved and respected Siabelle's fiery spirit but this was a time when caution had to prevail. "Unfortunately, if you did slay the Druid the Tribe would be terrified of the consequences and Kernack would almost certainly call for your own death in return. You would have to leave the tribe at a time when I have never needed you more and at a time when I could never desert them. Now, most importantly, how much can you rely on the support of the twelve warriors you command? Would they be prepared to forgo the Druid's ceremony in the woods and come to the Stones as our guardians?"

Siabelle did not even have to pause to think, "They would follow me into dragon fire if I asked them to."

"That's what I thought," said Chyrenia, but Siabelle could still hear the relief in her lover's voice. "We will need their help over the next few weeks before the ceremony and we will also need their complete secrecy. It is absolutely imperative that nobody apart from your warriors and my Priestesses know anything about what I am about to request from you." With these words of caution Chyrenia began to spell out her plans to an increasingly alarmed Siabelle.

13

As she had promised Chyrenia, Siabelle had been watching the trader selling the crystals and jewellery at the market. It was now just two weeks until Beltane and Siabelle and her warriors had been busy working with Chyrenia's Priestesses. They had had little attention from Kernack who was delighted with the prospect of standing with over a hundred warriors amongst the Oaks in celebration of Cernunnos. As chief of the warriors, he felt he was the God's representative amongst mortal men and fully intended to be the focus of attention in his increasingly lavish ceremony. When anyone did question as to why Siabelle's warriors were spending so much time with Chyrenia they were told that a completely new ceremony had to be designed so that the Goddess would not feel slighted. The villagers were told that they were to stay away from the Stones until the morning of the ceremony or they would incur both the Goddess's and Chyrenia's wrath and neither were to be taken lightly. An increasing number of wagons full of supplies were being discreetly taken up towards the Stones before the ceremony and people were looking forward to the feasting and lovemaking that would take place afterwards.

Just as Chyrenia had expected, towards the afternoon Siabelle observed a hooded and furtive looking Glannox make his way to the stall of the crystal trader. Glannox made a rather feeble show of looking at some of the stones on offer before slipping something to the trader hidden under the palm of his hand. Shortly after the exchange the trader began packing up his stall and soon his small horse drawn cart was winding its way slowly back down the track that led towards the lands of the Brigantes.

Siabelle stealthily followed the trader making sure she was well out of sight. She was an expert at tracking people without being seen, her life had often depended upon it. At first the trader was constantly looking back to check whether he was being followed but after the first couple of leagues he soon became satisfied and he seemed to relax. Although the cart was being pulled by the trader's horse, the track was so uneven that he could not travel much faster than walking pace without the risk of damaging his goods. Siabelle had decided to follow the trader on foot as it would be much harder to remain concealed if she had taken her horse with her, but she was extremely fit and had no trouble keeping up.

Just before dusk, after they had travelled about seven leagues, the trader reached the head of an estuary that marked the edge of the Gallancian lands and entered Brigante territory. They soon came upon a fishing village which, because of its position on the major route into the lands of the Gallencia, had a lodging house which had a stable for travellers' horses and sold food, ale, and mead. Siabelle had made sure that the trader had never seen her at the market so she was quite confident that he would not be particularly suspicious if she waited long enough before following him in. As an added precaution she skirted around the village and entered it from the Brigante side making no attempt to hide so that any spotters would not think the trader had been followed.

Upon entering she saw that there were about fifteen people plus the alehouse keeper and two serving staff inside. She took up a position on a bench with her back to the wall opposite to where the trader was sat and ordered a jug of ale and a bowl of fish pottage in exchange for a couple of small copper coins. It was not unusual for Gallancians to use the alehouse and Siabelle's appearance and obvious warrior status meant that only someone who was foolhardy or very courageous would intrude upon her without invitation.

She was careful to give every appearance of ignoring the trader who looked fidgety and uncomfortable. He was obviously waiting for someone, and they were taking their time in joining him which was increasing his anxiety. Finally, three people came through the door. One of them was a giant of a man and, although they were all dressed in Britonic tribal clothes it was immediately obvious to Siabelle that two of them were Romans. The huge Roman looked keenly at everyone in the alehouse and gave Siabelle particular attention, his military instinct telling him that she was the only threat in the room. Siabelle completely ignored the Roman and gave every indication of an exhausted traveller taking solace in a few mugs of ale. Although the Brigante's had been defeated they were far from being subdued and it would be reckless for two Romans to be alone in such a remote location. Siabelle was very sure that there would be others within calling distance should there be any altercation. Fortunately, neither she nor the large Roman were looking for unnecessary attention and after being briefly scrutinised she was left undisturbed.

The large Roman was speaking to the trader via a translator, the Briton who was accompanying the two Romans when they entered. They were talking far too quietly for Siabelle to overhear but she saw the trader hand over a folded piece of parchment, almost certainly the object that Glannox had palmed to the trader at the market. She had now finished her pottage and the ale and rather than stay and attract unnecessary attention she casually stood up, gave a weary stretch, and left the alehouse.

Siabelle left the village in the direction of the Gallancian territories and when she was safely out of sight, she skirted back to observe the alehouse from behind a bush on the slope of the hill that rose up behind the village. Although it was quite dark now, the night was clear, and the half-moon gave sufficient light for her to distinguish the movement of people and animals around the village. She heard the snorting of a number of horses a little way up the track on the Brigante side and smiled to herself. There was Roman cavalry in the village, close enough to intervene if necessary, should the Romans in the alehouse be attacked, probably as many as twelve from the sounds coming from the horses. This was no ordinary Roman interviewing the trader, whatever he had handed over must have had considerable value. A few moments later the two Romans and their translator emerged from the alehouse and a cavalryman holding three horses emerged from the gloom. They immediately got on to their mounts and rode quickly out of the village. Wherever they were off to they were certainly in a hurry.

Siabelle desperately wanted to interrogate the trader, but Chyrenia had been absolutely adamant that she should not interfere in any way. If the trader went missing it might be noticed by the Romans and alert them that their conspiracy had been discovered. Reluctantly she turned around and made her way back towards Gallanbhir.

Siabelle went directly to Chyrenia and explained everything that she had seen. Chyrenia listened without comment but everything she had been told reinforced her suspicion that the arrival of Glannox in the village was far from accidental. Glannox was without doubt a Roman spy, but she had no way of proving it and she knew that if she went to the Tribal Council with her suspicions she would only be met by anger and ridicule from Kernack. Glannox had completely gained the Chieftain's confidence and it would be Chyrenia rather than Glannox who would come under suspicion. The last thing she wanted at this critical time was for either Glannox or Kernack to take a keen interest in her movements.

Chyrenia did not know exactly what Glannox and his Roman masters were planning but it obviously involved separating the main body of warriors from the ceremony at the stones leaving the villagers and the priestesses dangerously vulnerable. The Romans were showing a surprising amount of interest in a small tribe that presented little threat to their ambitions and was at most a minor irritant on their western flank. There was more to this than the planning of a minor military expedition and Chyrenia had a grave suspicion of the true purpose behind all their scheming. She also knew that the future for the 'people of the Stones' would never be the same again. They were all facing much bleaker and darker times.

14

Marcus and his cavalry escort rode directly to Agricola's campaign quarters about twenty leagues from his meeting with the trader at the Brigante fishing village. Although it was now early morning with the first hint of dawn showing in the sky to the east, Agricola had given strict orders that he was to be awoken as soon as Marcus arrived.

Marcus handed over the folded parchment upon which was a drawing of a detailed map of Gallanbhir village, the path to the Stones and the location of the glade in the woods surrounded by the ancient oaks. He also detailed a little used track that passed close to the location of the glade that led directly to the shingled shore of the coast, avoiding the estuary which was the usual trading route to the village.

On the back of the map Drigwold had scribbled a few badly spelled words in Latin that he had learnt to write during his time in the Roman camp after the defeat of the Druids on Mona. This had literally been a painful experience for him as he was a dreadful pupil, and his frequent failings would result in a clout from a disgruntled Marcus who had been tasked to oversee the Druid's rapid education.

Agricola was delighted with the map and the information written on the back of the parchment. He learnt how Drigwold had persuaded Kernack to lead his warriors away from the stones to the Oak glade and the location where the Beltane ceremony would be taking place. Most importantly he had inscribed on the map in the middle of the Stones the word "Moonstone."

The Roman plan had three main elements. Firstly, in line with his ambition to continue his military conquest of Britannia he would make a big show of the legions marching north up the great valley between the mountains towards the lands of the Scoti. This would reinforce the rumours that had been deliberately spread to the local population that he was going to bypass the Western coastal peninsulas. This should reassure the Gallancia that the immediate threat to their lands had been averted and enable them to focus on their celebrations whilst hopefully dropping their guard.

Secondly there would be three galleys carrying three Centuria of legionnaires amounting to 240 men. These would be disembarked on the coastal shingle beach in the late afternoon the day before Beltane and make their way along the coastal track towards the oak glade. A short distance from the glade they would remain safely out of sight until the Gallancian warriors arrived for their ceremony dedicated to Cernunnos. These galleys were rowed by slaves and after disembarking the legionnaires, they would make their way back south to the Roman fort at Deva where they would pick up more supplies for Agricola's campaign.

Thirdly a small galley capable of carrying 25 legionnaires would travel up the estuary, disembark at the virtually empty village and make a dash towards the ceremony at the stone circle to capture the High Priestess and take possession of the Moonstone. This galley was rowed by handpicked Roman legionnaires as some of them would be required to take part in the mission and in all probability fight the unprotected Gallancian villagers if they showed any resistance.

15

The day before the Sabbat of Beltane, Chyrenia and Siabelle left their home before dawn and made their way along a little used shepherd's track until they came to two large ancient standing stones. The two stones were an ancient way marker that directed travellers who had been making their way along the coastal pathways to their settlement on the estuary, now the Gallancian village of Gallanbhir. The path was now seldom used, and the stones were largely hidden amongst the hawthorn, willow and elder that had grown up around them. The two women squeezed their way between the branches trying to avoid the worst of the prickly hawthorn thicket. Siabelle cut away the undergrowth to create a small clearing between the stones where Chyrenia could sit and safely go into a trance whilst Siabelle stood guard.

For an hour Chyrenia called on the Goddess to confer upon the stones the power of guardianship of a precious gift she was presenting on behalf of the tribe. She felt the energy surge up within her and transfer to the stones which seemed to shimmer as if in a response to a summons from the shamans of the distant past who had first erected them. At the foot of the largest stone, Siabelle carefully dug a small square hole the depth of her forearm with an old blade. Once the hole was completed, Chyrenia first lay down a pottery tile at the bottom onto which she placed a Cedar wood box covered in strange carved sigils. She then covered the box and the tile with an upturned thick clay cooking pot that Siabelle had carried for her. Chyrenia carefully covered the upturned pot with earth and as they left, they straightened any branches in the thicket they had disturbed when they had forced their passage to the stones. Satisfied that there was no evidence of their activity they made their way back to their home to complete the extensive preparations for the Beltane celebrations the next morning.

At first light on the dawn of Beltane, Kernack and Glannox led most of the warriors of the Gallancia to the sacred oak glade. There were over a 120 men and a dozen women in the great ceremonial procession who would be making their dedication to the great horned god Cernunnos, asking him to give them courage and strength in forthcoming battles against their enemies. The warriors were in great spirits, they sang songs about fabled warriors and victories of the past led by Kernack. Kernack was now proudly wearing a magnificent golden torc around his neck, its two ornate ends joined by twisted gold wires. Chyrenia would have cried in frustration if she had known just how many of the Gallancian's precious goods had been traded to fund this ostentatious symbol of the Chief's growing vanity.

When they finally reached the glade, Drigwold asked the warriors to sit in a ring and bow their heads in contemplation. The glade was not wide enough for them to all sit side by side, so the warriors made two concentric circles facing inwards towards Kernack who sat in the middle. To the west of the glade was a massive ancient oak that dominated the other trees around it and Drigwold left the ring of warriors to stand next to its huge trunk where he began to call out to the horned God to join them in his forest domain. He had brought a hand drum with him which he began to enthusiastically bang in time with his chanting making a cacophony of sound that echoed through the forest.

In the shadow of the trees shadowy figures began to move forward, their progress masked by the sound of the Druid's drumming as the Roman legionnaires encircled the Gallancian warriors whose heads were still bowed in dedication. With a signal prearranged by Drigwold, the drumming suddenly stopped to be replaced by the sound of dozens of arrows in flight thudding into the helpless exposed backs of the Gallancians. Those who had escaped the arrows leapt to their feet only to be met by a volley of Roman spears as the legionnaires closed in from the ring of trees surrounding the glade. The Gallancians had no protection from the deadly assault as they had left their shields behind in the village and they were only armed with their swords which offered little defence against the Roman spears. The massacre was over in less than a minute without a single Roman being wounded. Any Gallancian warriors who were still alive were mercilessly executed where they lay.

When the onslaught was over Drigwold walked out from behind his cover. He had protected himself from any accidental wounding from a stray arrow by nipping behind the huge trunk of the oak which had proved to be prudent as there were now two arrows firmly embedded in the front of the tree. The ending of the drumming was the signal he had written in his message to Agricola which gave him a vital couple of seconds to move to safety. Kernack was slumped forward in a kneeling position with a Roman arrow protruding from his back in the centre of the ring of the dead and dying. Drigwold walked over towards the Chieftain's body and, looking down on him with contempt, he bent down and with a great deal of effort he twisted the golden torc to part it enough to wrench it from Kernack's neck. He looked at the craftmanship in wonder as he held it up to the sun only to have it snatched from his hand by the centurion who was in command of the raiding party. Drigwold snarled in helpless frustration as he looked into the impassive face of the battle-hardened legionnaire who had taken his prize from him. With a smirk the Centurion threw a leather pouch into the Druid's hand containing a paltry ten silver Denarii. "Rome thanks you for your service" he said mockingly.

The Romans had no intention of burying the Gallancian warriors, they just left them in the forest where the wolves, bears and foxes would soon begin to feast, closely followed by the crows and buzzards. They did however collect the swords which would be either traded with loyal Britonic tribes or melted down to make new weapons for the Roman forces.

The disgruntled Drigwold then guided the column of 200 legionnaires along the track towards the village where they would offer additional support if necessary to the raiding party that had rowed up the estuary. By now it should be approaching the sacred stone circle of the Gallancians to capture Chyrenia, the tribe's High Priestess, although only Drigwold and Marcus knew about the existence of the precious Moonstone. They expected the raiding party to face little resistance as according to the plan all the Gallancian warriors should now be lying dead amongst the oaks. Only relatively few unarmed men and the women and children of the Gallancia should still be left alive. These would be no match for the trained Roman legionnaires to overcome even if they were relatively few in number.

16

Apart from their warriors, all the villagers of Gallanbhir had gathered in the meeting area in the centre of the village where the market was held. It was still dark, and the faces of the villagers were reflected in the flames of the torches held by Siabelle and the twelve loyal warriors from her war party. There were fewer people than usual for Beltane, as in more normal times delegations from other villages were invited to attend the ceremony and bear witness to the celebrations at the Stones. This year Chyrenia had, without Kernack's knowledge, sent her priestesses as messengers to all the settlements in Gallancia urging them to remain in their villages as the tidings were not auspicious.

The procession up towards the stones was very subdued, there was no drumming and no ceremonial maiden to consummate the renewal of the Goddess and God in ceremony. The joyous celebrations of the year before when Garraculous and Melesone had come together in love and conceived their beautiful daughter Daliphe now seemed a distant memory from another time. Instead of drums and torches, the villagers had been directed to bring agricultural implements, sickles, scythes and also, for those who had mastered them, their hunting bows. The Roman defeat of the once powerful Brigantes had caste a looming shadow over their lands. Despite their worries the villagers had responded to the call from their beloved High Priestess Chyrenia and were happy to put their trust in her guidance in these fearful times. Not a single woman, man or child was left behind in the village as they made their silent way up to the Stones.

To the villagers' surprise, instead of standing outside the ring of stones they were invited in and they gathered in front of Chyrenia who stood beside the sentinel stone that pointed the way to the north. Chyrenia held the ornate box with the Roman lock that had been so coveted by Drigwold when he had visited her in her woodland dwelling.

"Please listen to me carefully." she said. "Today we are facing a great danger and the divine Goddess Anu has told me that the day is not auspicious to hold the ceremony of Beltane in her sacred space within the Stones. She asks each of you to invite her into your hearts and place your faith in we her servants."

The villagers looked at each other with alarm. Nobody could remember a time when they did not secure their harvest with the Goddess's blessing at the Beltane festival and there was a growing sense of unease amongst them.

Glyderferwyn, the elder of the tribe then made her way forward and stood beside Chyrenia. "Listen to your High Priestess today for she speaks words of wisdom. Follow her guidance without question or argument because the lives of all of you and your children depend upon you following them."

Chyrenia had shared her concerns with Glyderferwyn after Siabelle had reported back on the movements of the trader and the implications for Kernack's trust in Glannox. The two women were distraught that they could not see any way in preventing the risk to the warriors. Any attempt to interfere in Kernack's plans would have ended very badly. If the women had been banished or perhaps even murdered, they would have been unable to take any actions to protect the rest of the tribe.

"A great evil is descending on our village today and we have to leave our homes behind us and travel into the mountains until it is safe to return. Over the last week we have been building shelters at the edge of the Lost Valley Lake and most of our sheep and cattle have been moved up to the high pastures on the slopes of the surrounding hillsides. We will be secure there until the danger in the village has passed and we can rebuild our community once again. Glydeferwyn will lead you on the journey to the lakeside, but we need to delay those that are pursuing us, so I need volunteers to stand with Garraculous and hold the pass above the Stones."

"Where are our warriors, why can't they stand with us?" cried out a voice which was quickly joined by a clamour from many others. Sons, husbands, brothers, and lovers were missing, and a terrible dread began to fill the hearts of the villagers. Chyrenia looked at the faces of the villagers looking at her for answers. What could she tell them? How could she acknowledge that she had failed to save them from the Romans and had allowed them to be sacrificed to Kernack's vanity and stupidity and Glannox's evil. What kind of high priestess could allow so many of her followers to perish? Tears began to flow down her cheeks as she looked at them helplessly. Adding to her misery was the knowledge that she would never see any of the villagers again.

Siabelle suddenly walked up to Chyrenia and stood by her shoulder. "The fate of your loved ones is unknown to us; they stand with their chief, and they face a great peril, but I trust in their courage. I trust in the strength of all the peoples of the Gallancia. I am a guest in your village, and I am proud to have been accepted, trusted and to be able to call so many of you friend. All the Gallancia have warrior blood flowing through their veins, every man woman and child. Now is the time to show that you truly deserve the trust and honour of your ancestors and to stand defiant against those who oppress you. Who will stand with me and Garraculous today and spit in the face of the Roman dogs who would take your lands and freedoms from you?"

A cry of anger rose from the villagers, and they raised their arms in defiance, waving sickles, scythes, and hunting bows in the air. Siabelle and Garriculous went amongst them and selected about forty men and women who would be able to make a stand with the eleven other warriors in Siabelle's raiding party. All the rest of the villagers including the priestesses of the Stones followed Glydeferwyn on the long trek up through the mountain foothills towards the hidden lake where they could hopefully evade the pursuit of the Romans.

The fifty defenders followed the villagers up the shepherd track rising up above the Stones as the track followed a stream that had scoured a v shaped cut in the rising hillside. This created a steep sided tree lined valley as the pass narrowed in on both sides, ideal for defending against a resolute enemy. They then split into two parties with six of Siabelle's warriors leading each side and they hid behind the trees, boulders and the tall ferns that grew amongst the rocks.

17

The centurion Marcus was standing in the prow of a small flat-bottomed galley that pulled up at the wooden quay at the side of the estuary where the now deserted village of Gallanbhir was located. By now the Gallancian warriors should be receiving their surprise welcome from over 200 Roman legionnaires. As he expected the villagers must have made their way up to the Stones and there was no activity apart from a couple of sheep hounds foraging for scraps from between the roundhouses. One of the large hounds growled at the sudden appearance of 25 armed Romans disembarking from the galley to be met with an arrow through its chest for its trouble. The other hound slinked off, sensing the danger from the belligerent strangers that had entered the village.

Marcus looked up the map and soon picked up the well-worn track that followed the side of a stream which led from the village towards the sacred stones of the Gallencia. The Romans formed into a column led by Marcus and force marched their way up the rising slope into the narrowing valley carved by the stream. They were eager to spring their own unwelcome surprise upon the celebrating Gallancians. Although the Romans would be heavily outnumbered, Marcus believed that there was little that the villagers could do against armed legionnaires in attack formation without their warriors. A few slaughtered children would quickly focus the minds of their parents allowing Marcus to strike out directly for the High Priestess and the prized Moonstone.

Within an hour they had reached a point in the valley where a left hand fork in the path would lead them towards the stone circle. As they climbed clear of the vegetation which lined the sides of the stream they had their first glimpse of the stone circle which, to Marcus's intense frustration, was completely deserted. He wished he had that treacherous Druid Drigwold with him so that he could take out his anger directly on the wretch. Cautiously the legionnaires came up to the stones and circled them to make sure that nobody was using them as cover. One of the legionnaires who was an experienced tracker saluted Marcus and pointed out that a large number of people had recently been gathered at the stones. The imprints of the footprints were still fresh, and they pointed back in the direction of the track that they had recently left which continued upwards as it climbed the hillside. Marcus decided to follow the villagers, and the Romans quickly set off again at a forced march in pursuit.

The track steepened and narrowed as it climbed the hillside and Marcus raised his hand in caution to stop the column. Suddenly two women appeared around a curve in the track about fifty strides ahead of them, one was holding an ornate box which matched the description of the Moonstone box given to Agricola by Drigwold. The other woman was dressed as a warrior in leather armour and had a sheathed Roman longsword at her side. She also had a large vivid scar running diagonally from her forehead down the left side of her face. The two women froze in alarm as they saw the Roman column just beneath them and immediately began to retreat back up the path. Marcus could not believe his luck, he thought he had lost his opportunity to get the Moonstone. He was already beginning to rehearse the excuses for his failure in his mind for what would have been a deeply unpleasant and probably fatal meeting with Agricola. Agricola was not noted for his clemency towards those who had failed him.

Marcus ordered his column forward sending two of his fittest and fastest scouts ahead after the two women who he was sure would be rapidly outpaced and captured. As they rounded the curve in the track the Romans suddenly found themselves confronted with a hail of arrows, some with narrow hardened steel tips that could penetrate their armour. Within seconds Marcus had lost half his column and under a canopy created by their raised shields, the Romans retreated back down the path as Gallancian warriors and villagers poured down the slope towards them. The Gallancians were led by a huge warrior carrying a massive war axe who was covered in wode paint and tattoos which distorted his face into a hideous vengeful mask.

As the Romans retreated back down the path, the huge Gallancian hammered on the shield of the rear legionnaire with such force that the man fell backwards and was immediately bludgeoned to death with a blow to the head from the heavy axe. As suddenly as it began, the pursuit ceased, triggered by a strange deep thrumming sound. Marcus looked up the slope of the hill to the crest to see the two woman they had first encountered, one of whom was holding the ornate box in the crook of one arm. With the other arm she was swirling a large shell around her head which was the source of the strange sound. The female warrior with the scarred face stood next to her and held up the stolen Roman spatha in defiance. Her eyes blazed directly into the eyes of the Centurion with pure hatred and Marcus gave a grunt of grudging respect. He would never forget that face. The women had neatly ambushed the Romans and, more worryingly seemed to have completely anticipated their arrival. Marcus had underestimated the Gallancians and Drigwold seemed to have forgotten to mention that not all of the warriors had been enticed into his carefully planned trap in the oak glade. If he ever got the opportunity, he would forcefully remind Drigwold of the error of this omission.

The Centurion faced the same dilemma he had earlier. The Moonstone was still out of his grasp and it would take at least two hours to gather sufficient legionnaires together to force a passage up the track to pursue them. He looked again at the two women on the hillside but to his surprise they turned their backs and continued on their own up the hillside leaving the Gallancian defenders to block the passage of the Romans. This did not make any sense to Marcus, why would they leave themselves so exposed without the protection of the remaining Gallancians? The only thing that made sense was that they somehow knew that the Romans were after the Moonstone, and they were trying to escape with it. The direction they were taking was towards the coast to the northwest and the direction of the Roman trading post at Glannoventa set up in agreement with the local Carvetti chieftain. It was just a hunch from a wizened old campaigner, but it was a hunch that he would be staking his life on. If the women were heading towards Glannoventa they might be able to escape on one of the frequent coastal trading ships from the Scoti in the north or from the island of Hibernia. There was no way they could catch up with them by land as they were blocked by the party of armed Gallancians, but there was just a chance they might be able to get there in time by sea.

Marcus and the remaining legionnaires quickly headed back towards the village only to find to their frustration that their galley was high and dry on a sandbank as the tide had gone out. It would be several hours before they could restart their pursuit of the Gallancian women. Marcus smashed his fist on the wall of an adjacent roundhouse in sheer frustration. The only consolation was that he had too few men remaining to adequately crew the galley and the closing sound of the Roman column approaching the village from the west would at least resolve his manpower issues.

Marcus thought about ordering the Romans to go in pursuit of the fleeing Gallancian villagers, but Agricola would not thank him for being distracted and there were other considerations. The slaughter of most of their warriors meant that the Gallancians posed no further threat to the flank of the main Roman occupation forces which were now heading to the north. In addition, Roman legions required a lot of feeding, and they would need the local populations to provide the crops and livestock to supply them. Although he was sorely tempted to pursue and slaughter the villagers and burn the village after his embarrassing rout in the pass, it was not a good strategic decision and Marcus was the consummate professional soldier. He would send the main column of legionnaires to march onwards around the estuary towards the land of the Brigantes to join Agricola's main force whilst he would pursue the two women with the Moonstone in the galley. Curse this damn tide!

As a vindictive parting shot, he ordered a party of legionnaires to head up to the Gallancians precious stones and pull a few of them over. Although it was unwise to physically break the bodies of the remaining Gallancians, he had no issue with further breaking their spirit.

Chyrenia and Siabelle looked down the hillside at the fleeing Romans and their Gallancian friends who they might never see again. Two days before, Chyrenia had asked Garriculous and Melesone to come to her home in the woods and there she had told them about her fears. Garriculous and the rest of Siabelle's close knit band of warriors from her raiding party had already been party to the covert building of shelters and the transfer of supplies to the shore of the hidden lake. What Garriculous did not know was Chyrenia's suspicions about the Romans' desire for the Moonstone of the Gallancians. She told them about Drigwold's interest in the Moonstone's box and this had forced her to take precautions to hide it in the hollow of an old tree to keep it safe. On more than one occasion she had come back to her home to find evidence that someone had been searching through her belongings and medicines. Chyrenia believed that if the Romans believed that the tribe still had the Moonstone with them, their pursuit would be remorseless and catastrophic to the fleeing villagers.

She explained to Garriculous and Melesone her plan to let the Romans see her leave towards Glannoventa with the box in the hope that they would follow the stone and not the villagers. This was the reason why they had to let some of the Roman column escape back towards the village instead of despatching them all, much to Siabelle's frustration. It was a big gamble, there was no certainty that the Romans would not wait for reinforcements and still pursue the villagers. If they did, they would eventually find their refuge at the hidden lake nestled amongst the mountains. The Romans had virtually unlimited forces available and there was no way the Gallancians could hold out against them if the Romans were determined enough.

There was also no certainty that Chyrenia and Siabelle would find a ship in time that would be prepared to take them to Hibernia. It would be night by the time they reached the trading post, and they would have to wait until the tide ebbed before any ship could make an easy passage up the river estuary and out to sea.

Chyrenia had arranged safe overnight accommodation with her dear friend Tanuw who was a medicine woman and with whom she had previously left money and instructions to try to secure them a passage. She had no way of knowing for sure if she was going to be successful. What Chyrenia had not told anyone, even her beloved Siabelle, was that she had had a powerful vision of the events to come when she was in a shamanic trance. Visions were unreliable, they could reveal one of many possible outcomes but the clarity of this one meant she felt she had no choice but to follow the path that had been revealed to her.

It was a difficult journey to Glannoventa, Chyrenia in particular was exhausted when they finally knocked on the door of her friend's roundhouse as the last glimmer of the late spring light faded in the northwest. Unlike Siabelle she was unused to travelling long distances and lacked her lover's fitness. Both women were covered in scratches from the rapidly growing bracken and the yellow flowered, but viciously spined, gorse bushes. There was no direct track linking the trading post with the Stones and they often had to forge their own route along stream paths and up over the hills to get to their destination.

Tanuw quickly ushered the two women into her home and then clasped Chyrenia in a warm embrace. She was introduced to Siabelle whom she had heard so much about but had never met. She must have made quite a startling figure in her battle worn leather armour and with her vivid facial scar but Tanuw also quickly embraced the somewhat awkward feeling Siabelle. Apart from when she was with Chyrenia, Siabelle was not used to unconditional affection and did not really know how to appropriately respond. Tanuw had prepared a delicious hot stew for the two women who consumed it with great gusto after their long trek through the hills, whilst they listened to her news.

Fortune had favoured them and there was a trader who was well known to Tanuw and in whom she had complete trust. The trader was leaving at first light and had said that he would be honoured to offer Chyrenia safe passage. She had arranged to leave the two women alone together that night and would wake them before the dawn. They could then slip down to the quay and get on board the ship before the trading post stirred into life. This was primarily a civil outpost and, as it was there by mutual agreement between the Carvetti and the Romans, the only Roman military presence was a quartermaster prone to overindulgence, and a couple of bored auxiliaries.

After they had eaten Siabelle was surprised and pleased that Chyrenia was eager to make love having assumed that she would have wanted to sleep after the ordeal of their journey. Siabelle noticed there was a special intensity, almost an urgency in Chyrenia's passion and she willingly responded to her lover. Afterwards Siabelle lay with her head on Chyrenia's full breast whilst her lover gently ran her finger down the vivid raised scar on her face. She looked into Chyrenia's captivating green eyes and saw a tear gently trickle down her face.

Chyrenia smiled reassuringly as she saw the flicker of concern appear in Siabelle's face and she tousled her hair playfully to dispel the intensity of the moment.

Before they bedded down for the night Chyrenia prepared a honey flavoured drink that she said would help them to sleep more soundly so that they would be better prepared to face the long day that lay ahead of them.

When Siabelle awoke it was fully light and Chyrenia was no longer lying next to her. She felt very lethargic and it took a few minutes to gather her thoughts. As she stood up, she momentarily lost her balance and had to grab one of the strong vertical beams that supported the roof of the roundhouse. After regaining her balance, she staggered to the door and looked out towards the sea. She saw a trader's ship just leaving the mouth of the estuary to begin its return journey towards Hibernia. She detected a movement from further down the coast in the corner of her eye, and she saw a small Roman galley rowing furiously up the coast in an evident attempt to intercept the ship. With a growing terror in her heart, she knew that her beloved Chyrenia was on board.

"I am so sorry." said an apprehensive looking Tanuw who had been warned by Chyrenia of Siabelle's terrible and frequently lethal anger. "Chyrenia swore me to secrecy, she had foreseen the events unfolding out to sea and she was determined that you should be protected. She loved you so much Siabelle. She gave you a potion last night that sent you into a deep sleep because she knew that you would never let her leave without you."

For the first time in many moons, tears began to form in Siabelle's eyes, she was not angry with Tanuw, she knew that once Chyrenia had set her heart on a course of action, nobody would be able to stand in her way. Tanuw was openly crying as well now as her heart was also breaking at the thought of the peril her friend was facing. There had been quite a strong breeze coming up from the Southwest that had allowed the trading ship to tack and gather some speed, but the wind was now beginning to slack, and the sail of the trading ship was now failing to provide the thrust needed to escape the oars of the galley that was rapidly closing in on it.

18

The crew of the Roman galley had spent the night anchored near the mouth of the estuary of the river that ran down to the now abandoned village of Gallanbhir. After the tide had eventually lifted it from the sand, the galley had painstakingly made its way up the meandering channel that the river had cut through the sand and shingle. Twice it had temporarily run aground and had had to wait for the rising tide to lift it up again, but it was becoming too dark to risk further travel. The mouth of the estuary was full of treacherous sandbanks and if the galley managed to run aground again in the ebbing light when it was near to high tide, they could be left stranded. Without the possibility of a rising tide to lift them free they would never be able to successfully intercept their quarry and there were rumours of deadly quicksand in the estuary.

As soon as there was sufficient light to navigate once more, the galley pulled itself clear of the mouth of the estuary and the crew rowed hard to the north towards the trading post at Glannoventa. Once they had rounded the headland which had concealed the mouth of the river leading to Glannoventa, they saw the sail of a Hibernian trading ship already heading out to sea. There was quite a powerful wind blowing in from the southwest which enabled the trading ship to gain significant speed even though the wind was not directly behind the vessel. If the wind increased much more the galley, even with its own sail would struggle to keep up and its relatively flat bottom meant that it was pitching about in the choppy waves. Unlike the Hibernian trading vessel which had ballast to keep it stable and a deeper keel, the small Roman coastal galley was not built to weather rough seas.

Drigwold, who had been taken on board by Marcus, went to the side of the galley and threw up for the third time although there was very little more left in his stomach. He was sporting several new angry looking bruises on his face after the angry centurion reminded him of his oversight in forgetting to mention that not all of the Gallancian warriors would be at Kernack's ceremony. This oversight had nearly cost Marcus his life and he was still unsure as to why the Gallancian priestess had called off the attack in the valley above the Stones. There was no possibility that the remaining Romans could have fended off the Gallancians if they had pressed home their attack.

Suddenly the wind began to fade, and the galley quickly began to close in on the trading ship. They were about two leagues from the coast so there was no possibility for any passengers on the vessel to escape through trying to make for the shore. Now all he had to know was whether the Gallancian priestess and her warrior companion were on board. He was particularly looking forward to taking out his frustration upon the woman warrior with the vivid scar who had glared at him with so much hatred after his humiliating defeat. She was not going to be allowed to die quickly. Like most Romans, Marcus was initially contemptuous of the Celtic peoples for allowing their women to fight alongside their men. Long experience of fighting against them had now taught him it was prudent to treat their female warriors with caution and respect. Many legionnaires had lost their lives to arrogant complacency and memories of Boudicca's campaign were still fresh in Roman minds.

The galley was now within the range of an arrow, but Marcus had given strict instructions not to shoot. He wanted his captives alive; Agricola and his strange Egyptian priest would want to interrogate the Gallancian priestess, and it would be adding to his triumph if he could capture her. Suddenly he saw the priestess in the stern of the ship, the wind still strong enough to make her long auburn hair blow around her. She had taken off her travelling cloak and woollen leggings and was now dressed in the white robe of the Gallancian High Priestess of the Moonstone and she was looking directly into Marcus's eyes. There was no anger on her face, in fact she looked almost blissful as the galley closed in. Suddenly she pulled out her hands from beneath the robe and held aloft the small ornate strongbox, smiled at Marcus, and threw the box overboard where it immediately sank beneath the waves. The galley could not stop, and its momentum quickly carried it past the point where the box had sunk whilst the crew began to rapidly back row to stop it crashing into the trading ship. Two grappling irons were thrown to lock the vessels together and as the hulls touched Chyrenia collapsed on to the deck.

19

Chyrenia had looked down on the face of her lover for one last time as Siabelle slept peacefully beneath the woollen covers. It could not be said to be the most beautiful of faces with its vivid scar, but it belonged to the person who had completely stolen her heart. She knew that Siabelle would find it hard to forgive her for what she was about to do but the High Priestess now knew that her premonition was true and the only way to protect the one she loved was to be forever parted from her. She gently kissed Siabelle on her forehead and slipped out of the door of the roundhouse where Tanuw was waiting for her. Tanuw escorted her through the trading post, making sure that none of the traders were awake and led her to where Eochaid, the Captain of the Hibernian trading ship was waiting.

Once on the quayside Tanuw handed Chyrenia a cloth wrapped bundle that she had been looking after for her since her last visit. Chyrenia smiled wistfully and gave her friend an intense hug followed by a kiss. "Ask Siabelle to forgive me, her story is far from over but mine must end today. Tell her that my love for her will remain in her heart to guide her when she needs it the most. In many generations to come I am sure that our love will bring us back together again and will be renewed once more. I would ask you to tell her to turn away from vengeance as there is great danger in following this path, but this would be a futile endeavour. The fire that burns within her cannot be extinguished by my words, as it could not be extinguished through my love. She will choose her own path and meet her own destiny." With a final smile the last High Priestess of the Gallancians turned and walked across the wooden plank onto the ship.

The ship was soon underway and as soon as it cleared the mouth of the estuary it picked up a vigorous south westerly wind and began to make headway out to sea back towards Hibernia. Chyrenia went to the tiny space behind a curtain in the hold that she had been allotted for her travel and took out the bundle that she had left with Tanuw. In the bundle was the white robe of the High Priestess of the Gallancia, guardian of the Moonstone and the Sacred Stones. This was the robe that she had worn the previous Beltane before the darkness enveloped them and changed their lives forever. She changed into her robe and then pulled her travelling cloak over the top to conceal it. She also took out a small package of crushed seeds and a drinking vessel with fresh water which she place into a pouch that she carried with a shoulder cord. She climbed up on to the deck and looked south toward the tiny outline of a Roman galley appearing around the headland.

She watched calmly as the galley slowly closed and waited until they were past the shallows into the deeper waters of the Hibernian Sea and then she closed her eyes and called silently to the Goddess Anu. As she felt the energy begin to flow within her she slowly held up her hands with her palms facing into the brisk wind. She felt the energy of the great Goddess, whose boundless form encompassed all-natural things, flowing within her until they became as one. Then gently, she asked the wind to calm. Within a few minutes the ship's sail began to flap as the wind struggled to fill it and it began to slow as the waves began to ease.

Chyrenia could have used her powers to whip up a storm to drive the galley to the shore, but she knew that those responsible for the presence of the galley were driven by a power possessed by insatiable ambition and greed. They would never give up on the hunt for the Moonstone, even if she fled to Hibernia, and their evil would harm everyone who gave her sanctuary. Now the wind had calmed to a gentle breeze, Chyrenia saw the galley begin to rapidly close on them and Eochaid came and stood by her side watching the Romans frantically rowing towards them. He was puzzled, the Romans relied on trade and goods from Hibernia, and he could not understand why they should be pursuing him with such determination. He had nothing on board of such a value that would command such interest.

"Do not be alarmed Eochaid" said Chyrenia calmly, "it's not you they are interested in, they are coming for me."

Eochaid looked at Chyrenia in alarm, "I don't know how we can protect you Priestess; we cannot sail fast enough to escape them, and we lack the weapons and crew to fight them."

Chyrenia smiled calmly at the captain whose face was wracked with concern, "You do not have to do anything Eochaid. I implore you to do nothing to antagonise them as I do not wish to be the cause of any harm to you or your crew which would result from any defiance. The only thing I request is that you give me a moment of contemplation and space at the stern of your ship so that I may be ready to accept my fate."

"Of course, Priestess." replied Eochaid and he gestured to a couple of his crew to move away to leave Chyrenia to face the Romans. The galley was close now and with relief she saw the huge bulk of the centurion who had been at the ambush by the Stones. Her plan had worked flawlessly and now she could meet her fate with equanimity. She reached into her pouch and took a small handful of the crushed seeds which she swallowed with a sip of water from her water container. When the galley was within arrow range, she threw back her cloak and the now gentle breeze rippled her long hair. She took a deep breath of the sea air and raised the Moonstone box in the air to show the Roman centurion his prize. She could clearly see his cold calculating eyes and she held his gaze as she suddenly threw the box over the ship's stern. The Roman cried out in frustration as the small heavy box disappeared beneath the waves.

As the Roman galley crashed against the side of the Hibernian ship Chyrenia fell to her knees and then tipped over onto her side and curled into a foetal position. The sound of the Romans coming on board and the sea began to fade and she no longer felt constrained by her body. Her spirit soared up until she was high above the deck, and she looked down dispassionately as two Roman legionnaires roughly grabbed her body under its arms and lifted it forcefully upright. There was a silver glow all around her and then she was not separate from the glow but part of it, her spirit becoming one with the great Goddess. She was embraced once again, wrapped in boundless love until the time should come for her spirit to be reborn again and she could walk once more upon the Goddess's earthly realm.

20

Marcus leapt on board the Hibernian trader and looked at the lifeless body of the High Priestess supported in the firm grip of the two legionnaires. By now both the galley and the ship, which were locked together with the grappling hooks, had drifted a considerable distance from where the box had sunk beneath the waves. He called for Drigwold who clumsily clambered over from the galley, still feeling sick and unsteady in the swell. "What's happened to her?" he asked gesturing with his head towards Chyrenia's now lifeless body.

Drigwold searched Chyrenia and found the small pouch with the remnants of the crushed seeds still inside which he sniffed and examined closely. After a short while he looked up at Marcus and casually said "Hemlock, she poisoned herself with crushed hemlock seed."

Marcus went over to Eochaid whom he towered over. "Where is the other one?" he demanded. Eochaid knew very little Latin, but Drigwold had now learnt enough to attempt to translate. Eochaid's Hibernian dialect was very different to Drigwold's Britonic but after years of trading Eochaid had grown accustomed to the speech and quickly learnt that the Romans were looking for another woman passenger.

Eochaid looked at Marcus and shook his head and gestured with open palms that there was no other woman on board, but Marcus ordered a thorough search of the ship anyway. If he had the scar faced woman, he could have had her tortured to make sure that the Moonstone was inside the box. Now he had no way of knowing for sure and he imagined Agricola would not be easily reassured by this revelation. He decided he would not rest until he had found scar face, not just because she could confirm the fate of the Moonstone but also because she had so openly defied him when he had been routed. Marcus was not the forgiving type, and the woman would be easy to find with such a vivid disfigurement.

Marcus ordered the legionnaires back on to the galley, leaving Chyrenia's body dumped unceremoniously on the ship's deck. Marcus ordered the galley to make sweeping searches for the sunken box, but it was a futile gesture, the water was 25 cubits deep and there was nobody amongst the galley's crew who could dive to those depths. Marcus knew there were specialist divers in the Eastern Mediterranean who collected sponges, capable of reaching this depth, but that knowledge was useless to him in his current predicament. The water was also cloudy, full of sediment that had been swept down from the mountains and out through the estuary so there was no chance of spotting the Moonstone's box. He was not even sure exactly where the box had sunk and after over twenty futile passes Marcus gave up his search. Once again, the Gallancian Priestess had outsmarted him, although this time it was at the cost of her life.

Marcus directed the galley south, past the estuary of the Gallancian's until he came to another temporary trading post that was being used as a supplies base for Agricola's legions. From there he, and an ever-reluctant Drigwold took to horses and headed for the Roman Governor's legions which were now moving closer to the lands of the Scoti. Drigwold was not used to riding and rapidly became very uncomfortable sitting on the hard saddle, a fact that brought only the smallest of consolations to a deeply troubled Marcus.

Agricola and the Egyptian priest listened impassively as Marcus relayed the events leading up to the loss of the Moonstone's box and the death of the High Priestess of the Gallancia.

Agricola turned to the priest of Seth and simply said "Is the Moonstone safe?" The power of the Moonstone was manifest in all those with love for the divine Goddess of nature and their actions were guided by the compassion in their hearts for all living things. If the stone was beyond recovery, then to all intents and purposes it was almost as good as if the stone had been destroyed forever. Not that the members of the Order of the Black Crystal would be content with this, and he knew that Marcus's failure would reflect upon him. His hopes of leadership of the Order might now be in question, but if the crystal were safe, he would rigorously argue that he had fulfilled his duties.

The Egyptian priest repeated the ceremony that he had previously used to detect that the last Moonstone was in the land of the Gallancians. In his trance he could feel the tiniest hint of the presence of the Moonstone, but it was far too weak to either be found, or to negatively impact upon the ambitions of the Order of the Black Crystal. As he came out of trance, he looked at the round pool of blood on the segment of the granite altar stone and there was also no detectable deviation suggesting the presence of the Moonstone. He raised his head and looked directly at Agricola. "The Moonstone seems to be safe." he said, "This would be consistent with the Stone being inside the box that was lost from the ship, but we can never know for certain. The Order must remain vigilant and be ready to act swiftly should the stone ever be found and re-energised."

Agricola looked at Marcus and pondered as to what to do about him. He had a sense of loyalty to the centurion who had served him so well in their many campaigns together. Treating him too harshly might also not play well with the legionnaires that had served alongside him and respected him. Equally, if his failure were not in some way recognised then there was the danger that Agricola could be seen as weak and that would have damaging consequences for his command. The loyalty of the legions was earned through respect and a significant aspect of this respect was out of fear. When on the battlefield faced by overwhelming odds it was important that the legionnaires knew the price of cowardice and held firm. Boudicca had learnt this to her cost when her army was defeated by a Roman legion that she outnumbered twenty times over but whose discipline held and rapidly triumphed over a disorganised and chaotic foe. Perhaps even more importantly, Marcus himself would not respect the Governor if his failure were completely overlooked.

Agricola spoke to Marcus who stood rigidly at attention in front of him. "Your mission was to recover the Moonstone, not just to render it safe. It would not be appropriate for you to retain the position of primus pilus of the legion but your long service to me and to Rome will not go without recognition. I am going to send you to look after my estates and administration in Londinium and you will retain the rank and privileges of Centurion."

Marcus had feared far worse, and he knew that Agricola had been more than fair with him after the unsatisfactory conclusion to his mission. In some ways he was pleased. He had spent 25 years in the legions and the constant campaigning had taken its toll. He was no longer young and the comforts of the Governor's residence in Londinium would be a welcome change to the hardship of constant marching and battle.

Agricola then turned to Drigwold who squirmed uncomfortably under the Governor's unblinking gaze. "I have to confess at being surprised at the ingenuity of your scheming and plotting." he finally said to the Druid. "You almost pulled it off but like Marcus there has to be a reckoning for the fact that the Moonstone was not brought back to me intact. I promised that you would be released from slavery if you served me well and on balance, I believe you have done so within the limits of your abilities."

Drigwold raised his head in delight at these words, soon he would be free again and he was already beginning to think how he could take advantage of his Druidic knowledge to prey on the weaknesses and gullibility of others. There was great wealth to be created in a land where Druids were now extremely scarce. He would have to be careful as the open practice of Druidic rights in territories under Roman governance was explicitly forbidden, but where there was a will there was always a way with a sufficiency of cunning and blackmail. Finally, his luck had turned!

As quickly as his hopes had soared, they were quickly dashed as Agricola continued.

"I have here a scroll which enlists you as a freed slave to the position of an auxiliary in the Roman legions for a period of ten years, temporarily posted to the garrison of Londinium. You have proved useful to me and may yet prove useful again. I am sure you will find service as a Roman auxiliary educational, and it allows you to maintain your fruitful working partnership with Marcus. I hope I do not need to remind you that the penalty for desertion from a Roman legion is execution or a short and very painful life working as a slave in the mines?"

Drigwold glared at Agricola and caught the smirk of amusement on Marcus's face. He had no doubt that life under the command of Marcus would be almost as miserable as life as a slave. He did however have the wit not to speak out against Agricola's decision as he knew that retribution would be swift. He gritted his teeth and bowed to the Governor in acceptance of his judgement.

"In recognition of your service I have a gift of ten gold aurei," Agricola threw a small pouch to the Druid "which will help you to satisfy your rather loathsome proclivities in the brothels of Londinium. I suggest you do not spend it too quickly as you will find that the salary of an auxiliary is far from luxurious. After deductions for food and equipment costs, an auxiliary typically earns less than 100 denarii per year."

After being dismissed a relieved Marcus and a fuming Drigwold walked away from Agricola's quarters and the huge Centurion put his arm around the diminutive Druid and squeezed him painfully hard. "I am sure you are as delighted as I am to be continuing our professional relationship together." he said cheerfully. "You will be delighted to know that I already have plans for you."

"I'm sure" said Drigwold miserably. His reply earned him a backhanded blow from Marcus that knocked him to the ground.

"I'm sure Centurio" growled Marcus, "you're in the legion now my lad so you had better get used to addressing your superior officers properly."

A dazed Drigwold dragged himself to his feet and slouched forlornly in the wake of Marcus who set about securing a passage for them both to Londinium.

21

Eochaid breathed a sigh of relief as the Roman legionnaires removed the grappling hooks from his ship and turned south. He was worried that the Romans might dish out some swift retribution after the death of the priestess and was glad to be met with complete indifference by the centurion in charge. With great care Eochaid and his crew lay Chyrenia's body onto a clean woollen cape and he pondered what to do next. His first instinct was to continue on his way and take the body to Hibernia with him but finally he decided that she deserved to be buried by her people and so he turned the ship around and tacked against the wind back to Glannoventa.

Tanuw and Siabelle saw the ship return and, with the help of a generous payment from Siabelle, they persuaded Eochaid to take them both with Chyrenia's body back to the village of Gallanbhir. As they neared the wooden quay Siabelle saw the bulky figure of Garraculous with his sword drawn, standing with three other surviving warriors. He was eyeing the approaching vessel with deep suspicion. He sheathed his sword with relief when the ship was close enough for him to recognise Siabelle, but the relief was short lived when he saw the body of Chyrenia lying serenely on the deck.

Garraculous told Siabelle that most of the tribe were still sheltering up by the hidden lake, but Garraculous had decided to follow the Romans back to the village. He had seen the main body of legionnaires arrive with growing concern and then was relieved when he saw them march on towards Brigante territory. He then watched the small Roman galley eventually drift off the sand by the quay as it was raised by the tide and made its way back up the estuary.

"What of Kernack and the others" asked Siabelle.

Garraculous told her of a scene of complete carnage in the oak grove. There were so many bodies, far too many for him to deal with and some had already begun to be eaten by the wolves. There was nothing he could do until it was safe to call back the tribe and for each family to try to find and bury what remained of their loved ones. At least the Romans had not torched the village but there were too few warriors left to safely defend it from raiders, let alone the Romans should they choose to return.

"Did you see the body of the Druid Glannox amongst the dead?" asked Siabelle.

Garraculous's eyes blazed with fury as he told Siabelle that the Druid had returned, unbound, with the main Roman force and had left with the huge centurion on the galley. "It was obvious that he was already known to them and that he had betrayed Kernack and the village by leading them into a trap."

"Kernack betrayed himself and the village with his greed and vanity." said Siabelle. She stopped short of telling Garraculous of the clandestine evening meeting between Glannox and the Roman centurion at the travellers' rest house. It would be hard to explain to him why Chyrenia and Siabelle had not raised their suspicions directly with Kernack at the Council. At least this way they had managed to save the rest of the villagers and a future for the tribe's children although it had been at a truly terrible cost.

The next day the villagers returned, and it was decided to bury the dead where they fell at the sacred Oak grove. Over the centuries to come the grove would gain a dark reputation. It was sometimes said that at the anniversary of the massacre, the sound of the clash of swords and the cries of dying warriors could be heard emanating from amongst the trees.

The remaining twelve Priestesses of the Stones with Siabelle, Tanuw, Garraculous and Melesone conducted a quiet burial for Chyrenia near her roundhouse in the woods. Some of the Priestesses argued that she should be buried in the centre of their sacred stones, but Siabelle felt that the Romans had desecrated the circle by toppling over some of the stones. She knew that Chyrenia had always been at her happiest at her home amongst the trees, and in the company of all the animals who used to come and visit her. As they laid her body in its woodland grave the tears poured from Siabelle's eyes, the agony of this final parting from the only person she had ever truly loved was far worse than any wound inflicted upon her in battle.

After they had buried their High Priestess the other twelve priestesses felt that there was no longer any future for the sisterhood. The Priestesses of the Moonstone had been formed long ago when the tribe had been presented with the Moonstone and now that the stone was lost and the power of the Stone Circle desecrated, they felt that it was now impossible to create the ancient magic. There were also immediate pressing needs that they had to focus on. The Priestesses were also wives, mothers, aunts, sisters, and daughters who also used their knowledge as healers. Many had lost loved ones after the massacre in the oak grove and the tribe had never been in greater peril.

Over the next few days, a new Tribal Council was formed and Melesone was elected as the new chieftain with Garraculous taking the role of the commander of the remaining warriors. Although still young, Melesone had been carefully selected by Chyrenia for her compassion and wisdom to serve the Goddess at the Beltane ceremony that had taken place just over a year ago. The remaining women of the tribe overwhelmingly backed Chyrenia's choice, and it was a time for reconciliation and the building of new alliances and relationships. With so many warriors gone, almost half the men of the tribe, and twelve of its strongest women, it was now a time to compromise if the Gallancia were to survive.

Siabelle was asked to join the Council and Garraculous suggested to her that she should lead the warriors as the few that were left had been under her command in her raiding party and had formed strong and loyal bonds to her leadership, but Siabelle declined. The loss of Chyrenia had broken her spirit and she became a bit of a recluse, spending much of her time alone at Chyrenia's roundhouse in the woods. Apart from sharing her martial skills with the young in the tribe who had grown strong enough to handle weapons, she mostly preferred her own company although she often talked to Chyrenia whose spirit still seemed so alive and present.

One of the first actions that Melesone undertook in her new role was to arrange a meeting with Connull, King of the Carvetti at the tribal capital of Luguvalos. Garraculous wanted to accompany her, but Melesone knew that difficult decisions would have to be made and she feared that Garraculous's pride and passion could prove to be more of a hindrance than a help. Instead, she was accompanied by Glyderferwyn and was granted a Carvetti escort to ensure her safety.

Connull knew of the massacre of the Gallancia warriors but rather than take advantage of the weakness of the Gallancia he was gracious and supportive when he met with Melesone. It was however clear that the Carvetti would be taking no action against the Romans in reprisal despite the fact that the Gallancia had an alliance with the Carvetti for mutual protection against aggressors. Connull was a courageous leader, but he was also wise enough to know that he could not defeat the Romans and the best course of action for the future of his people was to make peace with them. He was therefore actively providing support to Agricola and his legions in his campaign against the Scoti and the other tribes that inhabited the lands far to the north.

After some negotiation Melesone agreed to take back a proposal to the Gallancian Council which she had provisionally agreed with Connull. The Gallancia would become part of the Carvetti tribe although they would retain their own local Council and leadership. They must also pledge their allegiance to the authority of the Roman Governor, pay tribute to the Carvetti King and pay the taxes imposed by the Romans. In return Connull would continue to provide protection against the northern raiders and would send thirty warriors and their families to settle in Gallancia to provide immediate protection and help with the impending harvest and the management of livestock.

Whilst Melesone was in Luguvalos she met with a Britonic speaking representative of the Roman Governor Agricola. Using the authority delegated to him by the Governor, he accepted the terms of the alliance proposed by Connull although he seemed rather contemptuous of having to talk to a woman. He asked disparagingly if the Gallancian men usually deferred to women in matters of such importance? He did however share some important and also alarming information with Melesone. He revealed that he was no fan of the centurion Marcus who had treated the administrator contemptuously when Marcus was still primus pilus, the senior centurion of Agricola's legion. He therefore took great delight in telling everyone who cared to listen about the Marcus's dismissal to Londinium with his pet Druid. He also said that the Romans were very interested in a woman warrior with a pronounced facial scar and were offering a substantial reward for her capture, but only if she could be captured alive. Apparently, she held knowledge that was of interest to Governor Agricola.

Melesone returned to Gallanbhir knowing that her proposed agreement with Connull would be met with anger from many within the Gallancia who were a proud and independent people. They would now essentially be vassals of the Carvetti who in turn had accepted their fate as vassals of Rome. Most painfully she also knew that Siabelle could no longer stay with the tribe as they were in no position to offer her protection, and the Romans appeared to be only too aware of her associations with Chyrenia and the Gallancians.

The Tribal Council meeting was as Melesone predicted, extremely heated. Garraculous in particular was furious at the prospect of paying homage and taxes to the very people who had cynically slaughtered so many of the tribe. Melesone was breast feeding Daliphe who started to wail in distress as her father vented his anger and her anguished cries quickly stilled his shouting. In a calm and loving voice Melesone spoke to Garraculous as a father, not a warrior. "It's her future and the future of all the other children in the tribe that we are deciding here today." she said. "How are you going to protect her? Isn't it better to be vassals of Rome with a measure of independence than slaves of Rome? You can be sure that slavery is our fate unless you truly believe that you can both defy the might of the legions and the hostility of the Carvetti rather than seek their protection. Tell me truly Garraculous, can you and your warriors offer Daliphe a better future?"

The righteous anger within Garraculous had begun to subside, he loved Melesone and trusted her wisdom and Daliphe meant everything to him. His warrior code meant that he would fearlessly give his life to protect those he loved but the time had come when fighting would harm them, not protect them. When the vote came as to whether to support Melesone's treaty with Connull it was unanimous. After the meeting was concluded Melesone went up to her partner and lover. Raising herself up on her toes to reach, she kissed the lips of his bearded and tattooed face that brought such terror on the field of battle and yet shone with so much love for her. She passed Daliphe to him and the tiny figure fell asleep in the comfort of the crook of the mighty arm that held her.

A Carvetti messenger from Connull's personal guard had accompanied Melesone on her return to the village and he sped back to the King to relay the Council's decision. Within the next two weeks twenty sheep, ten goats and five cattle would be herded to Luguvalos as a tribute to their new King and protector. The King had been careful of what he had asked for as he knew that this was a time for the Gallancia to rebuild their community which was both in their interests and his own. In time they would be able to offer more, including young warriors who would be asked to serve as auxiliaries in the legions of Rome as part of his obligations to Agricola.

The only person with whom Melesone had shared the news about Siabelle, the centurion Marcus, and the Druid was Glyderferwyn. She now knew that Glannox, the Druid to whom they had offered refuge, was not an escaped Roman slave but a disgraced Druidic exile who had betrayed his own kind on Mona and whose real name was Drigwold. Word of his betrayal had now spread to the Gallancia, it seemed that his malign spirit corrupted everyone who came into contact with him. It had exploited the weakness in Kernack caused by his own greed and vanity and Kernack's weakness had nearly destroyed the tribe. It had only been Chyrenia's wisdom that had kept their hopes of a future alive.

Melesone and Glyderferwyn agreed that they should not tell the Council about the threat to Siabelle as she was sure that the warrior code would not be broken and that Garraculous and the rest of her loyal group would insist on protecting her. Melesone now faced the difficult task of telling a woman whom she loved and respected that she should leave the tribe that had adopted her. After the death of Chyrenia she was worried that this might be another crushing blow from which Siabelle might not recover. Love had shielded Siabelle when she first arrived and collapsed at Chyrenia's feet, and this same love was now going to drive her away.

As it turned out Melesone need not have worried. As soon as Siabelle heard about Marcus and Drigwold the anger that had kept her alive since she was enslaved and raped at the hands of the Romans at the age of fifteen erupted with renewed ferocity within her heart. She listened impassively as Melesone revealed that she now had a bounty on her head and that she was in considerable danger as it was well known that she had been adopted by the Gallancia.

"I leave tomorrow for Londinium" Siabelle replied with a voice that was as cold and emotionless as a block of ice. There were no words of comfort that Melesone could offer, and she somehow knew that Siabelle's fate was destined to be resolved in that distant town. She gave Siabelle a warm embrace to which the warrior gave a token response, but her mind was already elsewhere.

Before they parted Siabelle asked Melesone to relay a message to her brother and sister warriors who had fought so often beside her. "Tell them that my heart is broken with the memory of Chyrenia and that I can no longer stay where the people and places that she loved are a daily reminder to me that she is gone." She briefly smiled at Melesone, she loved this young leader of the Gallancia and would miss her. "It's not a lie," she said quietly, "I have been finding it increasingly difficult to remain amongst you with the constant memory of Chyrenia. If they know I have gone after Drigwold they would insist on joining me, and that would be a disaster for the future of the tribe I swore to protect." Melesone's eyes glistened with tears as she left Siabelle but for the scarred warrior the time for tears was over. Now was the time for retribution.

The journey to Londinium would not be easy overland if the word had spread that Agricola had an interest in her. Her facial scar made her dangerously recognisable and her status under Roman law as an escaped slave meant that everyone had an obligation to turn her in to the Roman authorities or face harsh punishment. She decided that the safest way would be to travel by ship, and she turned once again to Tanuw for her help.

Tanuw knew that Eochaid was planning a trading trip around the coast and eventually across the channel to Gaul. The respect that Eochaid had shown towards Chyrenia by returning her body to the Gallancia and the genuine sympathy he had expressed towards their plight at Roman hands made her optimistic that he would be prepared to take Siabelle to Londinium. Siabelle had also amassed considerable personal wealth as her share of all the successful raiding parties she had led against the Romans and other hostile enemies of the tribe. If Eochaid was prepared to take her he would be well rewarded for his troubles.

Tanuw hid Siabelle for three weeks until Eochaid next came in to Glannoventa and, after considerable negotiation, he agreed to take Siabelle to Londinium. The voyage took about four weeks as Eochaid was stopping on the way at a number of ports. Twice Siabelle had to hide in a tiny hidden compartment behind a false bulkhead near the bow of the boat as Roman administrators with local tribal officials searched the vessel for goods that could be subject to the portoria. The portoria was a customs tax paid on certain goods being imported into countries under Roman administration. Eochaid was taking a considerable risk, if Siabelle had been discovered his ship would have been impounded and Eochaid could have been heavily fined or imprisoned. Siabelle's fate would have been torture and death and she held her pugio to her own throat when the searches were taking place to ensure she could take her own life rather than be captured.

The risk of discovery and capture after docking in Londinium was also high as the Roman authorities in the town were far more thorough and efficient than in some of the more provisional outposts. Eochaid therefore anchored further up the estuary river known to Eochaid as the Tems that flowed through Londinium. Siabelle wore a hooded cloak that helped to shield her face from curious onlookers and also concealed her hidden spatha as she made her way into Londinium. Siabelle still favoured this Roman sword over the native Britonic swords, probably because of the familiarity of years of fighting with it. The spatha she now carried was her third, the first two having been ground to destruction through the frequent sharpening required to maintain a lethally sharp edge.

Londinium had been largely razed to the ground by Boudicca's revolt but in the more than twenty years since its destruction it had been rebuilt and had now grown even larger than before. It was estimated by Eochaid that the population had now risen to nearly 30,000 making it by far the largest town in Brittania. A stout wooden defensive stockade had been constructed around the landward sides of the town and entry points were guarded, with those desiring access frequently questioned and searched. Such was the new confidence in the primacy of Roman power after the ruthless subjugation of the tribes involved in Boudicca's revolt, that a substantial number of informal townships growing up outside the wall had been permitted. These were simply known as the

Settlements. They were largely ignored by the Roman authorities and had become lawless hotbeds of drinking, gambling, and prostitution.

There was no kind of formal council to govern the Settlements but there were two prominent gang leaders who dominated the others and who could afford to bribe the Romans sufficiently well to be largely left alone. The two leaders were Kystrachus, a Trinovante exile who had fallen out with his tribal council for thieving, and Strella, once a prostitute, who had slept, bribed, and murdered her way to power. Kystrachus and Strella switched between scheming against each other and cooperating, depending on which option offered the best return at the time. At this moment there was an uneasy truce between the two and the Settlements were somewhat quieter than usual.

Siabelle found a drinking house where she could get food and ale and where she hoped to engage a suitably intoxicated local in conversation to see if she could find any clues as to the whereabouts of Drigwold. Siabelle felt at home amongst this band of outcasts and to her satisfaction nobody seemed to react at her appearance or show any indication that they recognised her after she had lowered her hood. It seemed that Agricola's interest in the woman with the scarred face had not yet travelled as far as Londinium, or at least, for whatever reason, centurion Marcus had not yet put out word of the reward. Her scar was however useful to deter unwelcome advances from those who frequently benefitted from taking advantage of strangers if they detected any sign of vulnerability.

The drinking house had a number of long tables with benches at either side and it was not long before a young man sat down opposite Siabelle. He looked rather down on his luck and was drinking in a manner of someone seeking liquid solace rather than enjoyment. She asked him his name and was told that he was called Finiel. She asked him why he was looking so glum and then pretended to be interested as he told her how his girlfriend's father had found out about their affair and had banned her from seeing him. Despite her father's intervention they had managed a clandestine meeting, only to be betrayed by a jealous rival for her affection. She had been harshly beaten and her father had let it be known that he would handsomely reward anyone who did the same to him. His head told him to leave the town, but his heart refused to be separated from her and so now he sat and drank and awaited his fate. Siabelle could not have been less interested, but she made the occasional sympathetic remark and, as the effects of the ale grew and his reserves diminished, she began to gently question him.

"I have heard a rumour that there is a Druid in Londinium who is still practicing Druidic magic and giving prophesies despite the Roman ban." she said casually.

Despite the effects of the ale Finiel was still cautious enough to glance around to see if anyone was listening before whispering "You should not talk about such things, even in the Settlements the Romans have spies."

"It's probably not true anyway," said Siabelle, "the Romans would never allow it within the town limits, such goings on would mean certain death."

Finiel looked cautiously around again before replying, "Oh it is true, this particular Druid has Roman protection. He's the pet Druid of the new centurion in charge of the town's garrison and is therefore untouchable."

Siabelle feigned surprise, "A Roman protecting a Druid? I have never heard of such a thing!" After a long pause she said, "How would you get to see this Druid if you were interested in having a reading?"

"I don't see why anyone would bother." said Finiel, "What use have the Druids been in protecting us against the Romans? As far as I am concerned, they are a waste of time."

Siabelle said nothing but she placed a couple of copper coins on the table in front of Finiel which he quickly palmed and slipped them into his pouch.

"It's not difficult if you have money." said Finiel, "He lodges at one of the two brothels that are permitted within the town limits. Strella pays the Roman authorities handsomely to tolerate their presence, but it is money well spent. The wealthy traders, legionnaires and officials who frequent them make her a fortune. The Druid is in the biggest brothel opposite the grounds of the new Temple dedicated to Venus that the Romans are constructing. Rather appropriate don't you think?"

"Is it easy to get into the town?" she asked.

"It's not a problem if you have the correct pass." he replied.

"And if you don't have a pass?"

"There still might be a way." said Finiel.

Siabelle looked questioningly at Finiel to elaborate but he returned to gazing at his empty wooden ale tankard. Siabelle caught the attention of one of the women serving in the alehouse and soon there were two fresh tankards sat before them.

"Well?" she said.

"Strella can get you forged documents," Finiel replied, "but it would cost you."

"Could you introduce us?"

Again, Finiel returned to tankard gazing until Siabelle placed another couple of coins in front of him which he again quickly palmed. "Meet me outside this alehouse an hour after first light." he replied.

The following morning Siabelle met a very hungover Finiel as agreed, and he escorted her through the twisting paths that wound their way amongst the largely dilapidated dwellings of the Settlements. Soon they came to a heavily constructed compound fully twice the height of a person made out of stout wooden posts. There were a couple of guards at the door who showed evidence of their profession on their scarred and battered faces. Finiel went up to one of them and started talking to him and then pointed to Siabelle. The guard gestured for her to come over and he smirked when she dropped her hood to reveal her own scarred face.

"I hope you aren't looking for work in the brothels with a face like that." he grunted and then looked at his companion for recognition of his humour, receiving a smirk in response. "If you want to speak to Strella you had better make it worth her while."

Siabelle reached into the pouch under the cloak and produced two silver denarii. The guard held out his hand, but she closed her fingers over the coins. "You can have these when you have introduced me to Strella."

The guard's expression changed, and he moved menacingly towards Siabelle lifting a stout cudgel in the process. "I think I'll take them now." he said. As he clumsily took a swing at Siabelle she deftly sidestepped him, and the guard found the edge of a razor sharp pugio against his throat. He carefully dropped the cudgel and slowly raised his arms above his head.

"Are two denarii really worth dying for?" she snarled at him.

The guard very carefully turned his head towards the other one whose mouth had opened in astonishment at the speed with which the scarred woman had reacted. "Call Strella" he muttered.

After a few moments, a woman who looked about forty years old ambled out of the compound and emotionlessly observed Siabelle and the guard who was staying very still. "Can I help you love?" she eventually enquired.

"You are not going to upset me now?" whispered Siabelle into the guard's ear. His eyes confirmed that he would not and as quickly as it appeared the pugio was once again concealed beneath her cloak.

Siabelle opened her palm and said, "I wish to discuss business with you, but your employees here have shown a disappointing lack of hospitality."

Strella paused to assess Siabelle and then casually told her guards to stand down and she waved Siabelle into the compound. Siabelle briefly glanced at Finiel who looked as amazed as the guards at how she had dealt with their clumsy attempt to rob her. "Wait here" she said to him.

The defensive qualities of Strella's compound reflected her not infrequent quarrels with Kystrachus. Inside the compound were a number of timber dwellings and Strella led Siabelle into the largest one.

The two women had a grudging respect for each other. Strella had dragged her way up to a position of relative wealth and power through one of the toughest professions that any woman could follow by sheer force of will. Siabelle had followed an equally difficult and dangerous path and both women recognised and admired the survival instincts and determination of the other.

Siabelle explained that she wanted documents to gain access to Londinium and Strella said that it could be arranged but it would cost ten denarii. As a matter of respect for custom, Siabelle negotiated a price of eight denarii, half now and half on receipt, which was a lot for a relatively simple document, but which left both women satisfied. Strella also had the presence of mind not to ask Siabelle her name but suggested that the document be made out in the name of Hargwen, a seller of firewood for which there was a constant demand in the town.

When she came out of Strella's compound, she found Finiel waiting for her. He had decided that it might well be profitable to stay close to this very dangerous woman, with the added bonus that she might be inclined to protect him if anyone decided to take up the offer of his girlfriend's father's reward.

Two days later Siabelle sent Finiel off to Strella's compound with four denarii and he returned with a suitably stained and bedraggled piece of parchment which permitted Hargwen to bring firewood into the town. For a generous price Finiel had agreed to be Siabelle's guide when they had gained access to the town and to act as a liaison with the Druid to set up their meeting. As a resident of Londinium, Finiel already had the necessary permit to freely enter the town.

Siabelle bought a dirty peasant jacket and smeared her face with grime before approaching one of the entrances in the town just before dusk with a huge bundle of firewood on her back which made her stoop under the burden of her load and largely hid her face from observation. She could still not be certain that word had not reached Londinium of Agricola's interest in the Britonic warrior with a very distinctive scar. A very bored guard barely glanced at her permit before waving her through.

Finiel had already agreed a meeting for a "Refined Roman woman who was interested in pagan magic and would pay well for the privilege." They first went to Finiel's dwelling in the town where Siabelle dumped the firewood. Hidden inside the bundle was her spatha and her pugio. She had also brought with her the beautiful travelling robe that had been given to her by Marciana, the High Priestess of Venus when she had met her on the road so many years before. The robe was a bit creased and crumpled but she managed to get it looking presentable. It would pass as long as nobody noticed that she was wearing stout riveted leather sandals on her feet which were a bit incongruous with such an expensive robe.

22

Drigwold was rather pleased with his lot. His time as a Roman auxiliary in Londinium was nowhere near as awful as he had expected. To his pleasant surprise Marcus had virtually ignored him since they had arrived in the town and seemed completely disinterested in trying to train him up to be an effective auxiliary legionnaire. Perhaps the centurion had realised that it was a virtually hopeless task as Drigwold had neither the physique nor the mentality to undertake the duties of a legionnaire. He would have been an absolute liability on any field of battle.

To his even greater surprise Marcus had grudgingly permitted him to take up residence in a brothel and once his reserves of aurei had run out he had even let Drigwold earn money as a "practicing Druid" to finance his lurid lifestyle. This could be punishable by death in Roman law after Boudicca's rebellion but as a result it was also very profitable. Interest in the Britonic pagan Gods and practicing Druidic rights and divinations was still highly prized and there were very few Druids still alive under the Roman occupation. Drigwold had something of a monopoly, and he was exploiting it to the full.

Tonight, he was going to be entertaining a Roman lady who was titillated with the thoughts of meeting a "Real Druid." and was prepared to pay two gold aurei for the privilege. He had his own suite of rooms on the second floor of the brothel. It had a separate entrance via a flight of steps that led from an alleyway behind the brothel up the side of the building for the discretion of visitors. Strella charged him a fortune for the privilege. She also tolerated some of his excesses with the prostitutes although once he went too far, and he seriously hurt one of the women who could not work again for two weeks. One of Strella's henchmen painfully reminded him that it was unwise to damage Strella's employees and prevent them from earning. Stupidly Drigwold had complained to Marcus about his treatment and received another clout around the head from the surly centurion for his trouble.

Just after darkness fell there was a knock on the door, and he opened it to find the young man who had arranged the lady's visit standing outside. At the bottom of the stairs, he could see a lady in a very expensive gown, and he immediately started thinking of ways that he might separate her from even more of her evident wealth. He gestured for the lady to come up and she daintily climbed up the stairs, concealing her face in the hood which was entirely understandable as she was entering a well-known brothel and was sensibly concealing her identity. The young man remained outside, presumably to escort her safely back after her audience.

Drigwold had surrounded the walls of his meeting room with tapestries of exotic figures and symbols and had just a few candles around the walls giving off a low light. He had wanted to create an air of mystery and magic to impress his clients. In the middle of the room was a low table surrounded by comfortable pillows with a single white candle placed in the middle. He gestured for the lady to sit on the pillow and in his still rather faltering Latin he asked what he could do for her. In a gentle voice the lady replied that she was seeking revenge upon a man who had caused her a grievous injustice and asked whether he could help her.

Drigwold replied that he could cast a powerful curse that would undoubtably have terrible consequences for the man involved and could even offer to prepare her poison if she were in a position to use it. The woman still had not revealed her face to him, she was obviously shy about asking for such a service.

"That is not quite the sort of thing I had in mind." replied the lady in her gentle voice.

"I'm sure I can find some way to help you. Might I ask the name of the man who has so offended you?" enquired Drigwold.

To his amazement the lady leapt up, threw off the cloak and in a broad Trinovante accent said, "The name of the treacherous man is Drigwold and I am now going to disembowel the bastard."

Drigwold looked in horror at the scarred face of Siabelle who leapt across the table and plunged her pugio into his stomach. She placed her hand over his mouth to stifle his screams as she slowly twisted the blade in his bowel and sliced it open so that his intestines spilled out in front of him. He writhed in agony, vainly trying to escape the steely grip of the warrior who was killing him. As he started to pass out through the excruciating pain and loss of blood, he heard her say, "I heard you enjoy necromancy. Can you read your future in your own guts? The fresher the better they say. I'm no expert but your future looks to be full of pain and rather short." With that she thrust the pugio upwards into the Druid's heart and he left the world to face his own demons in the Otherworld.

Siabelle wiped her blade on the Druids cushions and spat at his body with contempt. She bent over to pick up her robe from the floor but at that moment the door crashed open, and its frame was filled with the enormous bulk of the centurion she had last seen in the ambush by the stones.

Siabelle leapt back with the pugio still in her hand and warily glared at the Roman who was blocking her exit.

Marcus slowly entered the room and glanced on the mutilated body of the Druid Drigwold which had slumped over after Siabelle had finished disembowelling him with her dagger. Keeping his eyes warily on Siabelle he pushed Drigwold's body over with his foot and looked dispassionately at it.

"He really was quite contemptible." said Marcus, "His character had no redeeming features at all so I guess you have done everyone a favour, although I am not sure Agricola would necessarily be pleased. He seemed to find the wretch's complete lack of integrity and loyalty useful and also manageable because we could also add cowardice to his list of dubious virtues."

Marcus was wearing his armour although he was not wearing his helmet and had a drawn and bloodied gladius in his hand. He saw Siabelle looking at the blood on the blade. "Oh, I forgot to mention that your escort has had an unfortunate accident and will not be able to join you, not that it matters because you will not be leaving this room alive. We have not been formally introduced, I am Marcus, the centurion in charge of the Londinium garrison and you are of course Siabelle, recently of the Gallancia. I am so glad you accepted my invitation."

"What invitation?" said Siabelle.

"Why the invitation that Agricola's representative in Connull's court left with Melesone? Agricola has no interest in you at all, in fact he is blissfully unaware of your existence. You were perfectly safe with the Gallancia, but I wanted to give you a little encouragement to leave and seek revenge on the person who had betrayed you. All I had to do was to set him up as bait in this brothel, in which he felt completely at home and wait for word from my spies that you had arrived. You might be pleased to know that Strella has been well rewarded for her services, which is just as well as she will no longer be able to benefit from her most profitable client." He kicked Drigwold's lifeless body again to emphasise the point.

"Now I am going to kill you for the embarrassing ambush you engineered with your dead Priestess, but before you die you are going to tell me everything you know about the Moonstone. I'm afraid you are not going to die quickly and there is no point in calling out for help as I have made it explicitly clear that our little meeting is not to be disturbed."

Siabelle knew she was in grave danger; she had left her spatha at Finiel's as it was too big to be effectively concealed beneath the elegant travelling robe and her pugio was little match for an expertly trained legionnaire with a gladius. She could see no way out but as always before a conflict, her mind cleared as she concentrated fully on the movements of the person trying to kill her.

Marcus gave a short lunge towards her and Siabelle nimbly stepped back, but this cost her distance and she was closer to the wall. She tried to feint to the right to draw Marcus, but he calmly held the centre and ignored her. Another thrust and more space lost, Siabelle's pugio just managing to deflect Marcus's blade. Now she was virtually against the wall, and she desperately slashed out with her pugio, but he calmly blocked it and delivered a crushing blow with the hilt of his gladius which knocked her sideways onto the floor and dazed her. As she tried to raise herself up, she received a powerful kick from a giant hobnailed military sandal, and she felt a couple of ribs crack. She rolled over with the power of the kick until she was on her back and saw Marcus standing above her with a victorious smile on his face. He knew that Siabelle was finished, and he would now begin to break her bit by bit until she had told him everything she knew. This would take time, this warrior was braver than many in his legion and she would not give way easily, but eventually even the bravest would succumb to an expert in torture like Marcus. Unlike many, Marcus took no great pleasure in torturing people for information, it was just a part of his job and the fear it brought was also a useful instrument of oppression.

Siabelle knew what was to come and desperately looked for a way out. Her pugio was still clasped in her right hand, she had never forgotten her training by the gladiators all those years ago. First and foremost was to never lose your weapon no matter how much you were wounded as so often it was the difference between death or survival. In one last desperate act she flung the pugio at Marcus's throat.

Marcus was amazed at the speed with which Siabelle reacted and only his instinctive combat training enabled him to move his head in time, he felt the blade brush the side of his neck as it sped past him into the doorframe where it remained embedded. He looked down at Siabelle who was still staring at him with hatred even though she had just carried out her last act of defiance. To his surprise he saw the expression on Siabelle's face slowly change from a look of defiance to one of triumph. He instinctively put his hand to the side of his neck where the pugio had brushed past it and he felt the blood spurting from the severed artery that had been sliced through by the razor honed edge of the blade. The strength in his legs started to give as he began to lose consciousness and he collapsed to his knees.

Siabelle hauled herself to her feet using one of Drigwold's tapestries and felt the agony of her broken ribs protesting in response. She looked down at Marcus's face which just reflected his confusion as his brain began to shut down through the loss of blood. She thought she would be elated at the defeat of her enemy, but she just felt physically and mentally exhausted. She was tired of fighting and killing, she just wanted rest, but she knew she was in great peril. The bodies of Drigwold and Marcus would soon be found and the search for their assailant would be remorselessly undertaken. The Romans would not take the death of the centurion of the town garrison lightly and there would be swift and terrible reprisals on the native population until the killer was found. She knew that Strella had already betrayed her once and would not hesitate to do it again and her spies were everywhere.

Siabelle had just one last hope, she painfully put on her Roman lady's robe and staggered down the steps and past the body of poor Finiel. She made her way down the alley and around to the front of the brothel which was bustling with activity and tried to walk as normally as possible across the wide main street until she was stood outside a large metal reinforced timber door. This was the compound where Finiel said the Romans were building a temple dedicated to the Goddess Venus. She painfully pulled at the chain and heard the sound of a bell ringing inside. She leant against the frame of the door for support and eventually a small panel slid back, and a female voice asked if she could be of assistance.

Siabelle reached behind her neck and unclasped her necklace and placed it through the aperture in the door where it was quickly taken. She heard hurried footsteps running off and then she heard more than one person returning. The large bolts that secured the door were drawn back and it opened inwards to reveal the beautiful kind and familiar face of Marciana smiling at her. "Welcome Siabelle, I have been expecting you." The woman standing next to Marciana gently took Siabelle's arm as she was led into the sanctuary of the Temple and the huge door was closed behind them locking out the dangers of the night. Inside the outer door was an enclosed corridor with a greeting room on one side and at the end of the corridor was a second door that led through into the Temple complex.

The Temple of Venus was separated into two parts. The first part, which was accessible from the outer doors via the corridor, contained a number of beautiful wooden buildings, largely constructed from cedar wood imported from Syria. The wooden buildings surrounded a courtyard full of shrubs and flowers and with a large rectangular pool in the centre. This was where the priestesses of the Temple and all their attendants lived. Only women were allowed into this part of the Temple, and men were forbidden from entering on pain of death. The exterior of this first compound was made from sturdy pine timbers which were closely planed and overlapped to prevent anyone from being able to gaze into it. Between the living quarters of the priestesses and the river was a large building site where the actual Temple of Venus was being constructed from large blocks of limestone that had been brought up the river by barge. The outer walls and the dome of the Temple were nearly complete, and this was where the Roman citizens and the dignitaries of Londinium would be able to worship and give tribute to the divine goddess. There was another iron reinforced door between the living quarters and the Temple itself which opened into a walled passageway that gave the priestesses access to the Temple without being seen.

Siabelle was gently taken to a building that was used for healing. She was stripped naked, bathed in warm water and her cracked ribs were strapped to prevent them moving. She was quickly overcome with fatigue and was led to a comfortable bed with warm covers where she fell into a deep sleep, calmed by the aroma of beautiful, scented candles. Siabelle awoke to the sound of the entrance bell which was being vigorously activated from outside the compound and she frantically looked for her old clothes and in particular her pugio. She was still naked under the covers, and she felt trapped and vulnerable. Marciana suddenly appeared beside the bed with a priestess's robe which she gave to Siabelle to cover herself. She sat on the bed in front of Siabelle and looked her directly in the eyes. "You are completely safe here Siabelle," she said "you are now under the protection of the Goddess and her servants, and no man may violate this sanctuary. Do you understand?"

Siabelle remembered the first time she had seen Chyrenia's eyes and the way that they had enchanted her and reassured her when she thought she was dying from the assassin's wound. Marciana's eyes had the same qualities of kindness, integrity and yet great inner strength and she realised that she could trust this woman with her life. "Yes," she replied, "I understand, thank you."

One of the Temple assistants came to find Marciana to tell her that there was a Roman officer at door requesting an audience. Marciana instructed the assistant to invite the officer into the greeting room near the outer door of the Temple and cordially greeted the decurion. She asked whether he would like any refreshments which he graciously declined and then inquired as to his business.

The decurion informed Marciana that there had been a double murder in the brothel across the way, and that one of the victims was the centurion in charge of the town garrison. They were looking for a fugitive and he had reason to believe it may have been a woman who was responsible.

"I can assure you that there is nobody in the Temple here who is not both familiar and welcome to me. I hope you are not insinuating that the priestesses of the Temple could be responsible for murders in a brothel?" Marciana reinforced her point by looking directly into the officer's eyes daring him to challenge her.

The decurion bowed again deeply, apologised for disturbing their sanctuary and left a generous tribute in the donation bowl that was next to a statue of Venus set into the wall of the greeting room. Marciana and Siabelle later learned that the Romans assumed the murders had been committed owing to a falling out between Strella and Marcus. Strella owned the brothel, and she was known to have had dubious dealings with both Marcus and Drigwold. They raided Strella's compound in the Settlements and executed everyone within. Strella had paid a heavy price for her betrayal of Siabelle.

Once Siabelle had recovered she approached Marciana to discuss her future. She no longer had her weapons although she had a little money left, and more importantly she had nowhere safe to go. Marciana had instructed one of the attendants to dispose of Siabelle's pugio into the waters of the Tems. No weapons were allowed in the Temple compound, it was a place of love and healing, not conflict. Marciana explained that many of the women in the Temple had run away from violent and abusive relationships. The Romans liked to think that the priestesses of Venus and their attendants were innocent virgins and that gave them a special insight into the nature of the Goddess. Marciana did nothing to dispel this myth but many of the priestesses had actually escaped sexual violence and Marciana herself had been raped at the age of twelve by one of her uncles. The Temple was a sanctuary from the violence and oppression of the Roman patriarchy, and she invited Siabelle to remain with them in safety.

Siabelle was tired of violence and conflict and instead she dedicated herself to healing. She shared many of the remedies that she had learnt from Chyrenia with her sisters in the Temple and eventually learnt to love again although nobody could fill the hole in her heart left by the death of Chyrenia.

A couple of months after Siabelle arrived at the Temple she had a vivid dream where Chyrenia came to her and told her that she must make a record of her life and the secrets of the Moonstone. In the dream she told Siabelle that her narrative should be buried for a time in the far distant future when the world would be ready to receive this knowledge. Siabelle discussed her dream with Marciana who immediately felt the importance of this message and the fact that it was delivered by a High Priestess of the Goddess. Although the Gallancia called the Goddess Anu and the Romans called her Venus she was the same goddess, the source of all living things, the womb of all life and the ultimate source of love.

In the quietness of her quarters by the light of a candle, Siabelle began to write her story.

"Greetings to my sister, for I know that the Goddess would only entrust these revelations to one of her daughters. My name is Siabelle of the Trinovantes, I am writing in the year given by the Roman oppressors of my people as DCCCXXXII, and this is my story."

To preserve Siabelle's story it was carefully scribed with a steel stylus onto thin sheets of copper and after it was completed it was sealed in a small lead chest and secretly buried. Only Marciana and Siabelle would know of the contents of the chest and its final resting place.

23

"You wouldn't be able to keep talking out of your arse with all this left-wing bullshit if I shoved my cock up there first, you stupid commie dyke bitch!"

"Well, you have to hand it to him. He has managed to successfully combine homophobia, misogyny, violation through anal sex, question your intelligence and condemn your political leanings with 154 characters to spare" observed Jess helpfully.

"Hmm, not very imaginative through, and with a supposed 34 followers he might not even be a bot produced by an algorithm" reflected Gem.

Jess and Gem were going through the painful ritual of looking at some of the replies Gem had received on social media after posting a link to her June article for Woke Media. The term "Woke" was turned into an insult by right-wing groups and their complicit media in late 2019. It was directed towards anyone who had the audacity to criticise the neo-liberal capitalist consensus that permeated through mainstream politics. Those who were impertinent enough to highlight examples of sexism, inequality, poverty, and institutional racism were condemned as "Woke people" trying to shut down valid freedom of speech by the entitled hatemongers serving the establishment. The fact that most of these "Woke" people were also burdened with a conscience and a capacity for empathy was even more enraging to those successfully dedicated to the development of a truly pathological society. A small group of activists and progressive university students decided to create their own media voice as their opinion was not reflected in any of the mainstream media outlets. They decided to use the term 'woke' as a badge of pride. It had the added bonus of really annoying most of the targets of their investigations and political commentary.

Gem had gone to an art college near her home in Peckham but had spent more of her time editing the student magazine than focusing on her studies. She left college in June 2022 with a 2.1 degree in creative design and a burning passion for tackling injustice through progressive journalism. To preserve the existing groupthink of the majority of establishment friendly media, the vast majority of posts for budding journalists were deliberately excluded from people like Gem. Internments for most media organisations were filled with kids from Russell Group universities with wealthy parents. These were the only young people who could afford to transcend the deliberately created barriers to entry such as the expectation of serving prolonged unpaid internships whist having to pay for staggeringly expensive property rents. This was why so many of the journalists in UK news media saw socialism and calls to tackle rampant inequality as a malign threat to their comfortable existence and entitlement. Not that it was as comfortable as it had been for the middle classes before the combined forces of Covid-19 and Brexit had successfully managed to further erode the UKs already faltering economy.

Gem had accumulated over £47,000 of debt after her three years at college and had been living with her single mum in a drafty, damp ridden flat for which the rent increased roughly in line with the spread of the mould caused by condensation and the leaky roof. When Woke Media placed an advert for a staggeringly rare paid internship, she was waiting outside the door of their portacabin in an industrial estate the next morning with CV in hand. She was waiting with 37 others and was amazed when they called her a week later to say that she had been shortlisted for interview. She was even more dumbfounded when they messaged her the next day to offer her the job. That was nearly eleven months ago and now she was a fully embedded member of the small but dedicated Woke team and had successfully attracted her own dedicated following of abusive trolls on social media.

Gem had first met Jess when she was reporting on a community demonstration against yet another tenant being evicted from her flat and being made homeless. There were hundreds of thousands of homeless after the economic collapse exacerbated by the Covid-19 pandemic that started in 2020. Jess at that time was working in a poverty action trust which was desperately trying to mitigate some of the worst excesses of the wave of poverty that was now the everyday reality of millions of people. Jess at 27 was five years older than Gem but the two young women had formed an instant bond and after several meetings first as activists, then as friends, they had now become lovers in a blossoming relationship. This had come as a bit of a surprise to Jess who had recently split up from a long-term relationship with her boyfriend Raul whom she had met in an experimental community called Consciência in Peru. She still loved Raul who was one of the kindest men she had ever met, but he did not share her passion for politics, and she did not share his passion for engineering. The distance was also a problem combined with the UKs growing problem with racism and bigotry. This was exacerbated by the tensions created in communities suffering from the effects of abject poverty, resentment from the growing wealth disparity in society and deliberately antagonistic Home Office policies. This meant that every time Raul came to visit her in the UK, he faced ever more intensive questioning about the purpose and duration of his visits.

Jess had never really acknowledged that she might be sexually attracted to a woman so the first time she kissed Gem after several drinks in a late-night wine bar, it came as a bit of a surprise, albeit a very pleasant one. Gem had never been attracted to men and happily identified as a lesbian and they had a steamy night of passion. Gem practiced taekwondo twice a week and Jess found her lithe strong body and her short spiky and currently pink hair, incredibly sexy.

The following morning as she lay next to Gem with her fingers stroking the ripples of muscle of her new lover's athletic abdomen, Jess had decided that she was probably pan-sexual. She suspected that she could be attracted to anybody from any gender whose sexual chemistry turned her on. Jess had felt her arousal building again and she mischievously tweaked Gem's nipple. Gem leapt on top of her in mock annoyance, straddling her body and holding Jess's arms assertively above her head enforcing a playful submission. Gem then began to kiss Jess on the lips and slowly the kisses descended down Jess's body. Gem released Jess's hands as she moved and these clasped the back of Gem's head, encouraging her on as her tongue and lips continued descending on their journey to their ultimate destination. Jess let out a groan of pleasure as familiar sensations started to build and when, after a tantalising delay, Gem's lips finally met their goal she lost herself to yet another moment of divine pleasure.

Gem's attraction to Jess was fully reciprocated and after six months together lust had started to be partnered by a growing love and respect between the two young women. There was also something very special and erotic about the atmosphere in the wonderful place where they were now both living that seemed to amplify both their desire and imagination. After many joyful visits to Jess's apartment, Gem had been delighted when she had been invited by Jess to stay with her in the 'Warehouse.'

The Warehouse was the aptly named building where a small group of residents lived together in an old, but thoroughly modernised warehouse, that had been converted into residential accommodation. It was situated on the riverside between the City of London and the Docklands. Jess had first joined the residents of the Warehouse in 2015 when she had come back from her visit to Consciência in Peru. Whilst she had been visiting Consciência, she had met Vanessa who had formerly been a trader in the City of London. Vanessa had once lived in the Warehouse where she had met Sensi, a Peruvian from Consciência who was a friend of the now renowned artist Alexandra Okereke who also used to live there. Sensi had persuaded Vanessa to come and join her in the community of Consciência, even though this meant that she had had to part with almost all of the wealth that she had accumulated during her successful career in the City. The founding ethos of Consciência was that the addiction to greed eroded the capacity for empathy and compassion and the pursuit of wisdom was impossible without the inner guidance provided by empathy. Anyone who wanted to permanently join the community with significant wealth had to give most of it away as a condition of residency.

Jess had been introduced to Consciência after she had met a wonderfully colourful lady called Roxie in a bookshop in Bath. Roxie lived in London at the Warehouse but was visiting the bookshop, which was owned by Ellen, an old friend of Roxie's. The two women were chatting at the back of the shop when Jess came in looking for inspiration. She was trying to understand why her degree in philosophy was completely failing to provide the answers she was looking for when trying to come to terms with her own life. Roxie and Ellen were impressed by Jess's sincerity and after setting Jess a challenge, Roxie had sponsored her on a visit to Consciência. Sensi had acted as her mentor and guide in Peru and it was there that Jess had met and fallen passionately in love with Raul who was Sensi's brother. Sensi's mother Lumi was a shamanic curandera. She had helped steer Jess towards a life changing spiritual journey and a commitment to fight for the survival of the Earth against the forces of greed that were rapidly destroying it. It was in Consciência that Jess met and became close friends with Vanessa who still had her old apartment in the Warehouse. Vanessa, with Roxie's blessing, happily handed over her Warehouse apartment to Jess so that she could move in on her return to England. That had been six years ago and in the intervening time Jess had quickly settled in and fallen in love with the other residents of the Warehouse who were collectively known as 'the Rabble.'

The Warehouse was a remarkable building with an extraordinary history. The main entrance was on the top floor, accessed by an open galvanised metal staircase. The top floor had a large, shared living space where the Rabble could gather and socialise with a large open kitchen at one end and a curtain wall at the other which led to a studio with a mezzanine floor. This had been Alexandra Okereke's studio when Jess had first moved in but now it was the mysterious Cyrene who lived there. Cyrene was the high priestess of a women's wiccan coven of which a number of current and former residents of the warehouse were also members. Cyrene earned a living through sales of her books on pagan traditions and witchcraft, by providing Reiki healing and divination readings through Tarot and stone crystals.

The front wall of the upper floor was pierced by a number of large windows that flooded the room with light through their south facing aspect. The back wall was covered by wonderful murals of Goddesses, animals and forest scenes that had been painted by Alexandra as a gift to the Warehouse community for taking her and providing refuge when she was escaping from a previous violent and abusive relationship. Alexandra now lived with her husband Richard who ran a very successful gallery which was also the sole outlet for the sale of all of Alexandra's paintings and sculptures.

The ground floor of the Warehouse was accessed by descending a spiral staircase and was split into six self-contained apartments where the residents lived, one of which was where Jess and Gem were now living together. The apartments led off a central corridor and at the end of a corridor was a ground level resident's entrance which opened up into a foyer and another exit door leading to a small, shared garden area and resident's car park. On one side of the foyer was a new set of stairs leading down into the basement and on the other side a small lift to give wheelchair access to the basement area. These had been funded by the Museum of London to give access to the most remarkable aspect of the Warehouse building. In 2014 the residents of the Warehouse had discovered a hidden basement and this basement revealed that the Warehouse had been built on top of the ruins of a Roman Temple dedicated to the goddess Venus. The Temple had been largely destroyed by fire in the 2nd Century CE, but the bottom of the large stone walls and intricate mosaic floor still remained intact after all this time.

By agreement with the Museum of London, the Temple area was open to the public between 9.00am and 5.00pm Thursday to Saturday. At other times, the residents could use the space for meditation and contemplation, often guided by Cyrene. On the eight main Sabbats at the solstices, equinoxes, Imbolc, Beltane, Lughnasadh and Samhain or at times when healing was required, Cyrene's coven would meet in the Temple and practice natural magic. The basement Temple still retained an amazing and essentially feminine sacred atmosphere which had formed since it had been consecrated in the first century CE. The Temple was also believed to be at least partly responsible for the exceptional libido exhibited by most of the residents of the Warehouse. Gem had discovered this to her delight that first evening when she and Jess had made love.

Apart from Gem and Jess and Cyrene, who lived in the top floor studio, there were eight other residents living in the Warehouse.

The matriarch and on-call agony aunt, beloved by all of the residents of the Warehouse was Roxie. Roxie was in her mid-fifties, her exact age being a closely guarded secret. She was, on the surface, a joyful and flamboyant personality with an energy and zest for life that defied her years. When Jess had originally moved into the Warehouse Roxie was very active in the swinging scene, no doubt augmented by the special atmosphere emanating from the basement Temple. At that time, she shared her apartment with her boyfriend Joris who was her junior by fifteen years. Now she lived alone with two cats that freely roamed the Warehouse and its small garden and had been adopted by all.

As Jess came to know Roxie better, she had discovered that her apparent joy of life was deceptive. Roxie was an empath and the hurt and cruelty of humanity's actions on the fragile Earth affected her greatly. On several occasions, Jess had found Roxie weeping as the emotional pain bubbled to the surface. She was particularly affected by the number of children growing up in extreme poverty and the harm being caused to so many animals that were being driven to extinction. She had written a couple of books railing against the evils of humanity's greed-based societies and although they were not commercially successful, she delighted in saying that every sentence was an act of defiance.

Jethro who was 35 and Max 32 were a gay couple who ran a gym and a company supplying door staff to a number of venues in London. When Jess had first moved into the Warehouse Max was quite successful in Mixed Martial Arts, but his fights were taking an increasing toll and his body was taking longer to recover. He had now retired from competitive fighting and had decided to focus on business although he was still incredibly fit. Jethro was larger framed than Max and at 110 kilos and 1.9 metres tall was an imposing figure. This helped him when working on the door if he had to stand in for one of his staff although he actually had a rather gentle nature. The couple had had to dig deep during the Covid-19 epidemic where the frequent government lockdowns caused havoc with their finances. Fortunately, after the crisis things were recovering and many of their previous clients had also somehow managed to survive the pandemic.

Fixie who was 28 had earned her name for her ability to secure tickets for just about any show in London or beyond. She worked as an agent for London theatres and her work had also suffered in the pandemic when she had been placed on furlough. She did however have a wealthy father, Frankie McNeal who liked to be known as a 'semi-retired businessman' but was regarded by the Metropolitan Police as a probably still highly active gangster. Fixie had a complicated relationship with her father who doted on her. She loved him as a father who had always been kind and loving to her, but she derided his criminality and the hurt he caused to others.

Fixie was now in a relationship with a lawyer called Luther who specialised in human rights and particularly the appalling treatment of asylum seekers and refugees by the UK authorities. Luther was also a rather good sax player in a retro ska band which was how he first met Fixie. She had taken pity on him standing in Tottenham Court Road trying to flog tickets for their next gig on a drizzly November afternoon. She had used her contacts and pulled in a few favours to help them out and ended up falling in love with both the music and the saxophonist. Luther had moved into the Warehouse with Fixie about twelve months ago and was rapidly adopted by the Rabble as one of their own.

Kaitlin and Julian were a married couple with a three year old daughter called Rowan. Kaitlin had now lived in the Warehouse for nearly ten years having moved in when she was just a nineteen year old student. She was now a researcher at the Museum of London specialising in the Roman period and was fluent in Latin which she had learned to support her studies. She had also been given the responsibility of looking after the basement Temple of Venus and its precious mosaics and arranging the supervision of visitors during opening times. Kaitlin was also a practicing witch and an active member of Cyrene's coven. Kaitlin had become firm friends with Jess and Gem and, although witches were sensibly cautious about their practices after centuries of persecution, Gem was also becoming increasingly interested in natural magic and Wicca.

Julian was a quiet and thoughtful man who was often absent as he worked for an overseas aid agency, and this was becoming an increasing strain since the birth of Rowan. Although Julian and Kaitlin both loved the rest of the Rabble, they were thinking of moving out if they could ever afford to do it. This was no easy task with the increasingly exorbitant London rents or the amount they would need for a deposit to secure a mortgage on their relatively low incomes.

The final and most recent resident was Dodi. Dodi stood for the "Duchess of Disorder" which was the stage name of Jacky Wetherall who had a stand-up comedy act. She was also amazing with computers and operated in the murky world of internet security and hacking. The other residents knew that Dodi had an extraordinary skill with computers, and she was constantly helping them out with building websites and setting up new smartphones etc.

Dodi also belonged to an amorphous group of hackers who called themselves Zeno. Zeno were called upon to help commercial customers protect themselves from cyber-attacks or deal with the consequences of one. They had on occasion also helped the police through a 'handler' in CEOP, the online child protection branch of the National Crime Agency, to track down child abusers. This was a very wary relationship because Zeno's group activities also involved exposing fraud and other embarrassing information about banks and corporations whose corruption had virtually undermined any pretence that the UK was still a functioning representative democracy. Some of the methods Zeno used in their investigations were of dubious legality and they were therefore keen to keep their relationship with CEOP a respectful yet distant one. In return for their help, CEOP did not ask too many probing questions about Zeno's other activities.

Zeno could be contacted on the Dark Web by those who knew where to look but they never met their customers in person. The people operating in this murky world could be very dangerous and Zeno had to take extreme precautions to preserve the anonymity of its members.

"Doesn't this constant stream of bigotry and misogyny ever get to you?" asked Jess as they finished the usually painful daily analysis of Gem's social media accounts.

Gem sighed and closed down her Twitter feed on the laptop. "It's starting to" she replied, "and I am really annoyed with myself because this is exactly what they want. Some of this is just the venting of the sick and inadequate hiding behind their screens who would shrivel up and die if they were ever confronted. There is also a much darker side to groups, paid for by vested interests, that act to deliberately shut down any progressive debate that might threaten their ability to exploit a sleeping population. It is also deliberately done to shut down the voices of women. I get ten times more abuse than any of the male journalists at Woke."

"Why do you think they fear women so much?" asked Jess.

"I have thought a lot about this." said Gem. "I used to think that all the vitriol, smears and lies faced by Jeremy Corbyn when he was the leader of Labour, and the deliberate obstruction of Bernie Sanders by the Democratic Party in the USA was because they were socialists. On reflection I believe it was because their policies were driven by empathy and empathy is an anathema to those who control the wealth in our societies. If a majority of the population were driven by compassion, we would never tolerate the obscene wealth of the few and extreme poverty of millions that we have today. The population would never put up with it but instead people are fed a constant barrage of propaganda designed to sow the seeds of hate and division between different groups in society. It's a classic case of divide and conquer and sadly a very effective one."

"What have Corbyn and Sanders got to do with the hatred of women?" said Jess.

"A much higher percentage of women than men voted for them because women generally have a greater capacity for empathy than most men." replied Gem. "Any woman who wants to gain high political office has to fight their way through the bear pit of a political system shaped by hundreds of years of patriarchy. The rules of the game are specifically designed to deter anyone with empathy and compassion from reaching the top and those who do pay a terrible price for their bravery. This is why many of the most prominent women who have reached the top in politics are every bit as pathological as their male colleagues. This is particularly apparent in the right-wing political ideologies that have dominated parliament for decades. Despite all the barriers to empaths, some amazing caring women are now reaching political prominence and are starting to fight back against the embedded culture. This is a threat to powerful vested interests as they resonate with many women voters and women are a majority of the voting population. As a female journalist supporting socialism, I am a natural target in this war against the promotion of empathy."

"Particularly as you are such a sexy young socialist too." said Jess and the girls embraced in a long and lingering kiss that they were both reluctant to end.

"Have you ever thought of talking to Cyrene about it?" suggested Jess

"Even Cyrene could not conjure up enough magic to stifle all that anger and hatred." sighed Gem.

"She might be able to help you to deflect it though." said Jess.

Gem did not know what to make of Cyrene and the witches. Although Jess was not a practicing member of the coven, she seemed to have no problem in believing in the reality of what was going on or the potential of natural magic to actually change reality in the material world. This may have been because of Jess's shamanic experiences with Sensi and Lumi in Peru that she had revealed to Gem. Gem had an open mind on such matters, but her rationality probably steered her towards scepticism. She was however quite keen to investigate whether there was any cross over of values between the pagan traditions that drew upon ancient wisdom and contemporary socialism. With her contacts in the Warehouse, she was in an excellent position to conduct such an investigation. She would have a word with Shelley who was in charge of the investigative journalism at Woke to see if they would be interested in such an article.

"That's not a bad idea," replied Gem, "it will certainly do no harm to ask."

24

The area where Cyrene practiced Reiki felt like returning to the comfort and security of a loving mother's womb to Gem. The area was created by carefully suspended rails from which hung colourful drapes. There was a large deep piled rug on the floor covered with figures and symbols that Gem guessed came from Iran or perhaps Turkey. There was a wide put-up massage table in the middle of the rug, covered in a soft blanket and in the background was the quiet haunting sound of music played on drums and pan pipes from South America. The air was filled with the scent of burning patchouli incense adding to the exotic atmosphere of the space. The light from the window was largely shielded by the drapes and the space was illuminated by the light of four large candles in stands which had been placed at the four points of the compass.

Next to the massage table was another smaller and ancient looking table. Carved into its top surface was a large pentagram within a circle surrounded by strange symbols and sigils. In the middle of the pentagram Cyrene had placed a number of crystals, some clear but mostly differing shades of blue.

There was a swish of a drape as Cyrene entered the space and gave Gem a beautiful smile. Gem was somewhat overawed by Cyrene's presence. She was tall, at about 1.8 metres she was a good five cm taller than Gem even in her bare feet. Both women had taken off their shoes before entering the healing space. Cyrene's green eyes seemed to peer deeply into Gem's soul, but this was in an enquiring rather than threatening way. Gem immediately felt that any attempts to conceal her true nature from this powerful woman would be pointless and also self-defeating if she was going to benefit from the Reiki.

Cyrene was dressed in a silky green gown, pulled in by a tie at the waist that accentuated her flaring hips. Her large curvaceous breasts, unconstrained by any bra, were partly exposed by the deep plunging vee shaped neckline of her gown. Gem was dressed in lightweight pyjamas covered in a butterfly pattern and she felt a bit like a gawky teenager in the presence of this elegant and sophisticated lady.

Both women were lesbians and as they stood closely facing each other they both felt the instinctive rising of sexual energy. This was a pleasurable feeling, an appreciation of beauty that was absent of any latent anxiety or tension. They both knew that their sexual appreciation of each other's form and nature would never be realised in sexual embrace, but it was joyful none the less.

Cyrene briefly turned her back on Gem to attend to the crystals, revealing her long straight dark brown hair which almost reached to the swell of her hips, and which gently swayed behind her as she turned. After a reflective pause she removed several of the blue crystals and replaced them with red ones.

"Do you mind if I ask you a question?" said Gem a little nervously, not sure whether it was appropriate to disturb Cyrene in her preparations.

"Please do." said Cyrene looking over her shoulder with a reassuring smile.

"Why did you decide to change the crystals?"

"Jess told me that you were receiving a lot of abuse online and she is worried about how anxious you might be feeling as the target of so much projected anger. I therefore started preparing on the premise of calming blue and clear crystals to relax you and ease away some of the tension. Now you are here I have sensed that it is not anxiety that is troubling you. You have a powerful inner strength and the fire of righteous anger, and you are seeking knowledge of how to channel this energy in a positive way. I am sensing frustration rather than fear and anxiety and I have altered the crystals to help this energy manifest itself. Part of you is trying to supress your outrage because your heart is guided by love, but your head is wise and together they will enable you to channel this energy well."

Gem reflected on Cyrene's words and sensed that the priestess was right. She was not afraid, but she was incredibly frustrated and angry at the stupidity of people who consistently voted for greed and power obsessed politicians. These politicians had no interest at all for the wellbeing of many of the people who voted for them. This was particularly true for those from poor backgrounds whose communities were constantly diminished by ever more draconian cuts in public spending whilst the wealth of a growing number of billionaires mushroomed. Gem could simply not understand why so many people were seemingly oblivious to their own subjugation and exploitation and yet continued to vote for their abusers. The growing global inequality came at the cost of the suffering of hundreds of millions and the insatiable greed of those that controlled global capital was now proving to be an existential threat to all life on Earth.

Being part of a progressive left-wing media organisation was certainly no place for the timid. Despite her frustrations, Gem generally relished the fray even if the chance of an ideological victory against the established order seemed as remote as ever.

Cyrene had turned back from rearranging the crystals and was looking at Gem, sensing the turmoil going on within her. Now was the time to calm her mind and to see what Reiki might reveal. She told Gem to lie on her back on the Reiki table and Cyrene gentle covered her with the blanket.

Gem did not have any expectations for Reiki, she just enjoyed being in the warm comforting atmosphere and her mind started to quieten as she listened to the music. Cyrene had placed a few crystals upon Gem including one on her forehead and had then left the Reiki area for a few minutes to allow Gem to relax. At first Gem was aware of the weight and coolness of the crystals but they almost seemed to dissolve into her body and become as one with her as she continued to relax.

Gem sensed Cyrene's presence again and experienced a brief tingle of arousal as she smelt her perfumed body pass nearby. Cyrene began to sense how the energy flowed through Gem's body and between her energy chakras, where it moved freely and where it was blocked. She placed her hands-on Gems body starting on her feet, then on her legs and arms and her sides before ending up with her hands each side of Gem's temple. At first Gem felt nothing but after about twenty minutes she began to feel a strange tingling in her fingers which grew in intensity and spread up towards her wrists. She had never felt anything quite like it before and instinctively she raised her hands palm upwards, and the feelings intensified. It felt almost like she was in a magnetic field as the energy pulsed and swirled around her.

Cyrene sensed the build-up of energy in Gem and began to chant strange words that Gem did not understand but somehow felt familiar as if of a distant memory. Cyrene gently removed her hands and picked up a hand drum and began to gently strum the surface of the drum with her fingers, increasing the speed and intensity of the drumming as she sensed Gem's energy field grow. Suddenly Cyrene stopped, she could see a pyramid of light hovering above Gem's body as if Gem were supporting it in her raised hands and then the energy gently dissipated as Gem's hands fell back to her sides.

Cyrene left Gem to relax for a few minutes and then gently helped her to stand up and drew back a drape so that they could move outside the Reiki area and sit down in a couple of comfortable chairs near the open kitchen. Cyrene made herself a fruit tea and brought Gem a mug of coffee that she had asked for.

"How do you feel?" she asked Gem.

Gem paused as she assessed herself. She had a lingering tingling feeling in her lower arms and hands and felt slightly euphoric and distanced from the world as if she had been visiting a better and more harmonious space and was now slowly returning. She explained this as best she could to Cyrene who listened patiently.

Cyrene explained that she was sensing the energy of the natural world that connects everything in the Goddess's realm. Some cultures called it ch'i other traditions know it as aether or even spirit. It acted upon and within all things, but most people had closed themselves off from it and could no longer sense or use this energy. This was the energy that was channelled by Wiccans through their will to influence and impact upon the world through the power of visualisation. Cyrene had sensed a number of blockages within Gem, but Gem had responded powerfully as Cyrene had channelled this natural energy through her hands and the crystals.

Over the next few weeks Gem had regular Reiki with Cyrene, becoming increasingly relaxed and comfortable with the Wiccan priestess as their familiarity developed into friendship. She also began to visualise places and figures that were unfamiliar to her but as her power of visualisation improved, she began to get quite vivid images in her mind of ancient Celtic and Roman figures.

One night she was laying on her bed next to Jess after they had made love together and she fell into a dreamy meditation sensing the energy beginning to flow within her. She could now switch this energy on almost at will which fascinated her, but she did not understand what to do with it or how to channel it to her will. As the energy swirled around her, she suddenly had a very clear image of a woman with a vivid scar crossing her eye and an overpowering feeling of familiarity. The woman looked anxious, and the shadow of a large figure loomed over her. The woman suddenly turned as if she had just seen Gem and looking directly into her eyes and with great intensity, she spoke some words in a foreign language. Gem sat bolt upright in bed, she had never experienced as powerful a vision like this before and she looked around the bedroom to see if the woman was actually in the room.

"What's up with you?" said Jess slightly grumpy at having been disturbed from her blissful post loving slumber.

"Just a very vivid dream," Gem replied, "probably nothing but it seemed so real."

"It's all this Reiki with Cyrene having an effect on you." teased Jess. "Were you fantasizing about her gorgeous body again?" This initiated a pillow fight followed by spooning as the girls fell back asleep.

The following day Gem was back with Cyrene enjoying her presence and the effects of Reiki when she suddenly sat bolt upright and in a very different voice cried out something that sounded to Cyrene like "wheram yasset de sepultuss suba."

The priestess quickly grabbed a pen and wrote down what she thought she had heard on a notepad that she kept for capturing thoughts during her work with clients. Gem was still sat upright on the bed in what seemed to be a sort of trance before blinking and looking at Cyrene in puzzlement.

"That was quick, is the Reiki over?" asked Gem.

Cyrene was far too experienced in magic to be fazed by what had taken place, but she was intrigued. She explained to Gem what had happened and read back what she had written down to find out if the words meant anything to Gem. Gem had no recollection of having spoken but she did tell Cyrene of her dream about the woman with the scarred face and the menacing shadowy figure. The two women had already discussed her visualisation of Celtic and Roman figures which Cyrene suggested might have originated from the powerful energy of the remains of the Temple in the basement.

On a hunch Cyrene suggested that they ask Kaitlin if the words meant anything to her as she was fluent in Latin and that they might have a Roman connection. Kaitlin looked at what Cyrene had written down in puzzlement at Cyrene's phonetic interpretation of the words Gem had spoken.

After repeating the phrase a few times to herself she said that it sounded a bit like "verum iacet sepultus sub."

"What does that mean?" asked Gem.

"Roughly it means 'The 'truth lies buried underground.' Does that make any sense to either of you?"

Cyrene and Gem were none the wiser, but both were fascinated by Gem's experience, and it was obvious to Cyrene that Gem was awakening to her hidden senses and capabilities at a phenomenal rate. Cyrene's intuition was telling her that Gem's experiences were linked to the Temple and wondered if it was finally time to allow Gem to be initiated as a novice into her coven. Awakening could cause a great deal of anxiety and could even be harmful if the person transitioning did not have a support group helping them through the process. Soon after moving into the Warehouse Gem had been delighted to know that she was living amongst practicing witches and had hinted that she would really like to join in. Cyrene humoured the young woman but gently discouraged her as her enthusiasm was more inspired by Hollywood than earnest conviction. Practicing natural magic in a Wiccan coven was not a frivolous entertainment but a serious commitment. Wiccans were drawn together by shared values, experiences, and beliefs and seldom advertised their presence.

Each of the women in Cyrene's Wiccan coven which, being one of the few women only covens was known as "The Sisters of Venus in honour of the basement Temple where they frequently gathered." Each woman had followed their own path towards the Craft. Once they had joined the coven, they did not overtly advertise the fact that they were practising witches. The terrible persecutions suffered by so many women accused of witchcraft by religious and secular authorities over the centuries was an unresolved burning injustice. In some parts of the world women were still accused and persecuted on charges of witchcraft, whether real or invented and even in contemporary society witches were looked upon by many with wariness and mistrust. As recently as the 2020 US presidential election, some on the more extreme fringe of the Christian evangelical right-wing supporters of Trump had sought to blame witchcraft for his defeat at the polls. It could still be dangerous for a person to come out as a practising witch which is why many practitioners of the Craft think it prudent to not advertise the fact.

Gem's capabilities were however developing rapidly, and Cyrene decided to ask her if she was still interested in Wicca? Gem was delighted to be approached, but before she could be initiated, she was tasked with reading a number of books written by witches. She was then extensively interviewed by Cyrene to see what she had learned and to test her commitment. Jess had at first been a bit lukewarm about Gem's interest in joining the Sisters of Venus as she thought this might just be another fad she was going through and some of the Sisters were precious to Jess. Once she understood that Gem was serious and she had seen for herself the speed and intensity of Gem's awakening, she was happy to support her. Jess believed that if you really loved someone you would do anything to support them on their path, even if this did not always mean you could join them on it. Jess greatly respected the Craft, there were many parallels to her own shamanic experiences in Peru but intuitively she felt that this would be Gem's journey. Her love of Gem and concern for her also meant that she took great comfort in the knowledge and friendship of those who were her fellow travellers.

25

Gem's heart was pounding with excitement and apprehension as, blindfolded, she was guided down the last few steps into the basement Temple. Although Gem was only wearing a thin gown it was not cold. The mosaic flooring was priceless and had been beautifully preserved as it had been covered over by ten cm of gravel, lime mortar and terracotta brick floor tiles when a warehouse had been built on top of the ruins of an older building after the great Fire of London in 1666. The current warehouse had used the existing 17th Century basement and foundations when it was rebuilt after the Blitz. The walls of the basement Temple were however unremarkable, except in the bottom metre of the four corners of the large rectangular space where evidence of original Kentish Ragstone used by the Romans was visible. The Roman Temple of Venus had been a large round construction and the 17th Century builders had used the hard Roman limestone as part of the foundations where the rectangle bisected the old circular construction. The fact that most of the walls had no archaeological significance allowed the residents of the Warehouse to fit radiators to them. These were powered by an electric boiler which drew energy form the large array of solar panels on the Warehouse roof linked in with a substantial array of storage batteries. This system enabled the Warehouse to be kept deliciously warm even in the depth of winter when the panels could often still produce more electricity than the residents needed.

Gem could hear laughing and singing from many women as she was gently steered into the middle of the basement area. She had taken off her sandals and she felt the warmth of a woollen rug under her feet as she walked. She could now sense that she was in the middle of the group of women as she could hear their voices all around her. Suddenly the singing and dancing stopped, and she heard Cyrene's wonderful deep voice demanding to know "Who has come into the sacred circle of the divine goddess?"

Gem had been prepared for the ceremony and replied, "I am Gem, a daughter of the Goddess, the divine mother of all life. I desire to dedicate myself to her service in the name of love and wish to be accepted by the sisters of this coven to learn the secret knowledge of her divine purpose."

"What values do you bring to bind you to this sisterhood?" challenged Cyrene.

"I come to this coven pledging perfect love and perfect trust." replied Gem.

"Those who are bathed in the love of the Goddess are truly blessed, her love is boundless." replied Cyrene. "Those who commit to her service with a false heart, who only wish to use her powers to serve their ego with selfish intentions will find that her retribution is swift and terrible. Now is the time to walk away if your heart is not true. You are blindfolded, as are all who walk this world without the love of the Goddess in their heart, their ignorance and greed destroying her priceless domain. If you choose to remove your blindfold, know that you cannot return to the comfort of ignorance. Only those with courage and strength should embark on this journey. Some cannot face the truths revealed and fail to transcend their own shadows and embrace the divine love of the Goddess. For those who falter, the veil of ignorance that protect the many will have been lifted and there is no path of return. If you have the strength of heart and courage to face the challenges that lie in your path you may remove the blindfold. If there is any shadow of doubt in your mind or in your heart, then it is far better to turn and walk away now."

Cyrene had talked at length to Gem about the dangers of exposure to the secrets of the Craft. She explained that all the women in the Sisters' coven were natural empaths which gave them the intuition and insight to follow the path of knowledge through embracing love. The World is in great danger and humanity is causing terrible harm to the fragile balance of nature that sustains all living things. Sometimes the suffering caused by human ignorance and greed is overwhelming. It was often impossible for empaths not to share the terrible pain being experienced by other beings and this could quickly overcome and destroy them. Millions of empaths are driven to suicide by being too awake and sensitive to the realities of living in a world where empathy and compassion are often treated with contempt by those without the capacity to understand love. The contemporary human world is driven by greed and empaths suffer terribly in such a hostile environment.

Gem had asked Cyrene why she followed such a path if it posed such terrible risks? Cyrene replied that once you had fully experienced the bliss of being at one with the love of the divine you always carried the strength and power of this love in your heart. It was the most precious possession anyone could aspire to. There were no guarantees, and the costs of failure could be severe, but uniting with the all-encompassing love of the Goddess was the most precious treasure of all. All human treasures were pointless worthless trinkets in comparison. For Cyrene, seeking such a prize was worth almost any sacrifice. This was why all those who followed the path of selfishness to seek fulfilment became soulless, empty vessels whose insatiable appetites and cravings harmed all around them.

Gem had been well prepared by Cyrene to consider the risks of the journey that she was about to embark upon and there was no wavering in her response as she quickly removed her blindfold.

Gem found herself standing at the centre of a huge circular olive-green rug fully nine metres in diameter. Woven close to the edge of the rug was a white circle and within the circle was a large black pentagram, the points touching the circle, which was surrounded by mysterious sigils. At the four points of the compass were large, lit candles and before the candle to the North was an altar. On the altar were a number of magical tools including a silver cup containing blessed water, a sacred dagger known as an athame, a bowl containing salt, an incense burner that had filled the air with a wonderful aroma and another lit candle. The flame, incense, water, and salt represented four of the sacred elements of fire, air, water, and earth. All the women were naked, or skyclad as was befitting of the daughters of the Goddess, blessed by the beauty that she had bestowed upon them. The shame of nakedness was a patriarchal oppression imposed upon women and the Sisters embraced the freedom of this safe and sacred place to practice their magic in their most natural aspect. Although some of the women in the coven were lesbian or bisexual there was nothing predatory in such a loving gathering and any sexual stirrings within them were happily embraced by all in the group as a natural gift from the Goddess. Sexual energy was a joy that should be celebrated and embraced not feared or shunned.

Gem was feeling self-conscious standing naked before these extraordinary women, but her anxieties were quickly dissipated as, starting with Cyrene, all of the women kissed and embraced their new sister and bade her welcome to their circle. Traditionally there were thirteen members in a coven, representing the approximate number of times the moon orbits the Earth in a year. The realities of life meant that, unless there was a specific magic to perform requiring a strict adherence to thirteen, the coven would often meet with whoever was able to make it. There were now nineteen members of the Sisters of Venus coven including Gem and fourteen had turned up today to greet their new member.

Gem knew some of the sisters very well. In addition to Cyrene there was Kaitlin from the Warehouse and she also knew Alexandra Okereke, the famous artist who had previously lived in Cyrene's studio space but now lived with her husband Richard. Although she no longer lived in the Warehouse Alexandra frequently visited her friends there and Gem had quickly succumbed to her warmth and sense of fun. Alexandra used most of the wealth raised by her paintings to help run a trust called Chalice that protected women and families that were escaping abuse and violence. Alexandra had once had to turn to Chalice for help and she never forgot the love and support she had been shown. Jess also worked for Chalice as a project manager and fundraiser and in the social fallout from the post Covid-19 recession the organisation had never had a greater demand made upon its services. They were just about to open their fifth home, and this would still be nowhere near enough to help all the women who approached them needing their urgent assistance.

After Gem's initiation Cyrene led the Sisters in an energy raising ceremony focused on Gem to see if collectively, they could visualise the influence that had been manifesting during her dreams and Reiki with Cyrene. Cyrene started by asking the Sisters to activate their energy chakras to create a flow of natural energy or aether that they could use to help amplify their visualisation. Gem had read about the chakras and had attempted this process on her own but to her disappointment it had always seemed more imagination than experiential. As part of the group, she immediately felt the collective amplification of the women around her, and she felt a surge of energy flow up from the base of her spine through her body and out through her crown.

Cyrene asked Gem to sit in the centre of the circle and the fourteen other Sisters walked around her in a clockwise direction chanting. The movement of the women and the slowly escalating chants had a soporific effect on Gem, and she fell into a kind of trance as if she were only partly present in the circle. Cyrene suddenly stopped the Sisters, and they all sat cross legged equally spaced around the inside of the circle facing Gem.

Images started appearing in their minds, of Roman priestesses within the Temple and the energy within the circle began to grow and spiral upwards towards the roof above until Gem was sat within a protective cone of energy. As the energy mounted, Cyrene had a stark vision of a ring of ancient stones and a gathering of what looked like some sort of Celtic tribe followed by visions of bodies covered in blood. Suddenly Gem started speaking forcefully in a voice that was not hers and in a language that none of them understood. Gem stood up and paced around the circle her forehead furrowed in concentration, until she froze on a spot just before the altar and pointed at the ground. It seemed that whoever had manifest within Gem could see the Sisters, and looked helplessly at them whilst pointing urgently at the same spot on the floor saying something unintelligible. Gem's arms dropped and she looked at the floor and stood motionless for perhaps ten seconds which seemed much longer to the Sisters watching her with concern. Cyrene was just about to intervene when Gem's head lifted and looked around the circle of witches, then with eyes blazing the strange intense voice repeated the phrase that Gem had spoken to Cyrene during her Reiki "verum iacet sepultus sub."

Gem's head dropped once more, but this time after a shorter pause it was Gem's smile that greeted the Sisters when it lifted, the powerful presence that had used her as a conduit was gone. Slowly the energy dissipated, and Cyrene took the Sisters through an energy closing ceremony. Many witches had found to their cost that it was not wise to walk around with open chakras as it could attract some rather unwanted attention. Open chakras acted almost like a magnet to others and this attraction was not always welcome. Some people whose energy was particularly disturbed or depleted would draw upon the energy of others and a witch with perpetually open chakras would find themselves feeling constantly exhausted.

Gem was completely unaffected by her experience except for a slight confusion as to why she had found herself standing in front of the altar instead of kneeling in the centre of the circle. It was obvious that whoever had manifested within her had meant her no harm and had no malicious intent.

After Gem's induction and the energy raising the Sisters sat on the rug and ate cake and biscuits and drank wine or herbal teas, exchanging their experiences. The Roman themes were very common when the coven met in the basement Temple of Venus as there was still a huge reservoir of stored energy from the time when it was a centre of worship in Roman Londinium. This had been refreshed and amplified by the Sisters when raising energy and practicing magic. For this reason, the Sisters sometimes met at other locations if they were focusing on visualisation as the Roman influence was so powerful. On the other hand, if they were looking to create and channel energy for magical purposes, there was no other site where they had met that compared with the energy raising potential of the basement Temple. The Celtic connection was unusual and seemed particularly linked to Gem's arrival in the coven. Cyrene's vivid visualisation of a stone circle was unique in her experience, and she therefore concluded that it was an important link to the evening's experience. Gem had visualised herself walking through mature woodland full of trees such as oaks, elms, and ashes. She saw a wooden roundhouse with a turf roof in a clearing and saw a woman, carrying a wicker basket full of various plants and herbs, who laughed when she saw Gem. By the woman's dress Gem felt that this all took place a long time ago and she felt an overwhelming feeling of love and delight in seeing her. Gem had no recollection at all of being in the circle and speaking to the Sisters during this period.

Once most of the Sisters had departed Cyrene, Kaitlin and Gem cleaned and rolled up the huge rug, pushing it against the wall so that it would not get in the way when the Temple was opened up to visitors. Cyrene made sure to note the spot on the rug that Gem had pointed to in her trance. As they rolled it up they could see that it was roughly in the position of one of the crescents of the stylised mosaic dolphins. These dolphins would have made a complete circle in the original Roman Temple but now the crescent ended against one of the later built walls. The three women then paused to contemplate what to do next. Their attention was obviously being drawn to the floor but why and what did this mean? As anything connected with the Temple would impact upon all of the residents, they decided to hold a Warehouse residents' meeting. As the residents collectively identified as the Rabble their 'house' meetings were called 'Rabble rousers'. By tradition it was Roxie, the matriarch of the little community that issued the convivial summons. She also decided to invite Alexandra who had been present in the Temple and who was also still considered to be an honorary Warehouse resident.

26

The Rabble rouser was held on the Thursday evening when most of the residents were available, although Max had to stand in on door duty at one of their client's clubs. Residents meetings were always accompanied by lots of communal food and drink and were a great opportunity for the residents to catch up with each other's news. The communal area of the joint living space was surrounded by comfy sofas and cushions and when everyone was relaxed Roxie started proceedings by having a bit of a chat on joint funding, outgoings, building maintenance and news from friends.

Unlike most household meetings, talk about magic and witchcraft was completely normal in the Warehouse so nobody present was remotely perplexed at the subject they had come to discuss. Alexandra was the first to say what everyone was thinking. She reflected that it would appear the woman who had been manifesting through Gem was trying to tell them that something was buried beneath the floor of the Temple. With the prior permission of all the Sisters, Cyrene had recorded the coven's meeting on her phone which she had placed outside the circle. This could sometimes be useful if someone were in a trance and started to speak and they wanted to hear what they had said. These recordings were usually deleted by common agreement after the meetings had broken up, but with Gem's permission Cyrene had kept the part when Gem was speaking and had created a digital audio file from it.

During the intervening time Kaitlin had shared the file with some of her colleagues at the Museum of London that specialised in languages and one of them had come to a quite fascinating possibility. According to one of the colleagues who specialised in British and Irish languages the words seemed to have some similarities to Welsh and Cornish but was dissimilar enough to be hard to understand. She had concluded that it might be a more ancient version of contemporary Cornish and Welsh evolved, possibly the Britonic language that was common before the Roman invasion and the later colonisation of the islands by others such as the Saxons. She was unable to accurately interpret what was said but it might have something to do with danger and finding the moon and a stone. This did not make sense to anyone, but Cyrene did ponder as to whether the reference to stone might be connected to her visualisation of the standing stones.

The Rabble agreed with Alexandra, but the question was what should be done about it. Jethro enquired as to whether they could just dig up the bit of flooring where Gem had been pointing to see if there was anything underneath, but

Kaitlin immediately interjected to say that it was out of the question. The mosaics were priceless, some of the finest that had been found in Britain and that they could not just speculatively risk damaging them because of what had occurred in the coven. They would need permission from the Museum to remove any mosaics and this was extremely unlikely without far more evidence to justify such a risky action.

The witches felt a bit dejected, the intensity of their experience made them all feel that whatever might be buried under the mosaic floor was important. Intuition was extremely important to witchcraft, but it was hard to justify acting upon it in a world that demanded tangible evidence.

Not for the first time it was Fixie who came up with a proposal. "Letitia, the singer in Luther's band, is a metal detecting fanatic in her spare time, always stomping over farmland and beaches hoping to find that golden hoard. So far, she has found many coins, a few musket balls and endless quantities of ring pulls from cans! Why don't we ask her to come over and see if she can detect anything?"

"She would have to understand that we couldn't share any finds with her." said Kaitlin thoughtfully. "Anything associated with the Temple would be covered by the preservation order. Would she be prepared to help us out of curiosity?" Fixie just smiled and winked, it was a pointless question, nobody could refuse Fixie when she turned on the charm.

The following Sunday morning Fixie, a slightly hung-over Luther, Kaitlin, Gem, Jess and Letitia were gathered in the Temple. Letitia had brought her metal detector with her, and she was absolutely fascinated by the Temple and its amazing mosaics. "Why haven't you ever brought me to see this before" she chided Luther. Its amaazzzing!"

Luther just grimaced a bit as a sudden sharp pain in his head reminded him of his overindulgence of the night before. He looked incredulously at Fixie who had been just as indulgent and was, as usual, as bright as a penny.

"How deep can you penetrate with this detector Letitia?" asked Gem with interest.

"It all depends on how big the target is." she replied. "I actually borrowed this one from a friend, it's a Golden Mask Deep Hunter Pro, made in Bulgaria and its especially good at detecting deeper finds. It should easily pick up anything bigger than ten cm to a depth of about a metre, smaller finds at shallower depths."

"It is unlikely that we would risk damaging the mosaics for anything as small as a coin as there could well be many dropped when the Temple was being constructed." said Kaitlin.

"Ok, that's useful as I can set the detector sensitivity to ignore small finds."

The Rabble had agreed not to tell Letitia where Gem had pointed to at the meeting and, wisely, decided not to mention that they were asking Letitia for help over a witch's hunch. Fixie had just said that it was a favour to the Museum of London and Letitia had been more than happy to help with that sense of excitement of an unknown discovery that drew detectorists out in all weathers.

Starting near the entrance steps Letitia carefully walked up and down the width of the Temple slowly sweeping the floor before her. Occasionally the detector would let out a small buzz but nothing significant enough to draw Letitia's interest. About a third of the way along the detector had a large hit and Letitia reported back that it was a large ferrous contact. This could be significant or might just be an old stone working tool such as a masonry chisel. Kaitlin got out a piece of coloured chalk and marked a cross on the floor. Kaitlin tried to hide her anticipation as Letitia worked her way along the floor towards the dolphin that Gem had pointed at during her trance. The detector was exactly over the spot when there was a significant reaction.

"Now that is really interesting," said Letitia, "a large nonferrous reading which I would guess is about half a metre down. Any ideas about what it could be?"

"It might be a hoard of silver or gold coins in an earthenware pot." mused Kaitlin. "These were not that unusual and its possible that it was buried before the Temple floor was laid, maybe just before Boudicca's raid on Londinium? Just speculation really, the question is whether it's worth the risk to the mosaics in order to find out."

Letitia found nothing else of significance during her sweep and Fixie offered to treat her to a pub lunch as a thanks. Luther just looked at Fixie in despair and declined her deliberately breezy invitation for him to join them. He was heading back to bed with the aid of paracetamol.

Kaitlin, Gem and Jess went upstairs, reported what they had discovered to Cyrene, and they all decided to seek out Roxie's advice. Roxie was not a witch; her mind was too wired to her rationality, and it fought against her intuitive impulses by constantly demanding evidence. The strength of the Warehouse community was that everyone had qualities that they brought to the whole and they had great faith and trust in each other. Roxie did not need to be a witch herself when there were witches in her little community. Just as the others often sought out Roxie for her pragmatic reasoning, she had the greatest respect for the intuition of the Sisters and time and again their magic had benefited the Warehouse and its residents. Kaitlin had just proposed that she make contact with her supervisor at the Museum, Dr Diane Evans, to get her advice and to seek her approval before taking any action.

"What if she says no and refuses permission?" replied Roxie. "Even with Letitia's evidence is she really likely to let you risk damaging the mosaics based on a witch's hunch? How would that leave you all feeling? We all decided at the rabble rouser that we needed to gain more evidence before taking further action and sensibly decided to stop Jethro grabbing his pickaxe! Letitia's findings were pretty conclusive, there is something substantial down there exactly where Gem was pointing. It is obvious that there is a very powerful dynamic behind this, and I would suspect that it would not bode well if we frustrated this dynamic through our inaction."

"I completely agree with Roxie" said Cyrene. "We need to think of Gem's welfare, this presence is acting through Gem and if it is frustrated in its task it may harm her. I don't mean this as a deliberate act of harm, I detected nothing malicious in the presence, but there is a powerful energy behind this and if we stand in its way there may well be consequences for Gem."

Everyone looked at Kaitlin who was divided between her professional instincts and her wiccan ones. It did not take her long to decide, Gem was part of the Warehouse family and family came first. She could not risk Gem coming to harm and besides, her curiosity would drive her mad if it could not be satisfied. She was an archaeologist, and the driving power of curiosity was what motivated her to take up such a precarious career in the first place.

"Ok, we'll do it" she said, "but I'll need everyone's help as we will have to do it when the museum is shut to visitors, which means we have from 5.00 pm on Saturday to 9.00 am the following Thursday morning to complete the job."

"Rabble rouser!" exclaimed a delighted Gem.

On the following Saturday afternoon, they started work under Kaitlin's supervision. It was not possible to exactly estimate the size of the object from Letitia's detection signals and Kaitlin felt it was better to remove more than enough rather than to get it wrong and have to increase the size of the area being removed. Kaitlin decided to remove a square area 60cm by 60cm. First, she cleaned off all the mosaics in the area and made sure they were completely grease free by wiping them with alcohol and then burning it off. She then covered the mosaics with a dissolvable adhesive and covered this with sackcloth. She then worked the adhesive through the sackcloth and covered it with a stout plywood board which had two wooden handles bolted to the top. This was then allowed to set overnight.

The following morning, Kaitlin with help from Jess, who had occasionally worked as a volunteer on various sites with Kaitlin, removed three rows of mosaics from around the edge of the board by hand. Then after protecting the edges of the mosaics that were still remaining, they used thin strips of steel with sharp edges to carefully work underneath the boarded area. This loosened the mosaic flooring from the Roman mortar and gravel underneath until it was free. With support from Kaitlin and Jess on the other two sides of the square board, Max and Jethro grasped the handles and carefully lifted the board with the mosaics securely glued to it and placed it on a large old carpet they had brought down for the purpose.

Taking great care not to spill any grit onto the other precious mosaics of the Temple floor, the team slowly dug downwards. It was obvious that there was an area of disturbed subsoil about half a metre in diameter just off centre in the hole and Kaitlin asked them to focus on this area. Meanwhile Kaitlin and Jess had the plywood board with the mosaics attached turned over and they cleaned off all the excess gravel and mortar until they had created a completely flat surface 5cm deep under the mosaics.

After carefully digging down about 50cm Max heard a distinctly metallic sound as the small excavation shovel he was using hit an object. They carefully brushed the top surface of the object and to Kaitlin's joy and amazement the top of a lead box was revealed. Max and Jethro dug around the box which was just under 30cm square and 30cm deep and then slipped some lifting irons under two of the corners and carefully, with considerable exertion, lifted it out onto another plywood board that had been hastily placed next to the hole. The team briefly stared at the plain lead box with wonder, it was fairly basic in construction, but all the seams had been carefully hammered and folded to ensure that the box was watertight. Whoever had placed this box in the ground had meant it to stay there and protect whatever was inside for a very long time.

They took the box upstairs to Cyrene's studio apartment on the top floor, but before they even started the examination Kaitlin ensured that all the mosaics were carefully replaced on the Temple floor. The hole was carefully filled with what had been dug up and with some extra loose gravel fill to take up the space occupied by the box which was pounded down to make a solid firm base. A thin layer of sand for laying slabs was then spread on the surface and the board with the mosaics fixed to the bottom was then replaced. They had to lift it half a dozen times as Kaitlin carefully examined the alignment of the bottom lip of the plywood with the surrounding mosaics and gently added more sand until she was completely satisfied.

The old carpet covered in the excess dirt was removed, the sackcloth was separated from the plywood and the adhesive cleaned off the surface of the mosaics. They then carefully replaced the mosaics around the edge, fixing them in place with a replica mix of Roman mortar which was then carefully discoloured to match the colour of the surrounding mortar. By the time they had completed the task they had been working on the project for four days. They had just one day left before it was to be opened to the public again. Kaitlin carefully examined the area they had been working upon to access the box and was rather proud of the teams' work. A trained archaeologist drawn to the area would probably identify that some work had been going on but there were other areas of the floor that had had to be repaired when it was first excavated so this would not cause undue concern. She was very pleased with their work and now desperate to discover what the lead box contained.

There was no lock, lid, or hinges on the box, it was just a roughly cubical container which had been sealed by carefully peening the overlapping edges of the box to cause a seal. At Kaitlin's direction Max carefully opened the seam around the top of the box using a chisel and some grips to unroll the edge. When he had worked around three edges, using the fourth rolled edge as a hinge, he prised open the lid to reveal the contents of the box. On top was a piece of carved olive wood, obviously imported from around the Mediterranean which had a depiction of the Goddess Venus. Underneath the wood, to Kaitlin's complete surprise, the box was filled with very thin sheets of hammered copper. Each sheet was completely covered in text that had been meticulously scribed into the surface with some sort of steel stylus. At first glance there looked to be over a hundred sheets. Kaitlin had never come across anything like it before. Someone had gone to extraordinary lengths to preserve this written legacy and Kaitlin could not wait to begin its translation so that she could reveal its contents to the rest of the Rabble.

27

The offices of Restitution Holdings were behind an unassuming door in a small lane in the City of London. Anyone passing by the door would not give it so much as a second glance. There were much grander buildings and doors in the Square Mile, but there were no doors that belonged to a more powerful and influential organisation.

Sir Giles Hemmingsworth nodded to the security guard who sat behind the screen in the reception as he passed through the hallway. He walked past the main lifts to the main offices above and the accompanying stairwell until he came to the end of the hallway where there was a reinforced security door with a biometric entry system. Giles placed his thumb on the reader and the door opened up to reveal a modern lobby area with the stainless steel doors of a lift in front. Giles got into the lift and entered a code into the touchpad underneath the lift buttons. The code took the lift fifteen metres downwards and the doors opened to a scene that would have looked more familiar to an Egyptologist than a city banker. Giles turned left into a leisure area which had a sauna, steam room, swimming pool and changing facilities where he changed into the elaborate robe that belonged to the Master of the Order of the Black Crystal.

Having changed, he made his way past the lift and entered a high stone vaulted corridor lined with carved hieroglyphs that had been pillaged many centuries before from Egypt. At the end of the corridor was a large round domed Temple, dedicated to the God Seth, also adorned with original, ancient Egyptian hieroglyphs. Under the dome were thirteen gilded ornate chairs arranged in a circle that were facing inwards towards a large granite altar with a large chunk missing from one corner. In the centre of the altar was an almost completely black, obsidian glass stone. The twelve other members of the Order were already sat in their chairs and Giles strode purposefully past the altar towards the largest chair which rather resembled a throne.

London was not the first home of this Temple or for the obsidian stone. The stone was older than recorded time but was first mentioned in Egyptian hieroglyphs dating back three and a half millennia to the reign of the King of Thebes, Ahmose I. The Temple in its current form had followed the scent of power through the centuries, starting in Alexandria and then relocating to Rome as it blossomed under the growing imperial patriarchal oppression of the Roman Empire.

After the collapse of the Roman Empire, the Order found a powerful new ally in the Roman Catholic Church. The Roman emperors recognised the potential of a religion that worshipped one tyrannical God whose rule was absolute and who had committed the most atrocious acts as the punishment of disobedient humans including mass genocide. The influence of a small Jewish sect who created an empathetic cult around a figure named Yeshua, who later became known as Jesus had been very effectively neutralised. This was achieved by associating Yeshua with the vengeful and judgemental Abrahamic God and thereby effectively neutralising any of his teachings of empathy and compassion by association with the totalitarian deity. This hybrid religion which became known as Christianity served the emperors well and it continued to serve the interests of many reactionary right-wing politicians, tyrants, and dictators. They use the example of God's ultimate power and vengeful nature to justify their own brutality and repression.

The Order thrived in Rome, working effectively with the Catholic Church and the associated secular feudal leaders who used the authority of the Abrahamic Christian God to justify their own power and omnipotence. The renaissance led to the gradual diminishing of the power of the Church and its pernicious Inquisitions through the growing influence of scientific thought. Ever adaptable to changing fortunes, the Order decided that its interests would be best served by embedding itself amongst the new powerful temples of Mammon, the worship of greed and avarice that was ballooning in the City of London. They recognised and admired the growth in power of the British Empire in the 18th Century and relocated themselves to its avaricious beating heart where the Temple had remained and prospered ever since.

The thirteen members of the Order also changed with the times as new members were sought out and inducted. The one overriding condition of membership was the desire for power and an insatiable appetite for the greed that underpinned it. Members of the Order could only leave it through their death or through incapacitating illness. For members that transgressed against the interests of the Order or disclosed its secrets, death could come far more quickly than nature intended. New members were sought out based on their ability and influence through their position in society to exercise power and the absence of any compassion that would constrain the Order's ambition. Whether it was within the Roman Senate, the Court of the Ottoman Sultan or within the liveried companies of the City of London, behind the faces of power were to be found the members of the Order, conspiring, influencing, and manipulating for its advantage.

There was a far greater power behind the Order than the coercive manipulation of influential people within the establishment. The Order had the service of a malign powerful entity, one that had grown through the malice of thousands of years of dedication and worship, focused through the Black Crystal. The Egyptians called this entity Sutekh, the Greeks named it Seth, but whatever the name given to this power, it was exercised and amplified by the directed malice of thousands of evil men. The most malign quality that grew with the accumulation of this malice within the Black Crystal, was the ability to constrain the ability of the majority of humans to discern the truth. Under the Crystal's influence, most of humanity was virtually asleep and largely apathetic as to how they were being manipulated. This inability of people to discern the truth or even care that their politicians and media blatantly lie to them meant that any dominant narcissistic charlatan or sociopath could easily rally millions to their cause. This was usually achieved by inciting humans to follow their darkest emotions, dividing populations, promoting hate at vulnerable minorities, and amplifying hidden biases without the impediment of any significant rational scrutiny.

The impact of the Black Crystal's influence throughout history was extremely pernicious and had literally plunged millions into wars and conflict. The latest fertile environment for the Order to exploit was the complete dominance of the neo-liberal economic model and the resulting unconstrained rapacious capitalism. Compliant unquestioning populations barely challenged the obscene accumulation of vast amounts of capital by global oligarchs, whilst hundreds of millions of people died through abject poverty, hunger, and disease. The Order's accumulation of wealth, which was held in thousands of shell companies located in tax havens across the world, amounted to roughly one trillion dollars. This continued to grow as exploitative systems and algorithms automatically extracted the wealth created by the labour of billions of people from global economies on their behalf.

This power of the Crystal to suppress the capability of most humans to discern the truth was the quality above any other that had best served the purposes of the order, especially when combined with their own directed malice. With the Crystal in their possession, the Order's ability to manipulate human affairs for its own ends was virtually uncontested.

The primary power of resistance to the Crystal's, and therefore the Order's, influence was the human capacity for empathy and the ability to love. At the Nuremburg trial of Nazi war criminals after the 2nd World War, Captain Gustave Mark Gilbert, the psychologist assigned to the Nazi prisoners had identified an important truth. This truth was the most important lesson that should have been learned from the terrible conflict and it was perhaps the one most quickly forgotten. The one common characteristic that all the Nazi prisoners shared was that they completely lacked the ability to empathise with their fellow man. Captain Gilbert came to the realisation that the evil they had unleashed on the World was defined by this the lack of empathy.

The glowing success of the Order was the fact that, rather than learning from the war against evil, rampant capitalism, devoid of empathy, had become the dominant global societal model. Societies had become pathological in nature and the evil of all-consuming greed had become the dominant global ideology.

The current life of any human with a developed capacity for empathy in this pathological world had become a life of constant torment. Millions of empaths have been driven to despair and even suicide. There was an epidemic of mental health issues amongst a generation of young people whose futures had been stolen and who could see no hope of life getting any better in the future. The suffering of empaths was a delight to the Order as empathetic beings had a natural resistance to the soporific qualities of the Black Crystal. If the capacity for love and empathy were to grow within the human population it would begin to threaten the obvious absurdities of predatory social models. In such a society the influence of the Order would come under threat.

Because of the dangers posed by the human capacity for empathy, any organisation that developed political influence and began to challenge the established order in a fight for equality, justice, and compassion became an instant target. They would become bombarded with a campaign of lies, hate and smears through the billionaire owned media and by the successful erosion of any objective scrutiny from public sector broadcasters. There were resistant movements and small progressive media outlets, but they found themselves fighting a constant war of attrition against the forces of evil. The power of the Black Crystal and the Order that channelled it had never been more powerful. The very existence of much of life on Earth was now under threat as the pursuit of greed required ever greater consumption of the Earth's resources and safe environments for all living beings were being destroyed at a terrifying rate.

Sir Giles had often reflected upon the purpose of the Order that he led whose ultimate nihilistic endgame would result in the desolation of the planet. The womb of the Goddess, the Great Mother of Nature would become barren and her beautiful realm, the tiny island of life in the vastness of the Universe would become a poisoned wasteland. This would be the ultimate victory for Seth over the Goddess Mut whose love had once been sought to constrain his powers. The order of the priestesses of the thirteen Moonstones had been formed in her name and for centuries their power had constrained the evil emanating from the Black Crystal. Through its agents the Order had actively sought out and destroyed these Moonstones and with the destruction of each Moonstone the power of the Black Crystal had grown. twelve Moonstones had been destroyed. Only one Moonstone remained, and this was safe. The Roman Governor of Britannia, Agricola, who was a member of the Order and who would ultimately become its leader had reported that this Moonstone was irretrievably lost beneath the waves. The fact that the last Moonstone was lost but had not been destroyed was a tiny remaining vestige of insecurity and vulnerability lurking within the Order's belief in its own omnipotence.

Sir Giles looked around the Temple at the other twelve members of the order. One or two were getting very old and their health was failing. It would soon be time to refresh their membership again. It was very unusual for all the members to be gathered together, many lived in other countries acting out their malevolent influence across the globe. They had been called together by one of the three permanent priests who interpreted and interacted with the will of Seth through the Crystal.

The Priests of the Order all came from an ancient cult dedicated to Seth that still existed in Luxor and had survived the rise of Islam within Egypt. They still served Seth or Sutekh, as the deity was still known in Luxor, by the followers of the cult. Through their devotion to their God, they had pledged to serve those who had the power to manifest his will upon Earth and this forged their bond with the Order of the Black Crystal. Every High Priest that ascended to prominence changed their name to Kharmudi in honour of the last Hyksos King who had built the first great temple dedicated to Sutekh and the Black Crystal. In a terrible ceremony each High Priest was blinded by their fellow priests to enhance their ability to visualise and interpret the will of Seth. In return for this sacrifice, they were given every earthly desire by the Order, every vice and perversity was catered for, and they had huge influence within the Order. The other purpose of this brutal ritual was a practical one for the Order, a blinded High Priest was also a more dependent and therefore dependable one.

Sir Giles banged his gold tipped staff on the Temple's granite floor to silence the Members. Even Sir Giles had not been informed of the purpose behind the summoning and he looked towards the shuffling figure of Kharmudi with interest.

"I have felt an ancient threat stir." said Kharmudi. The High Priest had been disturbed by a very ancient energy; a flicker of light that had flashed across his consciousness as he had sat in the presence of the Crystal. He sensed the presence of an energy that had not troubled any of the Priests for two millennia. "Something has been disturbed in the equilibrium, something linked to the Goddess."

Sir Giles and the other Members were stunned by this revelation. Usually, Kharmudi was alerting them to a current rise in a progressive and empathetic movement that had grown powerful enough to require the Order's attention. This was something completely different.

"What is this threat?" said Sir Giles

"It is not certain, but I saw an ancient chest being opened by one who serves the Goddess. The danger lies within this chest, but the nature of this danger is as yet unknown to me."

"Where is this chest?" asked Sir Giles.

"Its exact position is masked, an ancient protection linked to the Goddess is blocking my vision, the chest is protected by a sacred place, but it is close, it is in this City." replied Kharmudi.

"You must find out more." demanded Sir Giles.

"I will try offering a human sacrifice," said Kharmudi, "the ritual of anointing the Crystal with human blood as the spirit departs from the body will enhance my vision and perhaps give me the strength to see."

"See that its done," said Sir Giles, "and quickly!"

After the twelve other members had discussed their other business Sir Giles dismissed them leaving him alone with the three priests. One of the priests went to an intercom discretely placed near the Temple entrance and shortly after two assistants appeared. They disappeared for about ten minutes and returned with a young boy of about thirteen who was absolutely terrified but had learned through bitter agonising experience not to defy his guards.

Only a few carefully selected staff directly served the Temple and even fewer were privy to its innermost secrets although there were nearly a thousand people who served the Order. These were the staff employed through its corporation Restitution Holdings, or who were indirectly contracted to it. These other employees had no knowledge of the Black Crystal or of the existence of the Order, but they were complicit in the projection of its power. Nobody who worked for Resolution Holdings for any length of time could have been unaware of its ruthlessness, so it attracted a particular kind of employee who was comfortable with its commercial practices.

Apart from the leisure facilities and the Temple there was one other area in the basement that was accessed via another door with a biometric lock. This was where the members of the Order indulged their sexual deviancies and sadism on victims that were kidnapped from the streets of London. Hundreds of children or vulnerable adults, many who were in care or homeless went missing every year and most had nobody close enough to them to even notice their disappearance. Every year, dozens of men, women, and children disappeared into the Order's dungeon never to come out alive. The dungeon had another entrance that was accessed through a long tunnel hewn, two centuries before, under the streets of the City which linked it to the basement of a seedy nondescript hotel. This was where agents of the Temple would lure hapless victims, often with the promise of payment for casual sex that would ultimately lead to their deaths, often after terrible suffering.

Since its first inception in Alexandria in 332 BCE, the Order had always considered itself beyond any rules of society and no member had ever been held to account for their actions unless this was at the hands of the Order itself for an act of transgression. The members were unencumbered by any scruples having been deliberately selected for their lack of empathy or compassion and there was no thought of any sanction for their actions by their peers. Sir Giles himself was actually asexual and took little part in what went on within the dungeon. Sir Giles's pleasure was gained from the wave of misery caused to millions of people and other living beings by the actions of extreme financial and environmental exploitation. Some of the others had virtually insatiable sexual appetites and took great delight in the suffering of their victims, which also helped to fuel the growing power of the Black Crystal through its close proximity to this misery. From the dungeon side, the door that led to the Temple area was completely invisible, it just looked like part of a brick wall. Unless you knew it was there and were deliberately seeking it out you would never know of its existence.

The whole dungeon operation was undertaken and managed by a small and carefully selected group of Temple assistants, many with previous military training and mercenary backgrounds. The dungeon, and the hotel linked to it, was managed by a ruthless woman called Scara Hayes. She had previously been arrested by the police for modern slavery offences committed in a brothel run by a local crime syndicate. Her particular talents came to the attention of one of the Temple assistants, money passed through palms and soon she was employing her talents for the Order although she had no knowledge of their true nature.

The terrified young boy was taken to the altar where his head was forcibly held down and his throat was swiftly cut with an ancient sacrificial blade. The blood flowed down and pooled in a slight hollow in the altar that surrounded the inset Crystal. As the life drained out of the boy, Kharmudi cupped the Crystal in his hands and shook as the power raced through his body. His mind latched onto the disturbance he had detected in the Crystal and traced it backwards towards its source. He was in the mind of a woman; a powerful witch and he could see a room with candles and a massage table. His presence was immediately noticed, and he felt a powerful resistance to his intrusion, but the power of the Black Crystal was stronger and once again his vision began to form. He saw a table with a pentagram upon it and in the centre of the pentagram was the lead chest. Suddenly he felt another presence and a naked woman appeared before him, blocking his vision. She had long flowing auburn hair and piercing green eyes which stared defiantly back at him. She suddenly held aloft her hand from which came a blinding white light that drove him out of the witch's mind and threw him across the floor of the Temple.

Kharmudi had never been confronted by such a powerful opponent before and he took a while to lay on the floor of the Temple to collect his thoughts before putting out his hands to be raised up by the other two priests. Only a true high priestess of the Goddess could challenge his power but even then, he had doubted that any could withstand him when his will was amplified by the sacrificial blood ritual. This experience was a shock to him and for the first time in his life since facing the terrors of the blinding ritual, he felt vulnerable. He did not dare reveal this to Sir Giles, it was not wise to show weakness before the Master of the Order and he cursed himself for allowing Sir Giles to be present.

"The disturbance comes from a location where there is a powerful witch that practices magic here in London" said Kharmudi. "I do not yet know who she is or her location, but our spies will soon reveal her identity. A witch with her power will be very well known."

Kharmudi did not tell Sir Giles about the other woman who had driven him out, he was still smarting from the humiliation of being repulsed. He did however decide to reveal a powerful impression that he had experienced during the process. Part of the reason that he had been thrown across the floor was that the Black Crystal itself had recoiled from the light in the woman's hand. He had no idea how it could be possible but the only force that had ever had the power to cause such a reaction was the presence of one of the thirteen Moonstones. Somehow the last Moonstone was awakening and something in the lead chest had triggered this reaction. If the Moonstone had actually been found and used he would have sensed it immediately. He was sure it was still lost but there could be no doubt that this energy was connected to it and so was the spirit of the priestess who had so boldly challenged him in his vision.

"The disturbance is connected to the last Moonstone." he said to Sir Giles and for the first time since Sir Giles had joined the Order a shadow of uncertainty crossed his mind.

28

Cyrene, Kaitlin, and Gem sat in Cyrene's studio with the lead chest containing the copper sheets. Kaitlin was conflicted about what they were about to embark upon. She was excited to start translating the text but also felt guilty that she had withheld the existence of the chest from her colleagues at the Museum of London. As a trained archaeologist she felt she had a duty to rigorously follow established protocols for the examination of important finds and at this moment she was feeling more like a latter-day Indiana Jones. With some justification Cyrene had pointed out that established archaeological protocols were not drawn up in the context of following a witch's intuition. If they had followed the established protocols this chest would most probably still be firmly buried in the ground.

They had decided that the best way to undertake the task of translation was for Kaitlin to try to translate, and for Gem to use the typing skills she had honed as a journalist under the constant time pressure of deadlines for publication. Cyrene was going to supply copious amounts of coffee and reveal anything that she visualised during the process which might add context to the translation.

"Ok, here goes," said Kaitlin, "I just hope they are in some kind of order."

She picked up the first sheet and began to slowly read. The Latin was old, she estimated it to be from about the 1st century BCE with which she was fortunately familiar through her work at the Museum. The very first paragraph proved her to be right.

"Greetings to you my sister, for I know that the Goddess would only entrust these revelations to one of her daughters. My name is Siabelle of the Trinovantes, I am writing in the year given by the Roman oppressors of my people as DCCCXXXII, and this is my story. As these words have now been revealed it is a prophecy that the years of the controlling patriarchy, enforced at the point of the bloodied swords of the Roman legions, is coming to an end. You stand at the beginning of a new dawn. Fight my sisters, fight. Those who oppress your rights and freedoms will not easily relinquish the reins of power, you must prise it from their grip though the power of your wills."

"How could 832 be Roman?" asked Gem. "They were long gone by then; surely it was the time of the Saxons?"

"Our current BCE, CE dating system otherwise known as the BC, AD system was not conceived until the 6th century CE and not widely adopted until the beginning of the 9th. This writer is using the Roman system which dated the years from the perceived foundation of Rome. 832 would be 79 CE in our current calendar. This would be exactly when the Roman legions under the Governor Gnaeus Julius Agricola were campaigning in the North of Britannia."

Kaitlin looked at Cyrene and Gem in amazement. This was an incredible find, nothing like this had ever been discovered before from these times. It was the voice of a native Britonic woman from 79 CE greeting them in Latin from the distant past. The three women were completely captivated as the translation continued and it revealed the most extraordinary story that they had ever heard. The translation continued into the afternoon and revealed the existence of a powerful crystal called the Moonstone and of Chyrenia of the Gallancia, the High Priestess of the Stones.

Suddenly Cyrene held her head in agony and slumped forward. She had a blinding headache and at first she thought she must be having a stroke until her inner spirit reacted as she realised that a hostile entity was trying to take possession of her. She fought to drive it out, centring on her heart chakra and the power of the Goddess's love and for a few seconds she held it. She sensed a terrible presence, an ancient evil, and it was just too strong for her. She had never sensed anything so powerful and malevolent before and she felt her spirit slowly being crushed. Against her will her head began to lift, and her eyes looked around and centred on the lead chest on the table. As her eyes began to focus on the chest she was flooded with an ecstatic love, the pain disappeared and a voice within her said, "do not be afraid my sister for you are not alone." The malevolent entity was thrown out with tremendous force and for an instant Cyrene pictured herself standing in an ancient stone circle in the presence of a coven of other witches before the vision abruptly vanished.

"I think we should call an ambulance." said Gem with alarm as Cyrene's head lifted then slumped forward once more. Kaitlin had rushed to Cyrene's side, and she put her arm around her in support. Cyrene lifted her arm to stall Gem. She breathed slowly and then lifted her head to look at them both in wonder, she still had presence of a wonderful afterglow left by the spirit of the woman who had intervened to save her.

When she had gathered herself, Cyrene explained what had happened and that she knew that it was intrinsically linked to the story of Siabelle. Somehow she also knew the spirit that had intervened and saved her was that of Chyrenia of the Gallancia. They decided to leave the translation for the day to enable Cyrene to recover from her ordeal but resolved to meet again the following day to reveal the rest of the story.

The next day they continued, mercifully without another psychic attack. When they had finished translating Siabelle's story, they were overcome with the wonder of it. Siabelle had also revealed that she was the lover and partner of Chyrenia and that Chyrenia had told her of this malign power, that it was in the possession of the Romans, and it was aiding them in their conquest of oppression. It would seem that it was not only Chyrenia's spirit that had transcended a time span of nearly two millennia. It would also appear that this malevolent evil energy was still active in the 21st century and now seemed to be more powerful than ever. The questions they had to answer now were what were the implications of Siabelle's story being revealed to them at this moment in time, and what would be the reaction of the evil that had sensed its presence? What did it all mean to the small Warehouse community, and how should they react?

29

None of the residents of the Warehouse would ever forget the following Friday's Rabble rouser which would lead to a chain of events that would have such a profound impact upon all of their lives. Kaitlin had given them all a copy of her translation of Siabelle's story to read beforehand so that they would know more about the context of the meeting. To everyone's surprise, Roxie had also invited along another guest who none of them had ever met before.

When Roxie had read Siabelle's tale and heard about the attack on Cyrene something about it resonated with her and she recalled an intriguing story an old friend had shared about one of her customers. Her friend Ellen ran a quirky bookshop in the City of Bath that specialised in obscure and esoteric texts. One of her most regular clients was a complex character called Keith who would often come to her requesting her help in locating rare texts and historical documents. In particular he seemed particularly interested in Egyptian mythology and any references to the deity Seth and those who worshipped him. Keith was quiet and unassuming but over time Ellen and Keith had become close enough to exchange pleasantries. One day Ellen felt confident enough to ask Keith if there was a link between all the books and articles he was requesting from her? She felt it might enable her to be more helpful in aiding his search if she knew a bit more about what he was looking for and why. Keith had been a bit reticent at first, but he could see the sense behind Ellen's suggestion, and he shared with her a rather strange tale. He talked about an ancient order and a black crystal that cast a malevolent shadow over the world. When she asked him why he was so interested he had just revealed that it was connected to a childhood experience that had had a permanent impact upon his life. When she pressed him further, he clammed up and it was obvious that she would not get anything more from him on the subject.

Roxie and Ellen were the closest of confidantes and had known each other for more than half their lives. Such was the bond of trust between them that Roxie had no hesitation in telling Ellen about the recent events at the Warehouse. Roxie remembered this previous conversation with her friend and contacted Ellen to see if she could find out a bit more to see if it could be helpful. Ellen said that she was not sure as it seemed a bit of a tenuous link, but equally she knew the events at the Warehouse were connected to magic. Magic had its own synchronicity which often connected a sequence of events that seemed improbable. This made it easy for magical anecdotes to be dismissed by cynics as pure coincidence, which rather suited most of the magical community who did not welcome intrusion into their lives and practice. Ellen told Roxie that she would try to broach the subject with Keith, who was popping in to pick up an article the following morning.

Keith popped into the shop as planned and he exchanged the usual pleasantries with Ellen as she handed him the article he had ordered from her. Ellen then mentioned to Keith that she had a friend who was also interested in his area of research. She wanted to ask if his investigations into the ancient order and their crystal worship had revealed anything about the Romans in Britain and tales of a sacred Moonstone? To Ellen's shock Keith froze and his whole countenance changed. He looked at Ellen very intensely and she became quite alarmed at what he had to say. "Who is your friend? If you care for them at all you must let me speak to them, they are in grave danger. Please do not mention the Moonstone to anyone else if you don't want to also put your own life in jeopardy."

Ellen phoned Roxie whilst Keith was still with her and then passed over the phone to him. What he talked about alarmed Roxie enough for her to agree to meet him the following day in London. They met in a bar in Paddington Station. When he had told Roxie his story, she felt it was imperative that he should talk to the rest of the residents immediately and invited him to their Rabble rouser.

Roxie introduced Keith to the Rabble which included Alexandra as she was now intrinsically connected to the events that were developing, and her views were highly valued by the rest of the group. Roxie asked that they all listen patiently to what Keith had to say before deciding what to do about Siabelle's tale and Cyrene's disturbing experience.

Keith looked at this group of strangers gathered around him and wondered just how much he should tell them. Was he really about to trust a group of strangers with his story and would they even believe him if he did?

He caught Roxie's eye again and she smiled reassuringly at him. Decision made, perhaps it was this moment that was to be the realisation of his destiny? It seemed that many powerful dynamics were coming together at one place and at one singularity in time.

Keith began to talk, and he had an extraordinary tale to share. He remembered that he had always been troubled as a child and was often shunned by other children who seemed to sense that there was something different about him. He had also suffered from terrible nightmares about being constantly stalked by an evil monster that he could never quite see as it was always in shadow. On his 18th birthday his mother had felt that it was time her son knew more about his father whom he barely remembered, and she told him a frightening story about his early life.

His mother, Janet, revealed that she had been married to a very successful man, Richard Drayton, who was Keith's father. Richard had been a rising star in the City of London when she had met him. Keith's father had been incredibly charming, and at the young age of just 22 years old she had been flattered at being the centre of attention for such a popular and very handsome man. Richard was eight years older than Janet and had been to one of the top public schools followed by Cambridge University and an unpaid internship in a City trading bank that quickly led to a well-paid position. He was a rising City star, and their romance was a whirlwind of fast cars, luxury hotels and trips around the world, culminating in a glamorous and expensive wedding within two years.

Shortly after her wedding the gloss began to rub off Keith's mother's idyllic life. Richard had taken a job at a City firm called Restitution Holdings and almost immediately she started to see a change in his behaviour. She began to notice a cruel streak in Richard's nature that she later conceded had probably always been there, but she had chosen not to see it. To his mother's growing distress, he was becoming increasingly short tempered and controlling with her. He would be rude to waiters and staff in hotels and to her horror he actually beat their pet dog to death for peeing on the carpet. He was also becoming more brutal in their sex life, increasingly interested in aspects of controlling and violent sex which she did not enjoy, and she began to dread his advances. During this time, she actually became pregnant with Keith and it was after his birth in 1962 that things started to spiral out of control. Janet had been brought up as a Catholic and although they had had a secular wedding, she wanted Keith to be christened in a Church. Richard would hear nothing of it and the day she suggested it was the first time he physically hit her outside of the sexual context where she was still reluctantly acquiescing to his increasingly extreme appetites.

When Keith was just six weeks old, his mother revealed that his father had taken them both to the City and they had entered this rather decrepit looking hotel in a backstreet. As soon as she entered the hotel she was physically restrained and then blindfolded. She said they went down a lot of stairs and then along some sort of corridor that echoed with their footsteps on the hard stone floor. To her great consternation his mother had heard voices and cries of distress and she was becoming increasingly terrified as to what was about to happen to her and her baby.

When they took her blindfold off, she found herself in this large domed room that looked like an Egyptian temple with walls and pillars covered in hieroglyphs. In the centre of the room was a large granite altar with a large, virtually black crystal embedded in the centre. Around the altar sat thirteen men dressed in robes and headdresses, including Richard who had baby Keith in his arms. Standing in front of the altar were three priests dressed in strange attire and Janet noticed that the priest who was in charge of the proceedings was blind.

Janet was held just outside the circle of thirteen chairs by two large men whom she assumed were some sort of assistants. What followed was some kind of ritual ceremony akin to a Christening but seemingly to one of the Gods of Egypt. As the ceremony proceeded the thirteen men and two of the priests started chanting in a language that Janet did not recognise. Janet was then dragged forward, and her hand was held out in front of her. To her horror the blind priest approached her holding what looked to be an ancient dagger. Despite the priest's lack of sight, he seemed to know exactly where she was. Janet was terrified, convinced that he was going to kill her but instead he grasped her outstretched hand and cut her palm with the razor-sharp blade. Trickling blood was collected in a golden bowl held by one of the assistants for a few seconds and then the other deftly wrapped a dressing and bandage around Janet's cut palm.

Richard then stood up and walked forward, still holding baby Keith in the crook of one arm and offered up his other hand. Richards blood was also added and finally the blind priest added his own blood. He raised the bowl containing the blood and one of the other priests brought forward baby Keith. For one horrifying second Janet thought the priest was going to sacrifice her baby and she screamed and struggled against the men who were holding her. Instead, the priest trickled the blood over the Black Crystal and then with his finger he collected some of the blood from the surface of the crystal and anointed the baby. He said some words in the strange language and then in English said, "I name this child Nergal the destroyer, may he use his power to be a true servant of the Order, and to bring terror and retribution to all those who stand in its way."

After the ceremony Janet was again blindfolded and she sensed she was taken back the way she had come as her blindfold was finally removed outside the same grubby looking hotel that they had arrived at. Richard and Janet had a terrible row about what had happened, but Richard warned her that Nergal, he would never call the child Keith again, was a servant of the Order of the Black

Crystal. If she tried to defy him, she would never see the child again. Over the next two years of their increasingly strained marriage Keith became a troubled and preoccupied young child who struggled to find joy in life. The violence and abuse in the relationship got worse and one day Janet was so badly beaten that she had to get a taxi to take her to hospital when Richard had left the house. She confided what was going on to a nurse and she and the child were given sanctuary.

There was a police investigation, but Richard could afford the best solicitors and Janet suspected that the Order also had senior connections within the police, and it quickly became clear that no further action was going to be taken. It did, however, result in a restraining order which offered Janet some protection from Richard's violence. Janet immediately asked for a divorce which made Richard furious, but it seemed the Order had decided to act as they hated any kind of exposure, and he was forced to let Janet and his child go. Janet was warned that if she said anything about what she had seen or about the Order both she and the child would be killed.

Keith never saw his father again, his parents' divorce came through, and Richard's highly paid lawyers ensured that she was left with very little money from the settlement. A few years later his mother told him that she had received an anonymous note that his father, Richard, had died. He had apparently died in a boating accident on the Thames although Keith later suspected that he had been summarily executed for his weakness for failing to control his wife and risking the exposure of the Order.

It was not until much later in life, when Keith was in his twenties that he began to notice, with alarm, the impact he seemed to have on people who upset him. He was by nature a kind man and politically became quite a strident socialist. He hated greed and inequality and the unnecessary poverty resulting from a system that destroyed people's lives. Within him however he had the capacity for generating a terrible rage, although his heart, his conscience, and his memories of his mother never allowed the rage to resort to violence at those who had incurred his wrath. The rage seemed to almost have a substance of its own and when it became too much it just seemed to flow out of him like a stream of hostile malice over which he had no control. He then began to notice that the people who had instigated his anger started to almost immediately suffer misfortunes. Their health might fail, some would have accidents, or their business or employment might suddenly collapse. At first, he thought that this was just a coincidence and he just shrugged it off, sometimes even rationalising their fate in that they had created their own karma.

Eventually he realised that this was happening far too often to be purely coincidental. He began to suspect that during his evil baptism at the Temple, something malevolent had been embedded deep within his soul. He also researched the name they had given him and found out that it belonged to a Babylonian God of death and the underworld, an appropriate name for someone baptised to serve the brooding evil that was emanating from the Black Crystal. Against the odds he had become quite successful as an independent business consultant, but increasingly his conscience began to trouble him. He began to try to distance himself as much as he possibly could from people so that he could avoid situations that could trigger the destructive rage. He sold his house and downsized to a remote cottage that needed a lot of attention but released enough capital for him to survive without income if he was careful with his finances. Despite the fact that he was attracted to women and enjoyed their company he was too worried about the consequences his cursed nature could have on their lives to initiate any serious relationships.

In 2010 his mother had died and when he was going through her things, he found a book bound in an ancient leather binding that had obviously belonged to his father. It seemed to be his father's attempt to record some of the knowledge that underpinned the activities of the Order, a bit like a witch's book of shadows. In it he had written details of ceremonies and some of the history of the Order of the Black Crystal, secrets that they would be horrified to see disclosed to the outside world.

Keith had since spent much of his life trying to find out more about the Order and how they used their power to manipulate and corrupt society. In his book, his father had referred to the historical myth about how thirteen Moonstones, blessed by the Goddess Mut and infused with her love had once constrained the power of the Black Crystal and how the Order had destroyed all but one. It was recorded that the last Moonstone was irretrievably lost beneath the waves of the sea to save it from falling into the hands of the Romans by a Britonic priestess. This was why he was so concerned when his acquaintance Ellen from the bookshop, who knew something about his research, suddenly asked if he knew about a Moonstone from Roman times.

"If you were ever able to find the last Moonstone your lives would be in immediate danger." concluded Keith. "The Order will know it has been found, the priests serving the Black Crystal will sense it, and they would stop at nothing to destroy it. The only thing the Order fears is the healing power of love and the human capacity for empathy. The power in the hands of the Order and other parasitic oligarchs that corrupt and manipulate pliable and complicit politicians would start to crumble overnight if the malign power of the Black Crystal was overcome. People would rise up and stand against their subjugation if they were able to truly comprehend the reality of their situation. The majority of humanity now slumbers in apathy and ignorance whilst the World burns around them. The last Moonstone is probably humanity's and Mother Nature's last hope that the power of love can overcome the spreading evil, manifest in the selfishness and greed that is now consuming her World."

Keith sat down and hung his head with the exhaustion of a person who had had to carry a terrible burden of knowledge alone whilst helplessly watching evil spread. He had spent most of his adult life watching evil people destroy the planet. It was like watching a slow-motion train crash that he was unable to prevent, and the train was still accelerating towards its ultimate doom.

For a moment nobody said a word as they tried to digest the implications of what Keith had told them. In a few moments, an intriguing archaeological find had been transformed into a situation which could literally have a bearing on the future of most of life on Earth. The implications for the witches in particular, who had dedicated their lives to serving Mother Nature, the beautiful Goddess who had created the womb of life, were particularly stark. The power within the last Moonstone, if it even existed, served the Goddess as did they all. Who else but her magical daughters would be able to restore this power and challenge the growing evil of the Order and the priests of the Black Crystal? Were they strong enough to take on such a task? The Britonic warrior Siabelle obviously thought so or she would not have chosen to manifest through Gem, and Chyrenia's intervention when Cyrene was attacked, showed that even after all this time they were not alone.

As usual it was Fixie who took the initiative. "Has anyone even offered this poor man a drink yet?" she demanded with her hands on her hips. The spell was broken for the moment although they all knew that they would have to face up to the unanswered question of what to do next before the evening was out.

After they had all eaten and several glasses of alcohol in its many forms had been consumed Roxie called the Rabble to order. "The first decision, despite the enormity of its implications, is really quite a straightforward one. Do we take it upon ourselves to try to find the last Moonstone? In Siabelle's narrative she implied the box that was thrown into the sea may not have contained the Moonstone at all. Certainly, from what Keith has revealed, the Romans believed it was in this box but did any of them report that they had actually seen the stone? Why would Siabelle try to make contact after all this time if the stone truly was irretrievably lost? Why did she mention the burying of another box in the safekeeping of two giant stones as this seemed to have little relevance to any other aspect of her story? We need a vote, who here believes that the Rabble should take on the responsibility of seeking the last Moonstone?"

All the hands went up. "I know that the Sisters of Venus will support this enterprise too, this is a battle that we cannot avoid, the stakes are far too high." added Cyrene. The other three witches present nodded firmly in agreement.

"Everyone will offer support when they can" continued Roxie, "but we will need a small team to focus fully on this project and it will probably take a while. Who is in a position to make this sort of commitment?"

Most of the Rabble were fully employed with their occupations so it was not going to be easy. Cyrene was the first to speak up "With the forces we are dealing with and the way it all began I think it is imperative that an experienced witch is involved. I can probably reschedule my clients for three months and one of the other Sisters can preside over the coven, so I am happy to be one of the volunteers."

Kaitlin said that as an archaeologist she really would love to join the team but with her daughter Rowan being so young and at pre-school nursery she could not commit to travel. She would of course help the volunteers in any way she could.

Then Gem spoke, "Siabelle has chosen me to be the conduit for her voice so I think I must also be involved. I have already mentioned to Shelley at Woke Media about my wish to do a project about links between contemporary developments in feminist socialism and paganism. She was a bit lukewarm about my proposal but as there are no imminent elections looming, I shall try to persuade her that this is a good moment to take a few weeks out and explore the subject. I think I can convince her if I turn on the charm." She winked at Jess who looked back lovingly at her beautiful young partner. Jess had never been able to successfully resist Gem's charms.

Finally, Alexandra spoke, "I can take a break from my work, there is enough finished to keep the income stream flowing for the refuges. The Chalice Trust's bank balance is looking pretty good at present. One of the few positives of the appalling wealth inequality that has become steadily worse after the Covid-19 pandemic, is that the wealthy elite now have such ridiculous amounts of money that they don't know how to invest it all. They are snapping up any potential asset that they think might grow in value. As a result, my artwork is selling for stupidly high prices, which at least ensures that we have a steady stream of income to support Chalice. Jess can manage the Chalice finances and administration whilst I am away, and Richard has always managed to successfully look after the gallery and its website without needing my help."

"How wonderful, we have three witches taking up the challenge." said Roxie. "I think this bodes well but you must remember that we are all committed to seeing this through so you must ask if there is anything we can do to help."

"Please count me in too." said Keith, "I don't know what the Crystal did to me when they baptised me in blood, but I can somehow sense when the Crystal is energised, and I also probably know more about the Order than anyone else outside their number. This may be useful if they get a sense that you are close to finding the Moonstone. I have to reiterate that these are very dangerous people."

Keith's offer was very welcome, and everyone exchanged contact details so that they could keep in touch at all times.

Cyrene, Alexandra, and Gem agreed to start the following weekend to allow them to first sort out the practicalities of taking a break from their busy schedules.

Gem had a bit of a hard time persuading Shelley to give her the time off, but Gem was primarily paid by the article as Woke was always struggling to secure enough subscriptions to be able to pay salaries. She just told Gem that the article had better be worth the wait.

Jess was worried about Gem and the dangers that Keith had spoken about, but Gem was really excited and seemed oblivious to the magnitude of the responsibility that they were taking on. Jess was glad that Gem was with Cyrene and Alexandra who would look out for her as she knew Gem could be impetuous at times.

30

The three women met at Cyrene's early on the following Saturday morning and the first thing they had to work out was where Siabelle's story had taken place. There was no mention in any of the search engines they tried about a tribe called the Gallancia, and Kaitlin had also had no luck finding any reference through the Museum's database. They even asked Dodi to use her skills to search the Dark Web to see if she could find anything out about the Gallancia. She could not find any references, but she did find a couple of disturbing reports that might be linked to Keith's tale about the Order of the Black Crystal. There were an excessively high number of reports of missing teenagers from care and rumours of a sect of very wealthy and powerful paedophiles who would pay a lot for the right victims.

Rumours about high level paedophile rings were nothing new and some very public high-profile investigations had proved to be groundless causing considerable political embarrassment to the police. As a result, the threshold for the amount of evidence required to initiate police action against prominent figures in the establishment had been considerably raised. None of the material Dido had found was detailed or specific enough to initiate a police investigation but Dido had a nose for these things and her nose was telling her something smelt off. She determined to do some more mining in the dark spaces to see if she could find out more. With Keith's story, even though it had happened so long ago, she had a bit more to go on, including investigating anything that could be linked back to Restitution Holdings. Just to cover her back she let her contact within Zeno know that she had a sniff of a new investigation.

Despite their failure to find any information about the Gallancia, Cyrene, Alexandra and Gem did find references to the Carvetti and the Brigantes. After shuffling through often contradictory information about the historical location of these tribes, and using Siabelle's narrative, they concluded that the most promising location was around the northern side of the Duddon estuary. This was in Cumbria near the town of Millom. This was confirmed when they found references to a very ancient stone circle under the shadow of a hill called Black Combe which was called Swinside, also known as Sunkenkirk. The more they looked at the geography of the area and compared it to the events depicted by Siabelle the more probable it became that the Gallancia were a people intrinsically linked to the stone circle at Swinside in Cumbria. This would also be an appropriate location based on the records of Agricola's campaign in northern Britannia at that date in history. There was also a record of a Roman port called Glannoventa which is now the coastal village of Ravenglass. Although the first recorded use of this name was somewhat later than 79 CE this was not surprising as any records going back to Siabelle's time were extremely sparse. There were still some ruins of a large Roman bathhouse at Ravenglass, but these were from a later period after the port had been significantly expanded.

They decided that the best course of action would be to travel to the area, visit these key locations and allow their intuition to confirm whether they were on the right track. With the intensity of Siabelle's connection to Gem it would be extremely likely that there would be some resonance if they were correct in their assumptions. Cyrene initiated her Wiccan network, and a friend of a friend was a hedge witch who lived in a small village just outside of Millom who went by the name of Almeda. It was approaching the Spring equinox, one of the eight sabbats which seemed a propitious time to visit the stone circle at Swinside and Almeda arranged to meet the three witches there just after dawn on the 20th of March. They managed to book themselves into an inviting looking bed and breakfast called Herdwicks for a few days, with an attached bistro and bar overlooking the lagoon and the RSPB nature reserve at Hodbarrow. For a secretive investigation to seek out a magical stone the three witches were far from inconspicuous which was not the ideal start to their venture. The only car they had between them was the one that Alexandra had managed to borrow from her husband Richard. Richard had always had a passion for cars and had recently bought a black Maserati Quattroporte, much to Alexandra's disdain as she instinctively disliked any outward demonstrations of material opulence. She consoled herself that it was far better than Richard having a gambling addiction or being hooked on A class drugs. As he already had a Maserati when she first met him, she did not feel it reasonable to try to subsequently change the man she had fallen in love with. It did give them the problem in that it was not exactly the ideal vehicle for keeping a low profile. It also gave Richard the added anxiety of his pride and joy coming in close proximity to dry stone walls in narrow country lanes!

The morning after their arrival was the 19th so they had a spare day to absorb the atmosphere of the local area before meeting up with Almeda. After a hearty breakfast Cyrene, Alexandra and Gem decided to take themselves on a walk along the sea wall that separated a large freshwater lagoon from the sea. The Millom area had been heavily mined for iron ore and the landscape showed dramatic evidence of the impact of human hands on the landscape. This was quite concerning for their efforts to hunt for the Moonstone. If Chyrenia and Siabelle had buried the stone anywhere around the apex of the estuary it would almost certainly have been excavated and buried under thousands of tonnes of spoil from the mining operations and could now be lost for ever. Their hearts were lifted when they left the sea wall and rounded the tip of the estuary which was accessible via White Rock beach at low tide. The rounded pebbles near the rocks, ground down over centuries by the action of the waves and tides, led to vast swathes of sand that stretched right across to Askam on the other side of the estuary. The Duddon river meandered through the sand, and this was very reminiscent of the depiction of the estuary of the Gallancia described in Siabelle's tale. At high tide, the sea invaded the estuary and pushed back the river giving a navigable access to smaller vessels all the way up to Lady Hall and Foxfield at its head.

The three women walked along the sand at the side of the estuary and through the dunes to Millom Pier where they were greeted by one of Cumbria's most outstanding panoramas. The whole expanse of the Cumbrian fells from the Scafells to the Old Man of Coniston were spread out before them at the head of the estuary. They all sensed the magic in the air in this special place and as she looked at the stunning view Cyrene felt the energy start to tingle in her fingers. She looked at Alexandra who smiled back, words unnecessary between these two experienced witches. Cyrene was a high priestess and initiate of the 3rd order. In their tradition a 3rd level initiate was gained by taking on the responsibility of leading a coven in the creation of magic. Alexandra was an initiate of the 2nd order and was experienced and powerful enough to set up a coven of her own should she choose to do so. Gem was still very much a novice and was still learning how to sense and channel natural energy but her experiences as a conduit for Siabelle showed that she had a natural affinity for the Craft.

Tomorrow they would visit Swinside and meet Almeda.

31

Nobody at the Warehouse had heard the break in and it was obvious that the burglar was a professional. Two round holes had been cut through the panes of the sealed double glazed window unit which had then been unlocked and released. There was a rope still tied to one of the mounts for the solar panels on the roof which the burglar had used to access the window and to make good their getaway. As far as anyone could make out, there was nothing missing from Cyrene's studio apartment except for the lead chest that they had found buried in the floor of the basement Temple.

Fortunately, none of the copper sheets depicting Siabelle's story were still in the Warehouse. Kaitlin was still worried about how she was going to break the news to her supervisor about digging up the floor of the Temple, but as a precaution she had taken the copper sheets to work with her and safely stored them in the Museum's vaults. She had left the lead chest behind as it was unremarkable being devoid of any decorative markings and had been simply too heavy for her to carry. It was quite obvious that the burglar had been looking for the chest. It was always possible that one of the Rabble may have inadvertently revealed some detail about the chest, but nobody could remember doing so. The only other alternative was that their location had been discovered by the Order and this was a deeply concerning development. The Warehouse community was run on love and somehow everyone felt violated by this unwelcome intrusion. Roxie arranged to have the window replaced and everyone made sure that they now used the window locks when they left their own apartments rather than just closing the handles.

Roxie phoned Cyrene who had just left for Cumbria, and she was naturally alarmed at the news. It was a relief that Cyrene had not still been in the Warehouse as she may well have come to harm if the burglar had found her there. They had to be on their guard now even more than ever.

32

Sir Giles was deeply frustrated as he sat next to the lead chest that had nothing more than a few crystals in it. It had not taken their network of contacts long to identify the most likely candidate for the powerful witch they were seeking. The organisation's tentacles were pervasive and even reached into the inner esoteric domains of Wiccan circles. One of the sighted Temple priests had visited the Warehouse and booked a visit to the basement Temple of Venus through the Museum of London website. This had not been a pleasant experience as the priest began to feel nauseous even before entering the building and had been violently sick as he tried to cross the threshold. There was a powerful magical legacy in the building which was constantly renewed by the magical practice of the Sisters of Venus, and it would not grant access to someone so steeped in evil. The priest's reaction did however confirm to Sir Giles that they had almost certainly found the location they were looking for.

Cyrene advertised her Reiki sessions at her studio apartment, but the Order wanted to know the details of its layout and where it was in the Warehouse. They knew Cyrene would probably sense something was amiss if they deliberately sent in anyone directly associated with the Order. The intuition of such a powerful witch would immediately detect any deceit. The simple solution was to send along a completely unsuspecting junior employee of Restitution Holdings via a gift card for Reiki that was purchased from Cyrene's website. When the young woman came back, she was gently interrogated as to whether she had enjoyed the experience and what it was like. She was only too happy to chat about the exotic area with the drapes and incense and quickly the exact location of Cyrene's apartment within the Warehouse was known. After the reaction of the priest Sir Giles decided it was better to arrange for a professional burglar to be paid to steal the chest and the Order could easily afford the best.

Now Sir Giles had the chest, but it told him little more than he already knew. If he wanted to find out more about any connection of the contents of the chest to the last Moonstone, he would have to use more drastic tactics. He had the Warehouse put under surveillance and soon began to build a picture of everyone who lived there or was associated with it. He also knew from the testimony of the previous Master, the Roman Governor Agricola, that the Last Moonstone had been lost just off the coast of Cumbria at Ravenglass. If the insight from his High Priest was correct and Cyrene and her witches were indeed trying to locate the Moonstone, it was highly likely that one of them would put in an appearance. He decided to send one of his most skilled and trusted contractors to Ravenglass with orders to report back to him immediately if anyone of interest turned up.

33

Cyrene, Alexandra, and Gem took the turning for Broadgate off the main road that continued onwards towards Barrow and Kendal and found themselves going up a narrow country lane. It was so narrow that twice they had to reverse up and swing into gateway entrances to let a tractor and then a Land Rover with a trailer of sheep pass them. After about one kilometre they came to an even smaller road saying no motor vehicles, farm access only. They had just passed a small layby, barely big enough for three small cars to park. Alexandra winced as she heard the sound of brambles growing in front of the dry stone wall scraping the side of the Maserati's unblemished paintwork. The only other vehicle parked in the layby was a Triumph Bonneville motorcycle.

There was a small wooden sign directing them to Swinside stone circle as they started to walk up the track. At first it went quite steeply uphill before levelling off a bit. There was a pronounced hill on their left and as they climbed the gradient they could see a farm in the distance, nestled under the flank of Swinside Fell, which led eventually to the summit of Black Combe. It was a remote place, but it rewarded them with a wonderful view as they looked back towards the Duddon Estuary. They must have been walking for nearly a kilometre and were just starting to doubt whether they had followed the right track when the stones appeared before them in a field surrounded by a drystone wall. As they neared the stones, they could see a woman standing in the middle of the circle who waved to them as they approached. Apart from the woman and the dozens of grazing sheep they were completely alone.

As they walked into the field and crossed the boundary of the stone circle they were absolutely captivated by the setting. It was absolutely stunning and none of them could quite believe that there were not crowds of tourists and an entrance gate to access such a stunning site. The stones were impressive in size with the highest nearly three metres tall and the circle must have been nearly thirty metres in diameter. The circle was enclosed by hills from Swinside Fell around towards the majestic flank of the Old Man of Coniston and the hills that ran along the far side of the estuary. Cyrene and Alexandra immediately felt the energy of the place. The stone circle was acting like a giant megalithic capacitor for the storage of nature's natural energy. It was in every way the perfect place to build a temple dedicated to the Great Goddess and they intuitively knew they had found the ancient Stone Circle of the Gallancia. Gem had an even stranger feeling, a powerful Déjà vu, the site felt so familiar to her, as if she had been there before in a previous incarnation. She went up to the tallest stone to the north of the circle and placed her hand against it as if she were greeting an old and very loved friend.

Cyrene's first reaction to Almeda was lust at first sight. As Almeda described herself as a hedge witch, Cyrene expected to meet a woman wearing a flowing hippy styled dress with sandals. Instead, there was this wild looking woman in her mid-forties in a black leather jacket with leather trousers and muddy bike boots. Almeda had long wavy blond hair that was delightfully dishevelled after having been confined in her motorcycle helmet and she had mischievous twinkling blue eyes.

"Not bad eh?" she volunteered, "Knocks the spots off Stonehenge's setting."

"It's just amazing." said a round eyed Gem who was spinning around inside the circle trying to take it all in.

"I come up here a lot," said Almeda, "and there is usually hardly anyone up here apart from the families who live and work at the farm. You might get a handful of visitors at the solstices but for such an impressive circle it has surprisingly few visitors. Can you sense the latent power in the stones?" The women nodded in agreement. "Even the first time I visited them I sensed it, and I feel a powerful compulsion to try to re-energise them, although I am not entirely sure why. Imagine the energy there must have been when this circle was full of worshippers. I can only guess what used to go on here and why they built it. I come here at every sabbat and bond with them and I am sure they are starting to respond. Sometimes I sense I am drifting into the past and imagine I can see figures with linked hands dancing in a circle around me within the stones."

"It was built in dedication of the Goddess and as a Temple of fertility for the Gallancia." said Alexandra looking Almeda directly in the eyes. Cyrene and Gem looked at Alexandra quizzically, she was imparting a lot of information to a stranger they had only just met.

"How could you possibly know that?" said Almeda.

"That's what we have come to talk to you about." said Alexandra.

They followed Almeda the short distance to her home, a secluded old barn conversion, after executing a five-point turn in the Maserati as Alexandra tried to prevent Cumbrian slate from meeting expensive Italian paintwork.

Almeda's home was enchanting, there was a small intimate altar room with a large pentagram in a circle marked out on a black slate floor and the altar was covered with crystals and herbs. There were candles everywhere including four large ones on brass floor standing candlesticks that looked very old and had darkened with age. There was a large CD and vinyl collection in the living room with a predominance of punk and grunge. This was not the typically associated music of a hedge witch but by then it was quite obvious that nothing about Almeda fitted into convenient stereotypes. She had one wall of the living room completely filled with books on old antique pine shelving, many of them mystical or occult and some quite rare. On the other wall of the living room was a large grate with a real wood fire that had just been replenished with some dry logs, which warmed them all after the slight chill of the March morning air. In front of the fire were some luxuriant sheepskins and scattered around were a number of comfy cushions where they were invited to sprawl.

Almeda made them all tea and then went to change out of her bike gear. She came down in a pair of tight-fitting jeans, a black corset which enhanced and lifted her generous bust and an open crimson jacket cut in a style reminiscent of an 18th century pirate. It was also very obvious that she had detected Cyrene's interest and was responding to it. Alexandra and Gem could also sense the sexual chemistry building between the two women.

In the car the three witches exchanged what their intuition was telling them about Almeda, and they universally felt that they should trust her and share Siabelle's narrative. After they had drunk their tea, they took a stroll in the woods near to Almeda's home whilst she read it and then they all congregated around the welcoming wood fire in her living room.

Almeda was fascinated by the story of the Last Moonstone and the fate of Chyrenia and Siabelle. She also knew of a couple of nearby places that might possibly fit the description of the two standing stones that were shielding the mysterious box that had been buried between them. It was agreed that Gem and Alexandra would go to Ravenglass, grab a pub lunch, and explore the area whilst Cyrene stayed with Almeda to plan their trips the next day to possible locations for the Moonstone. Alexandra and Gem suspected that there might be another agenda on Cyrene and Almeda's minds. As soon as they pulled out of the drive Almeda walked directly up to Cyrene, put her arms around her neck and kissed her fully on the lips. Cyrene was usually the one to make the first move in such circumstances and she delighted in Almeda's approach. Soon two naked and hungry bodies were entwined in front of the fire and there were only a few glowing charcoal embers left in the grate when their lust had been satiated.

34

Alexandra and Gem drove up the coast road to Ravenglass which was a small picturesque coastal village at the mouth of the Esk river and a terminal of a narrow-gauge railway that headed up Eskdale towards Scafell Mountain.

They found the delightful Pennington hotel with a bar and restaurant in Ravenglass and had a lazy lunch. As they had rightly suspected, they were not exactly inconspicuous. The sight of a tall captivating black woman and her pink spiky haired lady friend climbing out of a Maserati had not gone unnoticed. As they were just finishing their meal, one of the guests in the hotel came over to their table and said to Alexandra, "Please excuse my interruption but are you Alexandra Okereke?" The man was dressed in casual but expensive chinos and shirt with a tweed jacket and looked to be in his mid-thirties.

Alexandra looked up from her coffee and truffle and immediately felt wary of this man. Although he had a friendly smile his dark, almost black eyes were as cold as ice and Alexandra sensed the presence of evil. Gem was still developing her senses and had not immediately picked up that there was something very wrong. She was very proud of her friendship with Alexandra, and she piped up, "that's right, the artist." The man turned his smile on Gem and enquired, "What brings you ladies up to Ravenglass?" Before she could answer Alexandra interjected, "Please don't take this the wrong way, but we have come to the Lake District to get some time on our own away from the crowds and would appreciate being left in peace." If possible, the eyes turned even colder, but the fixed smile remained the same. "Of course, please forgive my intrusion, I am such a fan of your work, and I just couldn't resist taking the opportunity of greeting you in person." Alexandra nodded and then returned her eyes to Gem who was looking at Alexandra quizzically. In Gem's experience, Alexandra was usually a very warm person and was more than happy to greet fans and even sign autographs or have selfies taken. Something was going on and Gem had sufficient presence of mind to wait until they had finished and paid for their meal before saying anything.

They left the hotel and took a path out the back that led through some woodland towards the ruins of the Roman Baths. When they were safely away from prying ears, Alexandra explained her feelings to Gem. After the burglary at the Warehouse, she was more on her guard than normal, and she thought it was highly likely that the man had some association with the Order of the Black Crystal that Keith had told them about. Gem was cross with herself for not being more alert, but Alexandra hugged her and told her not to worry about it. Alexandra knew that Gem's intuitive skill would develop over time, it was not a switch that could be simply turned on the first time an initiate entered a coven. It took time, practice, and perseverance.

Many of the thick Roman walls of the ruined baths had partially survived after withstanding nearly 2000 years of attrition from the elements. There was, however, nothing here to help their quest and neither of them sensed any special energy or atmosphere amongst the ruins. They walked back and ducked through a walkway under the coastal railway to come back down to the beach. From a distance a camera with a powerful lens was clicking away and soon digital images of the two women had been sent to London.

Alexandra stood on the beach and closed her eyes. To open up her senses and clear her mind of other thoughts, she visualised the scene of a Roman galley closing in on the trading vessel with Chyrenia standing on the stern and her hair blowing in the wind. If the last Moonstone really were out there buried in the sand under the sea, she was sure that she would sense something. Apart from the usual joyous feeling of standing by the sea as nature's energy swirled within her there was no sensation of any special powerful source of energy. She was increasingly convinced that whatever was in the box Chyrenia had thrown into the sea it was not the Moonstone and this filled Alexandra with both hope and consternation. Could it have possibly survived all the mining that had taken place around Millom and still be safe after such a long time?

Alexandra and Gem completed a full circle of Ravenglass and returned to their car through the centre of the village. As they passed the hotel Alexandra's eyes were drawn to the window of one of the guest rooms and she could see the stranger that had interrupted their lunch staring at them. This time the smile had gone and instead there was an expression of undisguised hostility.

35

Alexandra and Gem were getting out of the car after returning to Herdwicks when they heard the sound of a motorcycle coming up the lane and a familiar looking Triumph Bonneville, with a rider and pillion pulled up next to them. As the motorcyclists took off their crash helmets, they could see it was Almeda and Cyrene. Almeda had lent Cyrene a spare leather jacket and helmet and she was grinning with delight as she got off the back of Almeda's bike. This was the first time Cyrene had ever ridden pillion and she was still buzzing from the experience. She particularly enjoyed the fact that she had to firmly hold on to the rider's waist as the bike accelerated. Almeda was very well known at Herdwicks and she chatted happily to the staff in the bar while the others went upstairs to change.

When they came down, they sat at a corner table where Almeda could see everyone coming into the bar. All the other customers were local people and there was no evidence that anyone from the Order had yet discovered where they were staying. Almeda knew of two locations where there were significant pairs of standing stones but only one that really seemed to fit in with Siabelle's story. Based on everything she had read in Kaitlin's translation she guessed that Gallanbhir must have been located somewhere in the vicinity of the small village called the Green and the nearby cluster of dwellings at Lady Hall. The shape of the upper estuary and the position of the coast would have changed significantly over the 2000 years that had passed since Siabelle's time but the position of the stone circle at Swinside was a constant. A stream called Black Beck also ran from the hills, passed near to Swinside, and flowed into the estuary near Green Road Station. It was likely that the old path up to Swinside would have followed the valley carved out by the stream. Siabelle's tale revealed that Chyrenia had led her along a little used coastal path that led from the coast through a valley towards the village. At the coastal end of Whicham Valley at the village of Kirksanton were a pair of ancient stones, locally known as the Giant's Grave. These would be good contenders for the ancient stone protectors of whatever it was that Chyrenia had buried, particularly if it was the Moonstone.

They agreed that they would pick up Almeda the following day and visit the site she had identified. They had a lovely evening meal together in Herdwicks, delighting in sharing a number of delicious piping hot pizzas, baked in a clay oven. It was quite late when Almeda finally bid them goodnight and hopped back on her bike.

The following morning dawned bright and clear and after another hearty breakfast Alexandra and Gem picked up Almeda and headed towards the village of Kirksanton. They parked off the main road that passed through the village and Almeda took them along a back pathway so that they would be less noticed. Fortunately, there was nobody about as they made their way along the side of a field towards two large stones. They were still a good fifty metres away from the stones when Gem began to feel rather lightheaded, and she crouched down on one knee to prevent herself falling over. All three of the other women could sense the growing energy, it was almost as if they had been inspected, had passed some kind of spiritual test and were being welcomed back after a long time away. Cyrene and Alexandra each took Gem by the arm and steadied her as she walked up to the stones. The stones were impressive, the nearer larger one being approximately three metres high, the far one about half a metre shorter. Gem stood at the side of the stones near the middle, with the three other witches standing in a protective cluster around her and they all went through a grounding ritual to open themselves up to the nature's energy that began to flow through them.

Gem started to drift into a trance, and she visualised that she was flying backwards in time and space. She found herself standing as an observer watching a woman dressed in woollen and linen garments from the distant past kneeling before her. She had what looked like a broken short sword with a reshaped blade in her hand and was energetically digging a hole about half a metre in front of the largest stone. The ground was slightly raised between the stones in a slight mound and was completely surrounded by thicket. When the woman had dug a hole a forearm's depth into the soil she turned and looked towards Gem with a loving but sad smile and placed a clay tile in the hole followed by a small wooden box. At that point, the vision began to fade, and Gem felt herself flung forward again through time to the present day. She came out of her trance to find that she was being supported by her friends in the open field by the stones. She walked up towards the large stone and placed her hand at the exact point she had seen the box buried. The four witches linked hands until they were encircling the large stone and felt an overwhelming feeling of love and acceptance emanating from the spot. After they released their hands, they looked at each other in wonder and joy.

Cyrene was the first to speak, "I am sure this is the place that Chyrenia of the Gallancia buried the Moonstone; it is a miracle that it has not been lost or destroyed after all this time."

"The Goddess has been protecting it" answered Alexandra "but that leaves us with a dilemma. It has been safe here after all this time but even our presence here today has put it in danger. We have to think very carefully about what we do next." They looked around them to see if they had been observed but apart from a farmer on a tractor in a distant field there was nobody around. They retraced their steps and drove back to the safety of Almeda's home to decide what to do next.

The following morning Almeda dropped Cyrene off at Millom railway station and, after a long lingering 'see you soon' goodbye kiss, Cyrene caught the train back to London. She needed to update the rest of the Rabble and to flesh out the details of the plan the four witches had devised the previous evening.

Gem and Alexandra booked out of Herdwicks and booked themselves instead into the Pennington hotel where they had lunched in Ravenglass. The man who the witches had named 'Cold Eyes' was still in residence but apart from the tiniest nod of recognition from him when they met him in the lobby, he showed no overt signs of further interest. They made enquiries at the hotel reception about any local boat owners or fishermen who they could charter to take them off the coast for a few hours the next day. They were in luck and booked to leave when the tide was high enough the following morning.

They spent much of the afternoon walking along the beach with binoculars looking out to sea from various points and different angles. That evening they sat in the bar with a local Ordnance Survey map spread out in front of them arguing about where they thought they should be looking for something that had been lost. The following morning, they set out on the boat and headed out about three kilometres from the coast. Fortunately, there was not much swell, and the sea was uncharacteristically calm for late March. Alexandra had never suffered from sea sickness, but Gem's stomach was already complaining about the gentle rise and fall of the small fishing boat as it headed out to sea.

They stopped several times and on each occasion Alexandra and Gem stood at the stern of the boat and went into a meditative state before asking the skipper to move on. The following morning, they repeated the exercise a little further along the coast and slightly closer into land until at one spot after meditating, they appeared to be finally satisfied. They took careful note of the exact satellite position so that they could find the spot again and then headed back in. That evening in the bar they plotted the spot on the local map they had brought out the previous evening. They ordered some sparking white wine and drank a toast to 'absent friends' before getting an early night to rest before their trip back to London the following day.

None of their activities had gone unnoticed, Cold Eyes had been watching them closely having quickly driven to a shop near to Kendal to buy a telescope. He was irritated that he had to have them out of sight for several hours, and they were returning on the boat by the time he got back. He was somewhat relieved when they were poring over their map again that night in the bar and were out in the boat the following morning. This time he watched them as they moved the boat around and he could see them touching palms facing each other in deep thought in the stern each time it stopped. As the boat moved up the coast he had to jump in his car and drive quickly up the Shore Road as they were out of sight behind the dunes, but to his satisfaction, he quickly got them in view again. Shortly afterwards the boat stopped for a final time, and he could see the women go through their ritual once again but instead of shaking their heads in disappointment, this time they leapt up and did a little jig around the boat. He could see the boat's skipper lift off his cap and scratch his head at the antics of his two female passengers.

After the boat had come in to drop off the two women, Cold Eyes engaged the boat's skipper in conversation and made vague enquiries about his availability and rates of hire. As if in an afterthought he asked, "What was that all about today with the two guests from the hotel? They didn't look like the typical types to book a fishing trip."

"Mad as a box of frogs" said the skipper. "They were looking for some kind of lost box that they reckoned they would be able to 'feel' if they found it. Complete nonsense if you ask me but they were paying good money, so I was happy to humour them."

"Did they find it" asked Cold Eyes humorously.

"They reckon they did." replied the skipper. "They got all excited and started checking their phones to find out exactly where they thought the spot was. Won't be surprised if they're not up here again with diving gear to search for it when the sea gets a bit warmer."

That evening in the bar restaurant there was a brief moment when the younger woman got up to order some drinks and the artist went to the toilet leaving the map on the table. Cold eyes waited until the young woman was talking to the lady behind the bar then managed to quickly snap a photo of the map and the marked location on his phone before they returned.

Cold Eyes went up to his room and phoned Sir Giles back in London to explain everything that had gone on and send him the picture of the map. To his annoyance Sir Giles ordered him to stay put for another couple of weeks before he sent someone up to relieve him. Cold Eyes was a city boy at heart, and he was missing the night life and buzz of London. Still, he thought philosophically, the thousands of pounds going into his bank each week for his troubles was some compensation. Restitution Holdings was a very rewarding employer, particularly if you did not ask too many questions about the nature of their business. Cold Eyes had never suffered unduly from a troubled conscience.

36

Keith and Dodi sat in the empty space of a newly rented unit in a soulless block of offices opposite an uncharacteristically run-down hotel for this part of the City. The hotel was a curious entity, how could a shabby hotel afford to keep going in one of the most affluent areas of one of the most expensive cities in the World? Dodi thought she had found the answer. After tracing the ownership through a dozen shell companies, she had found a link to Restitution Holdings, the company where Keith's father had worked.

After Keith had told his story to the Warehouse residents, Dodi had talked to him about her suspicion that there might be a link to a paedophile ring she was investigating and the Order of the Black Crystal. Keith knew from his mother's tale about his sinister baptism that there was a physical tunnel linking a hotel with the Temple of the Black Crystal. He also knew from his father's employment that there was a plausible link between the Temple and Restitution Holdings. It was by no means certain that the Temple was located on the company's property, but it was a reasonable starting point. It took Dodi less than five minutes to find the address of the registered London offices of Restitution Holdings. There was no serious attempt to hide this as, on the surface, it was just another City trading firm, and like many others, the registered head office of the company was an address in the tax haven of the Cayman Islands.

It was now obvious to the Rabble that the Order were keeping them and their visitors under surveillance. The update from Cyrene, Alexandra, and Gem after their visit to Cumbria a couple of weeks before had revealed the lengths the Order were prepared to go to in order to find and destroy the Moonstone. Such was the concern that Dodi had organised for one of her contacts in Zeno to sweep the Warehouse in case some kind of bug or camera had been planted during the burglary. Fortunately, there was nothing found but everyone agreed that it was time to turn the tables. Contrary to the Order's perception, the Rabble were quite capable of protecting themselves if necessary, no matter how powerful the enemy and in such situations knowledge was power. The Rabble were about to go on the offensive.

Keith and Dodi had decided they would go to the City and try to locate the hotel that Keith had mentioned if it still even existed after such a long time. They dressed scruffily in hoodies and jeans to conceal their faces from any CCTV cameras that would almost certainly be positioned in the area around Restitution Holdings. They found the offices and the rather bland entrance door without any problem and there was even an unimposing company name plate on the door to confirm it. Keith felt something stir within him as they neared the building, a burning rage against those who had abused him was building up within him. Something in this building was reaching out to Keith and his spirit was railing against it in the only way it knew how. Keith felt by his reaction that it was highly probable the Temple also lay within. As they knew that the Temple was connected to a hotel by a tunnel it would be a logical conclusion that it was deep underground in a basement complex. Keith had the sense that whatever presence lurked within the Temple had also sensed him, the malice building in his heart felt at home and connected to this place. Fortunately, it was very unlikely that the evil lurking within him would be associated with any group protecting the Moonstone which thrived on trust and love.

After locating the offices of Restitution Holdings, they worked their way outwards around the block looking for a possible hotel that was close enough to be connected by a tunnel. It did not take them long to find it, there was no other similar hotel anywhere else in the City. The hotel's drab aspect and shabbiness, rather than making it inconspicuous, made it stand out in contrast to the expensive buildings and plush offices that surrounded it. The other striking aspect of the hotel was that it had no obvious name, just a grubby old red fluorescent hotel sign designating its purpose.

After the Covid-19 pandemic caused so many City workers to work from home, and the associated transfer of a significant amount of financial business to Europe after Brexit, many companies had decided that they could save a fortune on London rates by downsizing. It was therefore relatively easy to find an office unit to rent overlooking the hotel and for a very reasonable price.

Dodi finished setting up the last of the surveillance CCTV cameras and a device that she had obtained from Zeno that had managed to link to the hotel's Wi-Fi. She still had to break the code, which she hoped would not take long when she returned to the Warehouse. With a bit of luck, she might be able to gain access through the Wi-Fi to the hotel's computer system and anything else it was connected to. She looked at Keith with some concern. She had got to know him quite well over the last couple of days and she was becoming quite fond of him. He was a kind and generous spirit, but she could now see the torment of the conflict within him as an uncontainable rage grew and streamed out seeking its destination. Keith caught her looking at him and gave her a grim smile. "For once in my life I am not feeling guilty that someone who doesn't deserve it will come to harm through my damned affliction. The chickens are well and truly coming home to roost, Nergal the Destroyer is finally turning on his creators."

Back in her apartment at the Warehouse, Dodi started to decode the access link to the hotel's Wi-Fi link using Zeno's specially developed algorithm. Four hours after she had started it she checked back in and saw with satisfaction that she was now connected and had full access to the hotel's computer system. The Order had grown complacent through the arrogance of power and had carelessly used the Wi-Fi to wirelessly link the internal CCTV cameras to the host computer. Now Dodi was watching them and recording them remotely onto her own hard disk. She decided to leave it to record overnight, and she would catch up with it the next day to see if there was anything interesting. What she saw when she returned turned her blood cold.

37

Sir Giles did not really know what to make of the intelligence report he had received from his operative in Cumbria. After having secured the lead box from the Warehouse only to find it empty and its contents hidden, he was concerned that the witch and her friends might have found new information that would lead them to the Last Moonstone. To his relief it seemed that they had no more information than the Order and were searching for it out to sea where it had been reported to be lost two millennia before. The Order had always thought it was safe but the news that two of the witches had thought that they had located it was troubling. The Moonstone served the Goddess, and it was therefore quite possible that one of her daughters and devotees might be able to sense its presence where the servants of the Black Crystal were blocked. Somehow the witch Cyrene had managed to throw out the presence of The High Priest of the Temple and by doing so had gained Sir Giles's respect. The powers of these witches should not be underestimated.

The High Priest of the Temple had not sensed any rise in the power of the Moonstone, just the very faint presence that had existed since it first sunk beneath the waves in ancient Roman times. It was quite evident that witches had not yet been able to recover it as it would have been quickly re-energised. He had a rough location from the photo of the map belonging to the witches but finding anything would still be like looking for a very small needle in a very large haystack. If the witches could really sense the presence of the Moonstone he would use their powers against them to his own advantage.

Even if the witches did find the Moonstone and try to use it, it was unlikely that it would be able to stand against the immense powers emanating from the Black Crystal. If thirteen dispersed Moonstones had not been able to constrain the Black Crystal, what impact could one have? Was it really worth bothering about at all, he pondered, or was this all just an unnecessary irritation unworthy of his attention? He already knew the answer, the Order would not tolerate any defiance to its powers, no matter how small. It had always been completely ruthless in its ambition, and it was not going to change now. The Order had virtually unlimited resources that could be secured through its vast wealth. The small sums required to monitor and, if necessary, intervene on the activities of the witches were insignificant. If the witches found the Moonstone he would know immediately. Unlike Agricola, his illustrious predecessor, Sir Giles would succeed in destroying the last Moonstone and if necessary the witches and their friends with it.

He called his operative in Ravenglass and told him he was not going to be relieved after all. He quickly shut off the whinging by offering an extra £10,000 a week and Sir Giles ordered him to rent a property in the area that could accommodate at least five more people. He was going to send sufficient force to deal with any eventualities that might occur. If the witches really had located the position of the Moonstone they would soon be back to find it and the servants of the Order would be waiting for them.

38

Cold Eyes observed the diver re-surface for the third time that day through his telescope which was positioned on a tripod at his vantage point at the end of Shore Road north of Ravenglass. He withdrew his eye from the eyepiece and rubbed it, the strain of looking through the instrument for hours on end was beginning to tell on him. The famous artist, Alexandra Okereke, had returned to the Pennington hotel the day before with another friend of hers. Although Cold Eyes was no longer staying in the hotel, he always had one of his party watching the road into Ravenglass and an imposing looking black woman driving an expensive black Maserati was hard to miss in this sleepy coastal village. The artist's friend was also an imposing figure who obviously spent a great deal of his time in the gym. He was considerably taller than Cold Eyes and looked to weigh about 110 kilos. Despite her friend's considerable physical presence, it was obvious that the artist was in charge of the proceedings. Apart from his obvious physical strength the artist's friend also proved to be an adept diver. They had both turned up on the evening of the 28th of April and early in the afternoon on the following day they had set out in a diving boat that they had apparently arranged to hire beforehand. It was now about seven o'clock in the evening and they would have to come back in soon as the light was beginning to fade.

Cold Eyes looked wearily through the telescope again and the sight before him suddenly had his full attention. The diver had been taking a weighted bag down with him into which he could place any finds. This time when he surfaced he held the bag aloft and seemed very excited. After hauling himself up out of the water he handed the bag to the artist who pulled something out then did a little jig around the boat with something in her hands. The sun was now losing its strength and it was becoming too dark to see what it was from such a distance, but it was obvious that they thought they had found what they were looking for. Cold Eyes packed up his telescope and hurried back the short distance to the rented house he shared with the four other men. They were also contractors of Restitution Holdings with whom he had previously worked. He detailed one of the men to keep the hotel under surveillance and then he immediately phoned Sir Giles and told him the news.

Two hours later Sir Giles was joined by the three priests in the Temple of the Black Crystal in the basement of the Restitution Holdings building in the City of London. The High Priest walked up to the Black Crystal and carefully laid his hands upon it. His mind was immediately filled with an image of swirling flames licking around a bright white light that seemed completely impervious to their heat and fiery rage. He let go of the Crystal and staggered backwards. He had never seen anything like this before, but he knew immediately what the implications were. The bright white light in the black heart of the Crystal that was causing so much turmoil within it could only be one thing. Someone had found the Moonstone and it had been re-energised. For the first time in 2000 years the power of the Black Crystal was being challenged.

39

Alexandra handed Jethro the binoculars as she surreptitiously watched Cold Eyes speed away in his car, making very sure that he had not seen her looking at him. Jethro took the binoculars and saw the tail end of the car speeding around the bend heading back to Ravenglass. He smiled and, speaking quietly so that they would not be overheard by the diving boat's skipper and crew, said, "Now would be a good time to make the call. I'm glad all my hard work has paid off, it's still pretty chilly in these waters at this time of year." Alexandra gave him a big hug and immediately regretted her display of affection; he was freezing cold!

Cyrene, Gem and Almeda were sat in a hire car in a layby near Kirksanton all dressed in dark clothing and feeling rather anxious about the task that lay ahead of them. If they initiated the plan, there was no legitimate excuse they could offer if they were caught and challenged in the act. At 7.30 pm Cyrene's mobile rang and she heard Alexandra's familiar voice simply saying, "It's a go."

The timing was crucial, they wanted to have enough light to be able to see what they were doing whilst the onset of dusk made them as hard to spot as possible. They parked at the back of the village as before and just before 8.00 pm they were stood between the two imposing stones of the 'Giant's Grave.'

They took it in turns with one digging whilst the other two stood next to the nearby hedgerow to make it less obvious. They were relieved that the soil was not too compacted, it would have taken them an age to dig through the thick clay that was quite common in the area. The work of the two Britonic women who had dug down so many generations before had left its handiwork and despite being covered over for such a long time the soil came away relatively easily. They all felt like grave robbers, like latter-day Burke and Hares although fortunately the local name for the site was not realised in actuality by the discovery of any giant bones. After they had dug down about half a metre, the spade hit something hard. The three women gathered around and carefully turned on a torch within the hole to shield the light and they could see it was some kind of pottery. Their excitement was growing by the second, this was exactly as Siabelle had described in her story. With a small trowel they carefully cleared around the pot and then Gem who had the strongest arms after all her taekwondo practice clasped the edges of the pot and slowly lifted it. Underneath the pot, still virtually undamaged after all the passing years was a small wooden box covered in strange carvings. Gem carefully passed the box to

Cyrene and then Almeda and Gem carefully filled in the hole and scuffed over the top with their walking boots to disguise their activity.

They walked back to the car feeling that they must look incredibly suspicious, but their luck had held, and they had not been observed or challenged. They did not open the box in the car as they suspected that it might still have some residual magical ability to conceal whatever was inside from the Priests at the Temple of the Black Crystal. First they headed to a remote carpark by the church at Whicham which was nestled under the dark brooding mass of Black Combe fell. As they pulled in a dark figure moved out of the shadows, opened the rear passenger door of the car, and climbed in next to Gem. Gem lifted up the small cedarwood box to show her and Alexandra's beautiful teeth were lit up by the dim interior light as she smiled.

"How did it go?" asked Cyrene of Alexandra.

"I think we have bought some time" replied Alexandra. "As soon as we landed from the boat we went straight to the car and made a bit of a scene by dramatically speeding out of the village. Jethro has been an absolute star this weekend. I am sure we must have been seen by at least one of the Order's spies who have been watching us ever since we arrived at the hotel. If, as we suspect, their powers of corruption have secured the services of at least one pliable police officer they will know from the Automatic Number Plate Recognition on the motorway that Richard's car is racing back down to London. Hopefully, they will assume that I am in there with Jethro and a box containing the Moonstone. Jethro has arranged to rendezvous with Richard on the way back so that it looks like he is being dropped off at the Warehouse and hopefully they will assume it is me driving. If our luck holds it may just confuse them long enough for our plan to be implemented."

They then drove straight to Almeda's where they sanctified the circle in her altar room with salt, blessed spring water, fire from a candle and incense. They then cast a protective magical spell, asking for the blessing and protection of the Goddess, and called on the spirits of the four elements to assist them before carefully pulling the lid off the box. The wood had not swollen at all, and the lid came off readily, almost as if the box were expecting the hand of a daughter of the Goddess to caress it once again. Inside, nested in wood shavings was a beautiful Ethiopian fire opal the size of a large duck egg, and as Cyrene lifted it up in her palm it began to gently glow in recognition. After nearly 2000 years, the last Moonstone had finally been found. Their joy at finding this priceless treasure was however qualified by the knowledge that it was now in incredible danger as they were in no doubt whatsoever that the Order would stop at nothing to destroy it. They all now felt incredibly vulnerable.

40

Chief Inspector Rachel Davidson of CEOP's brow furrowed in concern as she saw the CCTV footage of a young girl who could not have been more than about twelve or thirteen years old being firmly gripped by a man and steered through the foyer of a hotel. Another camera showed an inconspicuous door with a frosted glass panel being opened revealing some descending stairs where the girl was taken. About three minutes later according to the time log on the video recording, a well-dressed man in a very expensive suit entered the foyer and followed the first man and the girl down the stairs. Ten minutes later another expensively dressed man followed. After more than two hours the two wealthy looking men came back through the foyer and exited the building a few minutes apart. According to her source at Zeno, more than twelve hours later the girl had still not reappeared.

Both of the wealthy men who had followed the girl had made no attempt to hide their faces, they obviously had the arrogance of familiarity with this place. Zeno had blown up the digital images of both men's faces. As they returned from whatever they had been doing they were both facing the foyer camera. One of these faces in particular looked familiar and it had taken very little time to realise that it was Lord Reginald 'Reggie' Mansfield, the industrialist who had been made a life peer for services to industry and, some would say, more than generous political donations.

Two nights later another young teenager, this time a boy, was captured in a video being taken through the same door, and again the child and his escort were shortly followed by two men. One of the men was new but the other one was unmistakably Reggie Mansfield who had been there two nights before.

Even more concerning was the recording from the CCTV camera that overlooked the service area at the back of the hotel. This revealed two men placing a long wooden crate into the back of a nondescript van. By having the street camera recordings analysed at the time of this incident they managed to obtain an image of the van's numberplate. It was registered to a company owned by the discreet but nonetheless extremely wealthy and influential Restitution Holdings corporation.

From her source at Zeno, Rachel Davidson had the address of the hotel and the exact times that these events had occurred. The methods that Zeno had employed to retrieve these recordings were however completely illegal and could never be used as evidence in court or to secure a search warrant from a magistrate. She also had details of a number of cars that had pulled up outside the hotel over the period of a week, taken from a camera that was obviously positioned in an overlooking building. Another aspect revealed by this other camera was that, although there was a grubby illuminated sign over the door of the building clearly advertising it as a hotel, there was always a 'no-Vacancies' sign underneath. It was not listed on any of London's internet hotel search sites either.

CI Davidson was becoming increasingly convinced that the hotel sign was just a deflection to provide an excuse for all the coming and goings so as not to draw attention. The legality of these external pictures was more arguable, but they were not in themselves sufficient to justify a search warrant and the individuals involved in the footage were pillars of the establishment. The shit would really hit the fan if the police moved too quickly, and their suspicions turned out to be baseless. All her instincts told her that something truly sinister was happening in that place but at this moment she just did not have enough legal evidence to take action. Even if she tried to use the illegal recordings she could not actually prove that either child was truly being taken against their will. Because of the camera angle in the foyer neither child's face was clearly visible as they were taken in, so it was also impossible to match the children directly with any missing persons on the police's Misper database.

41

Sir Giles had been updated on the suspicion that the Moonstone had been driven speedily back to London and one of his operatives who was keeping the Warehouse under observation confirmed that the car had been seen briefly at the Warehouse where the resident called Jethro had been dropped off. Firstly, he had taken his diving gear and overnight bag from the car and then he returned. The visibility from the quayside streetlighting was not brilliant but it had been confirmed that after reaching into the passenger well of the vehicle, Jethro had been seen carrying a small metallic looking box with him.

This was going to be problematic as Sir Giles was sure that the residents of the Warehouse would be much more alert to any attempt to burgle them again. Although he could probably force an access when the basement Temple was open to visitors this would be messy and could lead to a prolonged confrontation and even the involvement of the police. Before he would authorise such drastic action he would have to be absolutely convinced that the Moonstone was actually in the Warehouse. Despite all the evidence Sir Giles had a niggling doubt that something was not quite right. He was also concerned that two of the women who lived at the Warehouse had not been seen for three days. Where were they and what were they up to? They had not been seen either in the Warehouse or up in Ravenglass and he was fairly sure that one of them was the High Priestess of the coven. If the Moonstone was in the Warehouse, why was the High Priestess nowhere to be seen? Could the black Maserati carrying the Moonstone have stopped off on the way down? The ANPR on the motorway certainly did not indicate that this had happened unless some kind of exchange had taken place very briefly at a service station.

Sir Giles wanted to be sure. He had been reacquainting himself with the personal journal kept by the Roman Governor Agricola that was still kept on vellum scrolls in the Order's archives. Like many who were educated at public school of his age, Sir Giles had learned to read and write in Latin. Agricola had recorded how he had located the position of the last Moonstone using an ancient blood ritual carried out by the priest who was serving him on his campaign in Britannia. Sir Giles did not know what the ritual was, but he arranged to discuss it with the priests at the Temple the following morning.

Unfortunately, it was 10.30 am before Sir Giles entered the Temple of the Black Crystal as he had had to chair a board meeting for Restitution Holdings that morning. The High Priest knew of the ceremony which had been used many times when the other Moonstones were being traced and destroyed. The priests gathered around the Black Crystal at the altar and began to summon the spirit of Seth to help them in their task. The very air in the Temple seemed to thicken and the light from the candles noticeably dimmed as their chanting continued. Eventually the High Priest took an ancient dagger and cut the palm of his hand and, holding it just above the altar he allowed his blood to run onto a flat polished part of the surface, and pool. The sighted priests looked carefully at the pool of blood and, rather than pooling evenly, there was a small but pronounced depression in one direction.

"This is the direction where the last Moonstone is to be found." said one of the priests. The ceremony was far from an exact science, it was crude at best, but it was good enough to convince Sir Giles that his misgivings had been well founded. The Warehouse was located between the City and the docklands to the east of the Temple. The depression on the slowly congealing pool of blood was pointing roughly north-northwest. The witches had managed to trick him, the Moonstone was still in Cumbria but why keep it there? Surely they would have brought it back to the safety of the Warehouse where they could have used it to augment the power of their magic in the coven in the Temple of Venus. Why keep it in Cumbria?

Suddenly Sir Giles felt his heart racing, tomorrow was the festival of Beltane, he suddenly knew what it was the witches were up to. They were going to try to use the Moonstone on the sabbat that marked the beginning of the pagan summer at the ancient stone circle dedicated to the Goddess. Agricola had recorded that the Gallancia, who were known as the People of the Stones, were the tribe who had last possessed the Moonstone. It was the High Priestess of the Gallancia who had defied Agricola's centurion and thrown the Moonstone into the sea. What better place for them to challenge the power of the Black Crystal than in the Goddess's ancient stone Temple?

It was already afternoon on the 30th of April, the witches had bought themselves precious time and Sir Giles needed to act fast. The High Priest of the Temple had tried to again seek out the Moonstone using the power of the Black Crystal, but he felt a powerful resistance and could not penetrate the defences of those who defied him. They were already using the power of the Moonstone against him.

Sir Giles realised that he would have to take far more drastic and ruthless action if he were going to stop the witches and finally destroy the Moonstone once and for all. It was a Saturday and from the surveillance that the Order had carried out on the Warehouse, he knew where three of them were likely to be tonight.

He would teach them a harsh lesson that this was not a game and that they should never again interfere in the Order's business.

42

The four witches were taking turns shielding the Moonstone within the protected circle at Almeda's home. At first they thought that their elaborate distraction had worked as they had a quiet Friday night and Saturday morning. Early on the Saturday afternoon Cyrene and Almeda were sat on one of Almeda's large comfy cushions in the circle discussing the plans for the following morning. At least the omens were positive in one respect, the weather forecast was looking good. There was a ridge of high pressure coming in from the Atlantic and as a bonus it was drawing up some warm air from the Azores. The weather was looking to be set fair although it was going to be an early start if they were going to catch the sunrise at a little after 5.30 in the morning.

Suddenly Cyrene felt a familiar feeling in her head, the same feeling that she had felt in the Warehouse when she had had a psychic attack. The last time she was unprepared but now she knew who was behind it and they were expecting it. Almeda saw Cyrene's hands move up to her temples and immediately shouted for Gem and Alexandra to join them. Alexandra opened the circle by forming an arch in the air above it with her athame, a sacred knife used for magical purposes, and she let Gem in before closing it once again. The four witches sat around the Moonstone which was radiating light in the middle of the circle, and they could almost sense the light being sucked from the room around them as the power behind the Black Crystal made its evil presence felt.

The witches called on the power of the Goddess to join them in the circle and focused their thoughts on the love they held for her precious Earthly domain and for each other. They could feel the energy from the Moonstone grow, responding to the energy emerging from their heart chakras and flowing up through their crowns joining together in a cone of protection above the circle. As the cone grew, the light flooded back into the room. Cyrene felt her head clear, and she was just filled with the glow of love as she held the hands of her sisters in the circle. The attack was quickly over, and the power of the Moonstone had held. Far more worrying was the knowledge that somehow the Order now knew that the Moonstone was not in London, and it was quite possible that they had guessed what they had planned. They would have to be on their guard in the morning.

They called Roxie at the Warehouse and told her what had been happening. They expected the Order to respond but they were not sure how and would need to be on their guard. That evening as usual, Dodi, Fixie and Luther would be at the 'Stony Broke Bard,' a comedy and music venue above a local pub. The venue had been launched and named after the Covid-19 pandemic had taken such a dreadful financial toll on performers' incomes during the lockdowns in 2020 and 2021. Dodi was trying out a short new stand-up comedy routine on her local sympathetic audience and Luther was playing a short set with his band. Roxie suggested that they might think of calling it off and stay in the relative safety of the Warehouse, but they would not contemplate letting their audience down and the pub had already sold tickets for the gig.

The evening went well, the response to Dodi's set had been more enthusiastic than was required just to be kind, and Luther's band were on good form. Halfway through the set Fixie tapped Dodi on the shoulder and gestured that she was going to go to the toilet. Dodi thought nothing of it and turned back to watch Luther and the band. Fifteen minutes later Fixie had not returned, so Dodi went to the toilet to see if she was ok. There was no sign of her anywhere. Dodi went outside to see if Fixie had popped out to get some air and escape the humidity of the pub. As the noise of the music faded she heard her phone ringing. It was Roxie, the Order had taken Fixie and they were demanding that the Moonstone must be handed over if they ever wanted to see her alive again.

Dodi rushed back into the pub and interrupted Luther to tell him what had happened. Within twenty minutes they were back at the Warehouse. Dodi had a hunch where they might have taken Fixie and she rushed to her room and turned on the surveillance camera overlooking the unnamed hotel in the City. She watched the recording as she played it backwards and sure enough about twenty minutes earlier a car had pulled up and Fixie was dragged out of the passenger door and quickly into the hotel. Although she had her hands bound behind her back with a cable tie restraint, she was struggling furiously so at least they knew that she was still alright at that point. Dodi switched to the foyer camera and saw Fixie being forcibly taken down the stairs behind the glass panelled door. She picked up a burner phone that had one number on it and made a call. "Chief Inspector Davidson" came the reply. "This is Zeno." said Dodi using a voice distorter to mask her own. "I have just sent you a video clip of a kidnapping."

"Please hold." said Rachel Davidson as she looked at the clip on her phone. This was the evidence she needed. She would now be able to secure the warrant to search the mysterious hotel and find out what was really going on in there. This was kidnap and Zeno had given her the name of the victim, no matter how dubious the legality of the source of the CCTV clip, she now had enough evidence to act. "Please be quick." said the distorted voice. "Leave it with me."

said Rachel Davidson. Five minutes later she was on the phone to the on-duty senior officer of the City of London Police.

Shortly after Dodi had hung up the phone on Chief Inspector Davidson, Roxie received a call from the Order. She was told that if they ever wanted to see Fixie alive again they were to hand over the last Moonstone to an agent of the order at 5.30 am at Swinside stone circle. This was to be the final humiliation for the witches and the ultimate triumph of the inheritors of the Roman patriarchy that had been thwarted 2000 years before. The witches would have to watch as their precious Moonstone was smashed on one of the rocks at the Temple of their Goddess at dawn on their sacred sabbat. This would take place at the very spot where the High Priestess of the Gallancia had once defied Agricola's centurion. One of the priests of the Temple of the Black Crystal was already on the train north to meet with the Order's agents to verify the Moonstone's authenticity and to carry out its final destruction. Sir Giles would finally have succeeded where his illustrious predecessor had failed, and this would be his ultimate triumph. Once the stone was safely destroyed, he would have Fixie sacrificed in the Temple. This would be a fitting tribute to the God Seth and mark his ultimate victory over the Goddess and her servants who had vainly tried to contain his powers with the thirteen Moonstones. Tomorrow morning the cause of love would be lost forever upon the Earth.

43

At 4.15 am a coach pulled up at the Broadgate turning off the A595 and a strange looking party climbed out. There were nine women and thirteen men. All the women were dressed in green robes hidden under a variety of coats to keep off the early morning chill. They were met by four other women, three dressed in green robes under their coats and one in white. Everyone was solemn as it was known that a special soul who was dear to some of them was in grave danger and the morning's proceedings could end in either great joy or despair. The High Priestess Cyrene led the twelve other witches and thirteen men up the two kilometre walk that led to the ancient stone circle of the Gallancia. As she led the way Cyrene could feel the spirit of her predecessor Chyrenia growing within her as if they were joined together across the expanse of time on this special day.

They reached the circle just before 5.00 am and formed two rows in front of the stones, the men in front and women stood behind them. Two of the men walked forward and waited patiently. Twenty minutes later six figures appeared over the brow of the hill and began walking towards the stone circle. The lead figure had an arrogance about his stride although his pace slowed when he saw just how many people were gathered before him. He had been expecting to see just a couple of women holding a stone and he was now less certain about how easy this task was going to be.

Max and Jethro cautiously watched the party of men approaching them. At that moment Max's satellite phone rang. He held the phone to his ear, listened, and simply replied, "That's great" before hanging up. He turned to Cyrene and simply said, "They have her, she's safe."

Cyrene immediately lost interest in what was happening outside the sacred stones. All of the witches took off their coats and shoes so that they were barefoot on the ground dressed only in their robes. Two of the witches started gently strumming on two hand drums that they had brought with them, and they followed Cyrene as she began to walk around the circle in a clockwise direction. They circled the stones three times before entering through the portal and equally spacing themselves about halfway between the stones and the centre of the circle, facing the middle. The drumming started to grow as Cyrene began the process of greeting the spirits of the elements and calling on the power of the Goddess to join them. Cyrene had put on a twisted gold wire necklace and as she began the ceremony she pulled it out from between her breasts. Hanging safely in a cradle of golden wires was the Moonstone. As the power grew within the circle the thirteen witches dropped their robes and stood skyclad, like the priestesses of the Gallancia had before them, and twelve of them joined hands and began to dance and skip clockwise around Cyrene, whooping with joy and spiritual ecstasy.

At this moment, the sun climbed above the surrounding hill and flooded the circle with light. Cyrene took off her necklace and held the Moonstone aloft, she was no longer alone in her body, she had been joined by Chyrenia of the Gallancia and their spirits bonded in love. Suddenly the stones around them began to resonate and give off a low humming sound, revealing the purpose of the ancient builders. The stones were created as an amplifier to increase the magnitude of the spiritual energy being created within the circle and they were being triggered once again after being dormant for so long. The Moonstone was radiating a bright light and, as the ceremony reached its crescendo, Chyrenia guided Cyrene's hand as she passed between the dancing witches and placed the Moonstone in a notch in the top of the sentinel stone that stood at the north of the circle. The moment the Moonstone touched the sentinel stone a loud boom resonated around the circle of hills and mountains that surrounded the stone circle.

The ancients who had built this circle within the ring of mountains and hills had not chosen the spot by accident. A pulse of positive energy, powered by the witches' love, flew out from the Goddess's Temple, and rippled around the globe. It was simultaneously joined by hundreds of other ripples of energy. Cyrene had used the power of the internet to connect with a network of priestesses, pagans and shamans around the World who had also begun a ceremony in celebration of the Goddess's love at exactly the same time. The interlocking waves of energy bathed the Earth in their warm embrace and when they had finally subsided everything had changed. A great shadow had been lifted from the Earth and the power of love and truth could once more thrive in the nurturing womb of the Goddess.

Cyrene turned and faced Gem across the circle and the two women walked towards each other. When they were no more than three metres apart two white ethereal figures emerged from them, one a naked priestess with long flowing hair, the other dressed as a warrior with a vivid scar running across her face. The two figures embraced and merged into one ball of white light before gently fading. Two women whose love was powerful enough to survive for nearly 2000 years had been reunited for the one last time upon this Earthly domain.

The thirteen witches wept in the beauty and joy of the moment, they then hugged and embraced each other before quickly gathering their robes and coats as the slight chill of the morning air struck them once again.

44

Leaving Cyrene in charge of the proceedings in the stone circle, Max and Jethro walked forward to halt the party of men walking up the track. The stone circle was in a field surrounded by dry stone walls and Max and Jethro wanted to stop the men in the advancing party before they could access the field and disturb the proceedings. Cold Eyes glared at Jethro who was smiling at him although it was by no means a friendly greeting. Behind Max and Jethro were eleven hardened and experienced doormen from the pubs and nightclubs of London who worked for Max and Jethro's business.

Cold Eyes watched the developing ceremony in the stone circle and knew that something was wrong. "Give me the Moonstone." he demanded, but his voice lacked conviction. He was experienced enough to know that there was no way that the men in front of him were going to oblige him.

"Oh, I'm afraid that is not going to happen." said Max who was standing with his arm on Jethro's shoulder. Cold Eyes licked his lips, he had spent weeks stuck in this remote place and now it looked as if it was all for nothing. He was getting angry at the attitude of this cocky guy who stood in front of him taunting him. "You wouldn't be talking so tough if you didn't have your mates behind you." he snarled at Max. Max just winked at Jethro and slowly Jethro stood back and with the rest of the doormen created a wide circle around the Cold Eyes and the five very nervous men who were with him. Max stepped forward and stood in front of Cold Eyes gazing at him impassively. "Want to dance?" he said raising an eyebrow.

It was mercifully quick; Max may not have been fighting competitively in Mixed Martial Arts for a couple of years, but he still trained five times a week and it took him seconds to floor Cold Eyes. Just as Cold Eyes hit the ground an enormous sound akin to a massive sonic boom resonated around the hills.

"You'll regret that" said Cold Eyes, "you know you have just sentenced your friend to death."

"I think you had better discuss that with them don't you" said Jethro pointing at the two police vans dodging the bigger potholes as they drove up the track. "I think they want to question you about your part in kidnapping and attempted extortion." Just in case Cold Eyes and the rest of his party, which included a very nervous looking Egyptian priest, had thoughts of trying to escape the thirteen doormen closed in around them.

The walk back to the coach looking out at the stunning view across the Duddon estuary was a joyous affair with the two drumming witches merrily leading the way. Gem had rushed over to Max and Jethro after the ceremony at the stones had finished and, standing on tip toes gave them both a big kiss. Jethro squatted and Gem sat on his broad shoulders so he could lift her up and carry her back down the hill in triumph although he put her down after a few hundred metres as she was wriggling about too much. After dropping off the hire car, Almeda joined the others on the coach to return to London with them. That evening there was quite a party at the Warehouse.

45

At exactly 5.00 am the City of London Police with Chief Inspector Rachel Davidson from CEOP in attendance broke down the door of the unnamed seedy hotel and raced into the building accompanied by armed police officers. They went straight towards a glass panelled door which was swiftly opened with a ram and raced down the flight of stairs before them. At the bottom was a brick lined corridor with a number of cells sealed with locked steel doors. There was also a couple of rooms with beds, and a dungeon with benches, restraints, and all manner of implements for BDSM sexual practices. They arrested four men and a woman who were found there and also rescued three girls and a boy who had all suffered terrible abuse at the hands of their tormentors and a very angry young woman with a black eye and a bruised face. They also found a whole archive of appalling digital recordings of the abuse that had taken place within that awful place featuring some very prominent establishment figures.

Completely oblivious to the police operation taking place on the other side of the secret door that led to the Temple, Sir Giles, six members of the Order and two priests were holding a ceremony in anticipation of the moment the last Moonstone would be destroyed for ever. Sir Giles could not believe that this final moment of triumph was at hand. As 5.45 am approached, the time of the sunrise at the stone circle which was when Sir Giles had ordered the Moonstone should be smashed, the chanting of the priests reached its zenith. Suddenly the Black Crystal let out a deafening high pitched ringing sound and exploded into a thousand pieces. The two priests quickly died from the lacerations caused by the flying shards of volcanic glass. The faces and hands of Sir Giles and the other five members were covered in cuts, but they had been spared the worst because the bodies of the two priests had been shielding them from the exploding crystal.

For a moment Sir Giles and the others sat in shocked silence, their moment of triumph had turned into a scene of bloody carnage. One of the members had a splinter of volcanic glass in his eye, the blood running down his face and over his lavish robe. Suddenly one of the attendants rushed into the Temple, briefly pausing as he was confronted by the scene in front of him, before warning Sir Giles of the police raid taking place in the hotel. It would only be a matter of time before they discovered the concealed door to the Temple complex and Sir Giles and the other members would not want to be there when they arrived.

Sir Giles ordered the attendant to call his driver and car around to the front of the building before entering the lift. His mind was working overtime, he had never actually joined in with the sexual and violent abuse that had gone on in the dungeons and playrooms that were being raided. This was not through any moral opposition; it just did not excite him particularly although he had seen recordings of some of the more shocking activities that had taken place there. He saw them as reassuring evidence of the deviancy and cruelty humanity could descend to once the thin veneer of civilisation slipped. As there was none of his DNA there he could plead plausible deniability, he could afford the most expensive lawyers money could buy as he had the unimaginably large funds of the Order at his disposal. The criminal law and any vague notions of justice in a largely corrupted society was primarily for the poor, not the likes of Sir Giles. He would also make sure that he destroyed the lives of every single one of the witches and their friends at the Warehouse who had caused so much harm to the Order. His retribution would be swift and brutal.

He rushed past the alarmed security guard in the lobby of Restitution Holdings and, as he opened the front door, he was relieved to see his car already waiting for him. Looking up the street he could see the police cordons going up, blocking off the hotel and the flashing of a myriad of blue lights as the police raid continued.

Not waiting for his driver to open the rear passenger door as would be customary, Sir Giles ran across the pavement, leapt in, and shouted "Home, now!" The car did not move, suddenly the other rear passenger door opened and a man with a newspaper got in beside him. Before Sir Giles could express his outrage the newspaper was drawn back to reveal a sawn-off shotgun which was jammed into Sir Giles's ribs. A voice in an east London accent said "Please don't make me use this in here sir. It will make a terrible mess of the inside of this lovely motor, and I put on a clean shirt this morning."

"What do you want from me?" replied Sir Giles. For the first time in his life since his early days of experiencing the bullying and ritualised torment of public school, he felt completely helpless. All his wealth and power was completely useless to him in this moment when faced with the harsh reality of the two cold steel barrels of the shotgun pressed into his side.

"Me sir? Oh, I don't want anything from you, thanks for asking. Thing is my guvnor, a Mr Frankie McNeal, wants to know why you thought it was a good idea to kidnap his daughter and get one of your employees to punch her repeatedly in the face? He would just appreciate a quiet chat to straighten things out. He's very fond of his daughter you see, and I fear he has taken your interference in her life a bit personally. Frankie can get a bit emotional at times so if you wouldn't mind coming with us sir, I'd hate to disappoint him?" At that moment, the driver flicked the security switch and all the doors locked shut in the car. A stranger in his chauffeur's uniform turned around and gave Sir Giles a broken toothed smile.

Sir Giles was never seen again although his car did somehow manage to find itself in the service of a 'businessman' in Albania shortly after the incident. As the police investigation into the child abuse and the two bodies in the secret Temple expanded, they also began investigating the financial activities of Restitution Holdings. They discovered a web of financial fraud and money laundering spanning the global markets. This lead to the arrest and prosecution of dozens of directors and senior employees and the freezing of all of the corporation's assets.

46

"Your tits would look much better with my cum all over them!" Jess and Gem were once again undertaking the joyful task of going through the feedback on Gem's social media accounts. Today was a good day as the response to her article for Woke Media on 'modern feminism and the way of the Goddess' was at least three to one positive. "Block?" enquired Jess. "Block!" confirmed Gem giving her partner a peck on the cheek as the account of another pathetic troll was added to the long list of others that would no longer be able to access her postings. It was six months since the incredible events at the stone circle and the consequences of what had taken place were gradually taking effect.

The destruction of the Black Crystal and the rapid disintegration of the Order could not immediately overturn centuries of patriarchal oppression and all the structures that had been carefully constructed to maintain it. The embedded oligarchy of the wealthy plutocrats still dominated the media, politics, company boardrooms and the financial institutions. They were frantically trying to resist the unstoppable demand for change that was building as more people began to awake from their slumber and apathy and see the reality of their own slavery. The cracks in the system were widening but the whole corrupt edifice had not yet collapsed, and the media outlets of the press barons were screaming their indignation at the growing clamour for change.

In the last six months Woke Media had increased its number of online subscribers from 5000 to over 100,000. Along with a growing number of other progressive media outlets they were promoting the 'give it back' protest march which promised to be the largest since the protest against the Iraq war in 2003. People had woken up to the fact that trillions and trillions of pounds had been systemically extracted from global societies by a tiny greed obsessed minority into the opaque accounts of global tax havens. Now they were demanding the wealth be returned back to the societies it had been taken from. The vast extent of this systemic plundering had caused the stagnation of wages, the deterioration of public services, loss of social welfare and for many millions of people to be plunged into desperate poverty. The insatiable greed of the capital addicts had caused immeasurably more harm than the activities of all the drug addicts in the world combined. Some young radical left-wing politicians were even proposing that the hoarding of excessive wealth should become a criminal offence with unlimited fines and the threat of imprisonment. This was leading to a lively debate about how much wealth accrual should be deemed to be 'excessive.'

Things had radically changed in the Warehouse too. Since the disintegration of the Black Crystal, Keith no longer experienced the build-up of rage that had such potential for harming others and no longer felt the need to isolate himself. The end of the Black Crystal had seen the demise of 'Nergal the Destroyer' whose final victim had been the very organisation who had planted its malign presence in the soul of an innocent child. Keith and Dodi were now an item, Keith had finally opened up his heart and Dodi had rapidly stolen it.

Cyrene had now gone to live with Almeda in the Lakes near their beloved Swinside stone circle and they were now slowly gathering together a new coven which they had simply named 'Gallancia' in honour of Chyrenia and Siabelle. This meant that there was now a vacancy in Warehouse for the studio apartment. Everyone was looking forward to travelling to the Lake District the following Beltane where Almeda and Cyrene would be joined together in a handfasting ceremony. With Cyrene's departure, Alexandra had taken her initiation of the third grade and was now leading the Sisters of Venus coven which still met in the basement Temple of Venus at the Warehouse.

To the delight and amazement of the Museum of London, an amateur metal detectorist called Letitia had discovered some remarkably well-preserved ancient copper sheets in a clay pot after some restoration work in the carpark outside a building called the Warehouse in London. They detailed the remarkable story of a Britonic female warrior at the time of the Roman invasion. This was the only contemporary account of the impact of the Roman invasion from the perspective of those who had been oppressed.

The last Moonstone was kept safe and secure with Cyrene and Almeda who used its magic to heal and to challenge those who still promoted hate and division, with love, empathy, and compassion. The malice in the Black Crystal had been built up over the millennia by the egos of the men who had used it to fulfil the desires of their selfish ambition. When the Crystal had shattered a shadow had been lifted, but the conflict between wisdom and evil to win over the hearts of the peoples of the World was far from over. There was still much work to do for all those who served the Goddess in the cause of love.

Printed in Great Britain
by Amazon